Fired Up

Books by Mary Connealy

From Bethany House Publishers

THE KINCAID BRIDES

Out of Control
In Too Deep
Over the Edge

TROUBLE IN TEXAS

Swept Away
Fired Up

Fired Up

MARY CONNEALY

BETHANYHOUSE

a division of Baker Publishing Group
Minneapolis, Minnesota

© 2013 by Mary Connealy

Published by Bethany House Publishers
11400 Hampshire Avenue South
Bloomington, Minnesota 55438
www.bethanyhouse.com

Bethany House Publishers is a division of
Baker Publishing Group, Grand Rapids, Michigan

Printed in the United States of America

                    Library of Congress Cataloging-in-Publication Data
Connealy, Mary.
      Fired up / Mary Connealy.
          pages cm.— (Trouble in Texas ; Book 2)
      Summary: "Dare Riker is ready to move on from the Civil War, prefer-
   ably with Glynna Greer at his side—but someone dangerous is determined
   to stop him"—Provided by publisher.
      ISBN 978-0-7642-0915-4 (pbk.)
      1. Physicians—Fiction. 2. Texas—Fiction. I. Title.
      PS3603.O544F57 2013
      813'.6—dc23   2013017364

Scripture quotations are from the King James Version of the Bible.

Cover design by Dan Pitts
Cover photography by Mike Habermann Photography, LLC

Author is represented by Natasha Kern Literary Agency

13 14 15 16 17 18 19   7 6 5 4 3 2 1

Fired Up is dedicated to my daughter Wendy. When I talk about what inspired me to write a book, I always mention Wendy because she wrote a book when she was ten years old and it was really good. I asked her if I could take it and work on it, make it longer. (It was really short, but not all that short for a ten-year-old!) Wendy said, "Write your own book. Leave mine alone."

So I did. And here I am today a published author, thanks to Wendy.

Wendy has the sweetest heart of anyone I know, and a great sense of humor. She's also got an independent streak that I admire and she loves reading. When she got up to mischief as a kid, I'd say, "Go to your room!" And she'd perk up and ask, "How long can I stay in there?" She always had a book she wanted to read.

CHAPTER 1

NOVEMBER 10, 1868

Sitting high on the wagon seat, a breeze fluttered Glynna Greer's skirt. The near horse reared, sending the buckboard rolling backward. The other horse in the team whinnied and shifted nervously.

"Whoa there." Jonas Cahill dragged on the brake.

Glynna's blond hair whipped into her eyes and blinded her for a moment as she grabbed at her skirts to control them. They were a half mile down the trail heading for home, nearing a narrow pass.

"Mama!" Janet cried out from right behind Glynna.

Glynna had sworn she'd never let her children feel another moment of fear. A stupid oath to take as it turned out.

Janny and Paul were tucked into the bit of empty space in the back of the small buckboard. Glynna turned to ease their fears, and a gust of wind blew her skirt again and set the horse to rearing.

Dare Riker rode up to the wagon, wrapped an arm around Glynna's waist and wheeled his horse, carrying Glynna away. "Let Jonas calm the team."

Dare turned to Vince. "Your horse is as steady as they come. Switch that mare for your gelding."

"No, wait." Glynna was so eager to leave, she couldn't bear to have to wait around to change horses. "There's no need for that."

It had taken her weeks to come out and get her meager possessions from that house she'd lived in before her loathsome husband died.

She didn't want anything that was his.

Glynna hadn't thought to gather so much. But despite her protest, her friends hauled things out until the buckboard was stacked high with crates. She had to admit that the very sparse rooms she lived in with her children could use a lot of these things, detestable memories or not.

Redheaded Jonas, Broken Wheel's parson, quieted the horses. Dare, with his shaggy blond hair and droopy mustache, and Vince Yates, tidy and dark and too charming for his own good, each had a horse and rode alongside the wagon. These men had risked their lives to save Glynna from her husband, and they were still helping.

Glynna realized how nice it felt to be held in Dare's strong arms. She looked at her son, Paul, who sat beside Janny in the wagon box. Her young daughter's golden eyes were brimming with tears, while Paul's blue eyes blazed with fury that his newly widowed ma was so close to a man.

Quietly, Glynna said, "Put me down, Dare."

They exchanged a look. Dare glanced at Paul, gave a quick nod, and set her on the ground well back of the wagon.

"My skirts spooked the mare, but I've got a firm grip

on them now." Glynna looked from the horse to her young'uns. She had to sit up on the high buckboard seat beside Parson Cahill, as there wasn't room for her in the wagon box. "Changing the horse will take some time. I'd just as soon get going. Let's give the mare another chance."

Dare rubbed a hand thoughtfully over his mustache, then swung off his horse, handed the reins to Vince, and went over to the hitched mare's head and held her. He moved so his body blocked the horse's view of Glynna. "Okay, try it. Move easy now."

Glynna gathered her skirts securely against her body and moved toward the wagon. But the horse must have smelled her. It tugged on the reins, twisting its head to watch Glynna. Its eyes were white all around, wide with fear.

Stepping back until the horse calmed down, she crossed her arms, annoyed by the delay required to hitch up another horse.

"Can you ride?" Vince asked.

Glynna looked back at the handsome lawyer. "Yes, I've been riding all my life."

"Instead of switching teams, you take my horse. I'll go with the buckboard." Then he added the warning, "You'll have to ride astride."

The chance to leave this instant made her almost giddy. Glynna looked at Dare. She shouldn't look to him, she knew it, yet how often had she caught herself doing just that? "I'd enjoy riding. It's been a long time."

In fact, it had been a long time since she'd enjoyed much of *anything*.

She strode to Vince's big red gelding and swung up in the saddle, enjoying the feel of a horse under her. She adjusted her skirts. They were wide enough for modesty, also wide enough to scare a skittish horse, apparently.

Vince climbed up to sit beside Jonas, and soon the heavily laden buckboard was rolling again.

With the buckboard taking the lead, Glynna lost sight of the children. They sat on a bench right behind the driver's seat, surrounded by boxes and furniture and other leftovers from their miserable life with Flint, Glynna's late husband.

Her tension eased as they rode away. Dare guided his horse to her side, smiling. "You ride that horse like you were born in a saddle, Mrs. Greer."

A twist of humiliation surprised her. "Can we not attach the name Greer to me ever again? Call me Glynna."

"It ain't exactly proper, but I don't mind burying that sidewinder's name along with him." Dare's smile was gone. Glynna was sorry she'd had a part in wiping it away. Dare had killed Flint in a gun battle. Dr. Dare Riker wanted to heal, not kill, but Flint had given him no choice.

The buckboard creaked along. The weather had turned cool, as even Texas had to let go of summer at some point. Vivid yellow cottonwood leaves still clung to the trees lining the road to town. A few fell and fluttered down around them, dancing on the breeze.

The bluffs rose to the left and right. The edges were striped red, strange pretty layers of stone in this rugged part of north Texas some called Palo Duro Canyon. Juniper, cottonwoods, and mesquite were strewn here and there among the big blue stem grass and star thistles. Some places the trees were taller and thick, other places they were stunted and clung to patches of dirt over stone that didn't look deep enough to support roots.

Glynna looked at those highlands, remembering the guards Flint had posted to keep Luke Stone out and to keep her in. In the end, Flint had failed at both.

The bluffs were studded with boulders large and small. Looking ahead at the trail, she saw many had rolled down and been strewn about over the years. The bluffs got closer. A stretch not far ahead was almost a tunnel where the canyon walls nearly formed an arch over the road. It was a tight passage for about a hundred feet.

"Luke said he's going to start an avalanche deliberately one of these days. A rock comes down now and then. He'd like to wipe them out at a time of his choosing."

"He'll end up blocking the whole road if he does that." Glynna watched the buckboard ahead enter the narrow mouth of the canyon and realized she was mentally pushing it. She didn't like her children in there.

"If he does, Luke'll just clear the rubble. Not much backup in that boy."

Laughing, Glynna took a break from her constant worry, a sin she was working on with God's help. "Boy? Luke Stone has to be your age."

"Close." Dare was smiling again. "But still younger. The youngest of all of us."

Glynna was glad she'd teased. It put thoughts of Flint behind her. A sharp crack drew her attention forward, and she realized the buckboard was almost through the passage. She and Dare had just entered it.

The crack, though, what had caused . . . ?

"Ride!" Dare slapped her horse on the rump. "Avalanche!"

Her horse leaped forward as a rock struck the ground behind her. A low rumble pulled her eyes up to the bluff on the left side of the trail. Rocks were pouring down, rolling, crashing into others. Knocking them loose. Bouncing off the far side of the canyon walls, starting an avalanche on that side, too.

Her horse made a wild surge forward, changing from walking to a gallop in a single step. Glynna lost her grip on the reins and fell backward.

Dare caught her wrist and jerked her forward with a hard hand. "Stay with me!"

Clawing at the pommel, she leaned low over her charging horse's neck to make a smaller target. Thundering rocks sped up. One the size of Flint's fist hammered Glynna's shoulder, knocked her sideways and she lost her grip.

She fell between the racing horses and slammed into the ground. Crushing, iron-shod hooves thundered around her. The whole world was a tumbling whirl of hooves and blinding grit and falling rocks. She heard herself scream over the deafening noise that swamped her. Then her borrowed horse ran on.

She scrambled to her feet. A powerful grip sank into the front of her calico dress and she was airborne. Dare yanked her up in front of him. He'd spun his horse around, come back for her, and now turned again to the far side of the pass—closer than going back. Tiny rocks pelted Glynna's face. A boulder whizzed past her eyes, barely missing her.

She looked ahead to see stones tumbling down on the wagon. Jonas slapped the reins and shouted. Vince threw himself back, twisting his body, sheltering her children.

Vince's now-riderless horse sprinted past the wagon and cleared the narrow stretch. A heavy rain of dust and gravel cut off the world outside the deadly corridor.

"Hang on!" Dare yelled to be heard over the onslaught. Overhead, the rumble changed to a roar. He looked up as he spurred his horse forward.

One second they were galloping, the next Dare threw them off the horse and rolled with her toward the sheer rise of the bluff. Dare's weight knocked the wind out of her as he landed on top, shielding her. "Keep your head down!"

A boulder pounded in the ground only feet in front of her. Dare's horse reared and staggered backward, which saved it from being instantly crushed. As the boulder slammed past, the horse leaped forward and disappeared into falling stone and grit.

The huge boulder then bounced. How could something so enormous bounce? It hit the far side of the tunnel and ricocheted.

"Get up. Move!" Dare dragged her to her feet. The chunk of granite was careening toward them. They got past it just as it crashed into the spot they'd just been.

Staggering forward, raining pebbles hit like little bullets, cutting her face and neck. Choking dirt blinded them until they wouldn't be able to see the next boulder coming.

Dare picked up speed to a full sprint. He stumbled in the debris, went down, and she went with him. Soon they were back up, moving again. Surely they had only a few more yards to go. A jagged rock crashed into Dare's back and knocked him to his knees. Another cascade of smaller stones knocked him sideways.

Glynna snagged a handful of Dare's shirt and yanked him to his feet. She shouldn't have been able to lift him, but desperation somehow gave her the needed strength.

His knees wobbled. His head slumped forward, but he wasn't unconscious, just stunned. She wrapped an arm around his waist and plunged on through the raining stones.

Then out of the tumult, Vince and Jonas appeared. Jonas caught her. Vince got his arm around Dare, and they stumbled on.

The blinding debris finally thinned, and she could see again. A moment later the roar was behind them. They'd made it through.

Dare pitched forward. Vince held tight or Dare would've fallen on his face. Jonas had been hanging on to her, but he left and caught Dare to keep him moving forward.

The intensity of Vince and Jonas as they carried their friend brought tears to Glynna's eyes as she rushed behind them. They'd run *into* a landslide. They'd risked death to save their friend.

Glynna hadn't known men like this existed.

Her children shouted as they clambered down from the buckboard and hurled themselves at her.

"He's hurt. A big rock hit his back." Glynna stumbled and might have fallen except her children ran into her, holding her up just by being there.

Jonas and Vince knelt at Dare's side. Glynna saw blood. Too much blood.

His shirt had a huge tear right by his left shoulder blade. Jonas grabbed the frayed shirt and ripped it right off Dare's back.

"Ma, your face is torn up." Paul, his voice tight with fear, pulled out a handkerchief and handed it to her.

A crash shook the earth. Glynna looked back at the canyon pass. An immense red rock slab, taller than a horse, fell and crashed into the smaller stones, bounced and rolled straight for them, standing up on its side like a gigantic wheel.

"Run!" Glynna caught her children, saw Vince and Jonas drag Dare to his feet, one of them on each side, and together they ran. How far would that slab come?

Glynna heard an almost explosive thud and looked back. The stone rolled straight for them. The horses—those attached to the buckboard and the ones they'd ridden—were just ahead. The team would be killed, too. Rearing and bugling, the animals pulled the buckboard, but the brake was on.

"Glynna, get the children behind those trees." Vince shouted with all the force of a commanding officer. "Jonas, get that wagon out of here."

One glance told her he'd thrown Dare over his shoulder and was charging forward, running at her side. Jonas sprinted for the horses. He shouted at the saddle horses Glynna and Dare had ridden, and they bolted. Jonas threw himself onto the buckboard seat and jerked the brake loose. With a roar at the horses and a slap of leather on their backs, the horses lunged forward.

Glynna veered for the side of the canyon, hard on Vince's

heels. Her children needed no urging; they were outpacing her now, dragging her along.

As they reached the trees, Glynna glanced back to see the slab of stone coming straight for them.

They reached the shelter of a clump of undersized junipers and dashed behind them just as the huge rock hit. The slender trees bent backward, and for a few terrible moments they seemed about to snap and crush all of them.

Janet flung herself against Glynna's legs. Paul grabbed her too, coming from the other side.

The trees held. The rolling stone stopped at last, then tipped over to land flat on its side with a thud that seemed to shake the ground.

Vince charged out of the trees, still carrying Dare. He took a fierce look at the avalanche.

The pass was choked with dirt, and stones still trickled down with a grating racket. But the worst seemed to be over. Some of the tension left Vince's shoulders.

"I think it's done." Glynna emerged from behind the trees, the children still clinging to her. She inhaled silted air and coughed. "Of course I thought it was done before."

"Yeah, me too." Vince, his face coated in dirt, flashed his glowing white smile. "But this time I'm sure."

His words were casual, but his actions said he wasn't being careless. He walked well away from the pass before he crouched, easing Dare off his shoulder to lay him gently down on a grassy stretch alongside the canyon road. Blood flowed from several scrapes on Dare's face, and two big knots were visible on his forehead. But the ugliest wound was on his back.

Jonas had left the buckboard again, shaking his head. "How much control you got over that horse of yours, Vince? We need the water in your canteen."

Vince saw puffs of dust in the air where his horse had galloped away. He paused from examining Dare, lifted his fingers to his mouth, and blasted a deafening whistle.

Dare flinched and his eyes flickered open, then closed again.

Glynna wanted to go to his side with an urgency that was shocking. Her children held her back. She realized blood was dripping onto her dress and that she still clung to Paul's handkerchief.

Dabbing at the raw scratches on her cheek, she watched Vince and Jonas tend to Dare.

"What's going on?" Dare slurred his words and tried to roll over.

Vince's horse came trotting around the corner toward them. Glynna noticed its flank was bleeding. Then, far behind, she saw a second horse—Dare's—coming much more slowly, acting skittish, and who could blame it?

A gasp of pain from Dare got her full attention.

Vince, on his knees, tore what was left of Dare's shirt off. Dirt stuck everywhere. Vince grabbed the remnants of Dare's shirt, folded it roughly and pressed it against the gash above his shoulder blade.

Dare groaned in pain and pulled both arms up so he wasn't quite flat on the ground anymore. He propped himself on his bent arms enough to lift his head.

Running footsteps turned their attention. Luke Stone appeared at the other end of the canyon's narrow neck, barely visible through the thinning grit. "I heard the avalanche."

"Can you get through?" Vince yelled.

Luke paused and studied the hillside. "Yep, I'll have to do some climbing, but I can make it."

"Wait," Vince shouted, "bring us water. We've got some on our horses, but we might be a while rounding them up."

"Hang on." Luke turned and ran as if his friend's life depended on it. Another decent man.

Glynna turned back to Dare. "He saved me."

CHAPTER 2

Jonas and Vince looked up at her tearful statement. Their faces were smeared with dirt, their clothes and hair gritty with dust and gravel.

Glynna felt her eyes burning. "And you both came back for us. You got my children to safety and then came for me."

A trickle of blood ran down Vince's neck. He'd been hurt pulling her and Dare out of the avalanche and protecting her children.

She'd cried a lifetime's worth of tears in the last year. She'd hoped, with Flint dead, maybe she wouldn't need to shed any more for a while. But this generosity touched her so deeply. "I didn't know there were men like you."

"'There is a friend who sticks closer than a brother,'" Jonas said. He heard footsteps again and spun around.

Glynna saw Luke, canteen in hand, charging toward them, running flat out to help his friends. Despite her struggle to stop them, tears ran down her cheeks. She swiped at them.

"Now's no time for crying." Vince sounded aggravated

by her tears, almost past bearing, which oddly made Glynna want to smile. "We got work to do here. You can cry when you've got nothing better to do. And I think it's best that you pick a time when you're alone. For right now, I need something bigger to stop the bleeding, and you could better occupy your time by helping me."

Jonas threw off his coat, tore his shirt open, ripped it off and handed it over. In the chill November breeze, Jonas dragged his coat on over his long-sleeved undershirt.

Glynna took a step toward Dare. Only when she tried to move did she realize her children surrounded her still and held her fast. She wondered if they were clinging to her in fear or did they, especially Paul, want her to stay away from all these men?

Vince fought Dare's fast-bleeding gash. Jonas had given up the shirt on his back. Luke was clambering through a dangerous canyon gap. Glynna saw their bond, and because they'd mentioned the war, she assumed they'd met there, but she knew little about these men who were so loyal to each other.

Dare propped himself up a bit higher.

"Lay down," Vince ordered.

Dare ignored them. His eyes were clearer and focused, though he moved slowly.

Glynna pressed the kerchief against her cheek. She wasn't that steady on her feet, and although she wanted to go to Dare and help care for him, she wasn't completely opposed to her children holding her upright. "Parson Cahill, you said, 'There is a friend who sticks closer than a brother.' What does that mean?"

"It's from the book of Proverbs," Jonas answered.

Dare added, "Jonas is fond of quoting it when he thinks about us."

"Us?" Glynna knew they were friends, but this sounded like they were more than that.

"The Regulators." Flinching as Vince pressed down, Dare didn't say more.

"What's a Regulator?" Glynna should probably leave him alone.

"It's how we all met." Dare winced.

Then it occurred to her that he might want to distract himself from what was going on. She knew she'd rather forget the pain of being stoned half to death. So she kept talking. "But what does it mean, Regulator?"

"Luke, Jonas, Vince, and I and a whole lot of others teamed up to keep the peace in Andersonville Prison."

"I've heard of that. It was a prison camp during the War Between the States. In Georgia, wasn't it?"

"Yep," Dare said. "And as mean and hungry a place as has ever been known on earth."

"Well, I've heard there were some awful prison camps in the North, too." Glynna hadn't meant to sound indignant, but she was a daughter of the South, after all.

"True enough, the North had their camps and their harsh treatment, no doubt about it. Anyway, in Andersonville, they called those of us who were in charge of law and order 'Regulators.' It is a bond between us. It's why we came down here. Luke is one of us. He needed help when he found his father killed and his ranch stolen, so we came and fought at his side."

"And saved me in the process by killing my no-good husband."

Dare turned his head enough to look her in the eye. "It was always going to be a fight, we knew that. But our hopes were to lock Greer up for what he did to Luke's father. We didn't go into it hoping to kill."

"I'm sorry it came to that, but you rescued me from Flint's brutality as surely as you rescued me from this avalanche. Thank you for—"

The sound of stones rolling turned her attention, and she could tell they'd all braced themselves to run. Luke was across the rubble and climbing down. He got on level ground and rushed for them. "How is he?"

"His shoulder is cut and he took a whack on the head. He needs stitches, but he's the only one around here that knows how to set them."

"I can do it." Glynna's stomach twisted as she remembered the stitches she'd sewn into human flesh in the past. And the price she'd paid for helping a deserter.

Vince gave her a sharp look. She could feel herself being assessed. At last he jerked his chin in agreement. Which might mean she'd passed whatever test he'd been giving her. Or it might mean he realized their choices were very limited. "We don't have any supplies to do it here."

"There's a sewing box in my crates." Glynna pulled away from her children and hurried to the buckboard. Most of the crates were open, as there'd been no sense in nailing them shut for the ride to Broken Wheel. She identified the right one and clawed through the packed clothes until she found the small satchel containing needle and thread.

Whirling back to Dare, she rushed over. "These are silk threads."

"Let me see 'em."

Glynna found treating a doctor was more of a trial than treating someone who had no idea what she should be doing. She handed over the thread.

"These aren't as heavy as they should be. Where's my horse? My doctor bag is on it."

Vince glanced in the direction the saddle horses had run. "I see him and my horse. I can probably catch mine, even spooked like this. He's a mighty well-trained critter. Yours isn't so well behaved, though, and not likely to know my voice. If I catch mine, I can use him to lasso yours, but I'd be a while."

"No. Let's get this sewed up. This silk thread will do. Just double it."

"All of you get away from Dare for a second." Luke held the canteen but didn't hand it over. "You're covered in dirt and sand. Knock it off yourselves before you touch him again."

"Yep, there's no sense sewing gravel into my back."

Glynna backed away, as did the rest of them, except Vince, who kept holding down the compress. The rest of them shook the grit off. They kicked up quite a cloud.

Coming back to Dare's side, she knelt across from Vince and held down the pressure bandage while Vince dusted himself off.

"Okay, let's see if the bleeding's stopped."

She lifted the rags and saw the rest of Dare's back. Three ugly scars. Stab wounds. Old ones. One on each shoulder and another lower down. She had to clench her jaw to keep from asking about them.

"Dare's covered with dirt, too," Glynna said. "But most of it's been washed off his back by the blood."

"Lucky me." Dare twisted to look.

"There isn't any chance you might feel a bit faint, is there?" Glynna would have preferred him unconscious as she needled him in the back. But she had no hope. The man was wide awake and that was that.

"Nope." He looked at the needle she was threading. "Are you any good at this at all?"

"*Good* is such a vague word." Glynna took the canteen.

"So be specific. I don't mind putting off the minute you plan to—Ouch! That's cold."

Glynna let the water from the canteen flow over the injury. "You've got one main cut on your back." She thought information might make him feel more in control. "But the skin all around it is scraped and bleeding. The skin is kind of ragged, not like a straight . . ." She felt dizzy for a second and decided to shut up before she talked herself into fainting.

"A straight what?"

"I'm ready now. Be still." Glynna reached for Dare's back, then paused and looked at Janet and Paul. Janet was pale, her hazel eyes riveted on Dare's back. Paul had his arm around his little sister so tight he might have been holding her up. Glynna's eyes shifted to Jonas. "Can you take the children away? They don't need to see this."

"I'm fine, Ma," Paul said, his usual sullen attitude on full display.

Glynna met his glare, worried about her son more every day. "I want Janny to step away. And I don't want her alone. Go on now."

Jonas rose and went to the children. "I'm going to need help clearing out the back of the wagon so we can carry the doctor to town. C'mon, let's go." He urged the children toward the buckboard.

"I'll round up the horses," Luke said and then walked off.

Vince stayed on his knees beside Dare.

"I can ride," Dare said. He narrowed his eyes, tough guy to the bitter end.

Watching until the children were well away, Glynna bent close to Dare's ear and whispered, "I can do this a lot better without them watching."

Dare nodded. "Get on with it. You're right it needs to be cleaned before you sew. I'm not sure if that means you know what you're doing, or it's just common sense and you've got some."

"Well, you're the doctor. Feel free to dispense advice."

"I'm not a doctor."

Jonas dropped the tailgate with a sharp clink of the metal chains and started lifting crates. The children pitched in.

It took a long time for Glynna to be satisfied with her efforts in cleaning the wound, but finally she drew the skin into place. "Vince, can you hold it for me?"

Vince, cool as ever, replaced her hands with his.

There was no way around it, so Glynna went right through with the needle in Dare's poor, already-violated flesh. She flinched.

Dare didn't even react.

"You're tough," she said.

Dare gave her a half smile. "Don't ever forget it." He then folded his arms so he could rest his head.

Glynna turned to the next stitch. A wave of nausea surprised her. She'd always kind of enjoyed sewing up her first husband. Of course, he'd deserved being stabbed in the back. Which reminded her. "Did someone stab you in the back?"

Looking over his shoulder, his lips curled without a speck of humor. "Yep, I got all three of those in Andersonville."

"I thought that was where you learned to be a doctor. Who stabs a doctor?"

"You'd be surprised. The list was pretty long."

"Yeah, we stopped a whole lot of them," Vince added without looking up from where he held his friend together.

"Were you a bad doctor?" Glynna asked, trying desperately to distract herself from what she was doing—to stave off an unfortunate graying of her vision and buzzing in her ears.

Vince found a real smile. "He was about the worst doctor you've ever seen at first. Not as bad as Luke, though. They found Luke another job."

"I'm not a doctor." Dare sounded disgruntled.

"And yet you have a doctor's office and dispense treatment to everyone in the area."

"There aren't many folks who need anything fussy done. I can handle the basics."

"You just described about every patient who goes to a doctor," Vince said with a disgusted shake of his head.

"Why don't you just admit you're a doctor and quit caterwaulin' about it?"

"Can we tend this wound and get to town?" Dare, sprawled on his belly in the grass, glared at Vince over his shoulder.

"I'm going to be at this for a while. Why don't you tell me more about the Regulators and how you became a doctor. I could stand the distraction. Unless you want to talk about me opening a diner. I'm slow getting it opened."

"You needed to heal up first." Dare turned to her. His voice was deep with a hint of roughness, like he had some of the grit and gravel from the air stuck in his throat. His blue eyes were kind.

"Broken Wheel is going to be glad to have that diner open again." Vince seemed willing to talk even if Dare wasn't.

"There'll be nothing fancy. I'm a decent cook, but it's not my greatest gift."

"Most likely the cowboys you'll be cooking for are worse than you. And they like a meal cooked by a woman. Besides that, a lot of the time they're about half starved, so you'll be okay."

Glynna didn't think Dare's expectations were overly high, and that was just as well. "So who stabbed you?"

"Just finish up." Dare quit watching her as if he could put distance between them. All things considered, that wasn't likely.

"Listen, my hands are coated in blood. I almost got buried under a rockslide, and all my earthly possessions are right now being set along the trail to be abandoned. I don't really mind; they remind me of that no-account rattlesnake I was married to. But I think I deserve something for sewing you back together. You could tell me who planted a knife in your back. Was it one person who stabbed you three times? Or did three people attack you all at once, or—"

"Three different times," Dare cut her off. "Those are from three different people on three separate occasions."

"Were you really that bad of a doctor?"

Dare let out a chuckle, which moved his shoulders.

"Stay still." But the distraction was helping. Glynna's stomach quit fluttering like laundry in the wind, and she went on sewing with a steadier hand. She wasn't sure how many stitches to put in. In truth, she had no real training. Instead, she sewed Dare up like she was hemming a skirt. "There. That's the last." She hoped. "And the bleeding has finally stopped."

"Mostly." Vince dabbed at the jagged cut.

"Bandage it tight and let's go." Dare muttered out his doctoring orders, then raised his voice so it reached the buckboard. "You don't have to unload. I'll ride my horse."

Jonas ignored him and kept working.

In the distance, Luke was riding Vince's horse, which he'd managed to catch, and was now easing toward Dare's, shaking out a loop from the lariat hanging from the saddle horn.

"Let's get going." Dare shoved himself up until he could sit back on his knees. He wobbled and fell to all fours. Shaking his head, he said, "Give me a minute."

"I'll get a bandage on while your head clears." Vince sounded mostly reasonable, but Glynna heard the sarcasm

28

beneath it. Only a true friend could comfort you and mock you at the same time.

Dare nodded, which meant he'd probably missed the sarcasm, which meant he was close to unconscious.

Vince wadded up the remnants of Dare's shirt and pressed on the wound. "Hold this in place, Glynna."

The groan of pain when Glynna pressed the makeshift bandage down tore at her heart.

Vince jerked his own shirt off his back, twisted it into a thick rope of cloth, then used the arms to bind it around Dare, going over his right shoulder and under his left arm. Vince knotted the wrists on top of the bandage to hold the cloth in place and keep pressure on the wound. Now Vince was left in his long woolen undershirt for the ride to town.

"We've got space cleared. Let's get him loaded up." Jonas came walking over. Luke rode up, leading Dare's horse, dismounted and lashed the horses to the buckboard. The children had climbed in the wagon and were perched on the bench seat behind the driver's seat.

Dare wasn't paying attention. When Jonas caught him under one arm and Vince under the other, he shook his head again like he didn't need help. Then his knees turned to jelly.

"He blacked out." Jonas looked across Dare's body at Vince.

"Be careful of his stitches." Vince shifted his grip to draw Dare's arm across his shoulders. "We haven't even tended the goose egg on his head. Let's get him back to town." They walked him to the buckboard, bearing all of his weight.

"Facedown." Jonas was practically speaking in code, he was so terse.

"You know you're bleeding, too, Vince." Glynna came along carrying her thread.

Vince glanced back at her. "You too, ma'am."

Glynna had forgotten about that.

They got Dare in, and he took up every available inch of the half-emptied wagon bed. Vince fastened the tailgate. "Jonas, you drive. I'll watch from my horse."

Vince eyed the children. "You holler if you think he needs help."

They exchanged a nervous glance and looked at Glynna. She shrugged and nodded. "Just watch him. Honestly you young'uns are as close to being doctors as I am."

Looking at the stack of crates being abandoned by the side of the road, she knew it wouldn't break her heart if they got left there permanently.

"Is he going to be all right? Do you want me to ride in with you?" Luke looked over the edge of the buckboard as Jonas climbed up to the wagon seat.

"I hope he's just fainted." Vince clapped Luke on the back, then mounted up. "Most likely he'll come around when he's ready. Doubt there's much you can do. Ruthy's most likely fretting by now, so go on home."

Nodding, Luke said, "When you come back for the crates, holler at the house. I can help you load up. In the meantime I'm going to get my men busy opening that pass. No wagon is coming through for a while, but I'll clear a passable trail right away if I have to hack it out with a hammer and chisel. I may need dynamite to break up some of the larger boulders."

"What do you think caused the avalanche?" Glynna looked at the bombarded trail. In all the madness they hadn't talked much about the rockslide.

"I dunno. I reckon one boulder broke loose and started the whole thing going." Luke studied the top of the bluff. "How'd it come down all along that canyon neck, though? It seems to have swept the whole length of it clean. Almost like it started in more than one place."

Vince reined his horse away from the rockslide. "I'll be out to pick up those crates and help you clear the gap tomorrow."

Glynna swung up on her horse. "Be careful going back through it, Luke. The avalanche may have knocked more stones loose that are just looking for an excuse to come rolling down."

"I won't linger, that's for sure. But it looks mostly clear up there. I hope we won't have to worry about rockslides anymore. Strange that it happened right while you were riding through it. That was a long shot." Luke tugged the front of his hat and turned to cross the mess of rocks and get himself home.

Jonas threw off the brake, slapped the reins, and the buckboard rolled forward with a clatter. Vince rode alongside Glynna, just feet from the back end of the wagon, until she noticed her children. Janet's little brow was furrowed with worry as she looked between Glynna and Vince. Paul scowled.

"Think those young'uns can burn me to the ground with their eyes?" Vince asked quietly.

"They're certainly trying." Glynna gave Vince a worried glance. "I'm sorry. They've been through so much."

"Haven't we all, Mrs. Greer. Haven't we all. Why don't you lead this little parade? It'll ease their minds. I'd do it, but I want to keep an eye on Dare."

Glynna should probably stay and Vince go. The children would appreciate it. They didn't like letting her out of their sight. But she knew Vince would never leave Dare. She gave her horse a kick and took the lead.

Dare shook awake when his head bounced off a rock.

His first thought was war. He remembered how he'd felt when there'd been cannon fire. Like the very ground was bouncing around.

Then he woke up a little more. No, not cannonballs, boulders. He worked his way through a barrage of pain and remembered the avalanche that had done a mighty good imitation of the Confederate army overrunning Dare's Union lines.

His back was on fire.

His head throbbed.

He felt like a mountain had come down on top of him. Which it had.

He needed a doctor, but too bad for him, for there wasn't one within a hundred miles, or maybe two hundred. It might as well be the other side of the earth because none were anywhere close to hand when Dare needed one.

Doctors were rare in north Texas, for a fact, especially in Indian Territory, which was where Broken Wheel was situated. That was why the townsfolk put up with Dare's uncertain treatment. It was him or nothing. Yet nothing might be a better choice.

Forcing his eyes open, he saw little Janet frowning down at him, worried, sweet. Looking sideways, he found that grouchy son of Glynna's. The boy acted like every man who came near his mother needed to die.

Or be buried in an avalanche.

"Where are we? Are we getting close to town?" He wished for his bed. His head wasn't resting on a rock; it was on a board, which wasn't much better. He preferred something softer than wood under his head.

Paul gave Dare only sullen silence.

Janet shrugged.

"We're almost there." Jonas's voice drew Dare's attention farther forward and up. Just moving his eyeballs almost made his head fall off from the pain.

"Glynna took a needle to my back, right?" Dare was only talking to Jonas now, as he didn't think he was going to get much from the youngsters. "How did it look when she was done?"

"It was an improvement over an open wound. And face it, Dare, your back is already ugly. It didn't much matter if she made her stitches pretty or not."

"For a parson, you've got a mean streak."

Jonas looked over his shoulder and smiled, but the humor didn't reach his eyes. "I think we all oughta pick up and move to someplace that lies flat like the world oughta do. I think we oughta try Kansas. I bet there hasn't been an avalanche in that state since the first mosquito hatched."

"We got the bleeding stopped. You'll be fine if you don't get an infection." Vince was riding right behind the wagon.

Raising his aching head to look at his friend, Dare said, "We need to—"

"Don't turn your head to look at me." Vince's voice had that tone he could use, the one that could make General Robert E. Lee himself back down. The Regulators hadn't been officers, though there had been a battlefield promotion a time or two that ended up being rescinded. But Vince would've made a fine officer if he had a lick of ambition. In fact, Vince had the raw material, the brains, and a willingness to work hard that went with a man who achieved a lot. And yet he'd become a lawyer by reading law books, then came to this far-removed corner of the world and proceeded to be mostly idle.

Dare too could give an order if he was in the mood, but he rarely was. He preferred to do things himself.

Since it hurt to move anyway, Dare laid his face back down on the board that kept whacking at him. "Why?"

"Because the left side of your face is scraped raw. If you look at me and rest that side of your face on the wagon box, you'll be regretting it for a long time to come."

"Kansas doesn't sound so bad. It's nice in Indiana too, where I come from. No rockslides in Indiana. The summers don't try to roast you like a chicken. Lots of thick grass and tall trees that make house building and wood for the fire easy to come by. You think Luke would mind if we left him and Texas far behind?"

Vince rode up beside the wagon so he came into Dare's

view. "Luke's mighty attached to that ranch of his. I think we're stuck together here in Texas."

"Stay still, Dare." Jonas could give an order now and then, too. "I know it goes against the grain, but could you do it just this once and give yourself a chance to heal?"

"Right now, staying still is about all I'm capable of. I'm gonna close my eyes for a bit. I'm not passing out." Talking hurt. So did thinking. So did breathing. Since breathing was unstoppable, he cut everything else out.

"Here's town, just ahead." Jonas nodded forward. "You spent most of the trip unconscious. Aren't you supposed to stay awake after a head injury?"

"I don't know." Dare didn't bother to look. He'd seen Broken Wheel before.

"I thought you were a doctor," Paul said. "Aren't you supposed to know things like that?"

"I am indeed." Dare wished everyone would just quit talking. He was finding out that listening hurt, too.

"We'll get you settled, and I'll stay with you awhile." Vince was more than willing. He lived in a small upper room above his law office, while Dare had a house with a spare bedroom.

"I'll take my turn," Jonas said.

Hoofbeats almost made Dare look, but the pain stopped him. "I'll come in and cook and clean for you, Dare."

Glynna. Her pretty golden hair coated with dirt. Her golden eyes red-rimmed and gritty. The side of her face bleeding. The same side as he'd gotten scraped raw. He needed to doctor her.

"I've got carbolic acid in my office. We need to swab our wounds with it."

"What's that?" Glynna shook her head violently and wrinkled her nose. "Acid eats things away, doesn't it?"

"This is something real new I read about and ordered. I had it shipped all the way from England. It's supposed to stave off infection." Dare lifted his head, and his stomach lurched so dramatically he lowered it again. "I want some on my back for sure. Stitches can get infected easily." He wondered if his face looked as bad as hers.

She was sitting up, riding, while he was lying flat on his face. Even so, she needed a few days to heal. "You're not going to be able to run your diner tomorrow. You'll bleed into the food. Even starving cowpokes'll balk at that."

A tiny sigh caused his eyelids to open. He glanced at the children. They both looked strangely relieved. Dare wondered why they didn't want their ma running a diner.

CHAPTER 3

When she woke up the next morning, Glynna hurt so bad it was like she'd taken a beating.

She knew what that felt like.

Just as well she'd put off opening her diner yet again. This time she had a good reason, but there'd been plenty of lesser reasons, all conjured up by her children. They just wouldn't cooperate and were forever coming up with delaying tactics.

They must want her to themselves for a while longer. The diner, with its rooms upstairs, had come to her free. Abandoned and with no one to buy it from, she just moved in. Kindling kept showing up at her back door, along with haunches of antelope and bags of potatoes and buckets of milk. There was something new there nearly every morning. She'd gotten flour and sugar and just anything she might need to live. No idea who was leaving it, but she suspected it wasn't one man but in fact several of them. Every one of the men in town had taken the opportunity to greet her and tip their hats.

Dare Riker had even given her a stack of clothes. He

said they'd been left in his home by whoever moved out, or maybe by several families who'd moved away from Broken Wheel and hadn't been able to haul everything.

He'd brought clothes in many sizes for her and the children, as well as some furniture and assorted other things, and he'd done it all as if she were doing him a favor to take it. Considering there were a fair number of women's and children's clothes, perhaps he was telling the truth.

Between the food and the firewood and the clothes and all the things left behind by the former owner of the diner, Glynna and the children wanted for nothing. So there was no rush opening the place. It appeared she could live there forever for free.

Still, she should open the diner and stop depending on the kindness of others — and she would, just as soon as she stopped hurting.

She dressed with excruciating slowness and thought of poor, battered Dare. Maybe she should cook a meal and take it over to him.

The children were nowhere to be seen, so she headed downstairs. Paul was reading one of the *Leatherstocking Tales* to Janny. Glynna remembered when she was a child, her father had held her on his lap and read that very book to her, and then later she'd read it to Paul. Now Paul was reading it to Janny. The books were the one thing Glynna was glad to have from Flint's house. They belonged to her. Not Flint, and not her first husband, Reggie. Neither of those two nitwits had done much reading.

Paul closed the book. "How are you, Ma?"

"I'm feeling like a mountain slid down on my head yesterday." She smiled and found that it was a true smile. Despite the avalanche, she thought maybe her family was going to be all right. She wondered if she ached too badly to hold Janny on her lap, with Paul close beside her. She would love the normalcy of reading a book to her children.

A sharp rap on the door stopped her from spending any great stretch of time being optimistic.

She walked to the door of the diner, ready to shoo away whatever man came asking if she was open yet, which happened several times a day. Hungry men came to her front door, food and kindling came to the back. Life was taking on a rhythm.

She saw through the window that it was Dare. Standing upright. His face scraped, but otherwise the scoundrel looked just fine, while she'd barely been able to crawl out of bed.

Glynna felt like a weakling by comparison and straightened her shoulders as she reached for the doorknob to let him in.

Paul was at her side, glowering, before she got the door open.

Dare's eyes slid from Glynna to Paul and back. "How are you this morning?"

"I'm getting by. I've no need of a doctor, but thank you for inquiring. What in the world are you doing up and about? I thought you were going to rest for a few days."

"May I come in?" He shoved his right hand in his pocket. "I find myself in a strange situation this morning, and I think your family can help."

Glynna stepped back to let him in.

For a second, Paul didn't. There was a hostile silence, but finally her son gave way. Dare came in and firmly closed the door behind him with his right hand. His left was held close to his body, mostly unmoving.

He was acting very strangely, even for constantly moving Dare. Maybe the blow on the head had done some damage to his reason.

"Janny, you come over and hear this, too," Dare said. Frowning, he waited until Janny came up and the four of them formed a tight circle. "I've got a problem." Dare looked between all of them, smoothing his mustache almost as if he were trying to cover his mouth and hold the words inside. "Um . . . can you all keep a secret?"

Glynna nodded. "We lived with a man who terrorized us for a year and none of the men who worked for him ever knew. I won't even start on my first husband. Yes, we can all keep secrets. All too well."

"Right," Dare said. "Fair enough. Well, I'm not sure if I'm right about this, but I think I am, so . . ." His voice faded to silence and he shoved his right hand back in his pocket, then bounced one knee.

"Has something happened?" Glynna had never seen Dare act so uncertain. "Something awful?"

"Not awful, no. Um . . . the thing is . . . Vince and Jonas are riding out to help Luke clear out that narrow trail today. I'm going, too."

"Dr. Riker," Glynna snapped. "That is just pure foolishness. You aren't in any condition to—"

"Stop." It was an order, as if he thought she were a private in his ranks and he, of course, the general. "That's not what I came about. I know I'm not going to be much help today. I'm afraid I'll tear out my stitches if I do any bending and lifting."

Glynna heaved a sigh of relief. "Then why are you going?"

Dare shrugged his left shoulder, and the smallest possible flinch of pain crossed his face. He didn't move that side of his body again. Glynna realized that although the man was up and about and he couldn't quite keep from fidgeting, he wasn't moving like usual. He stood rigidly erect, and while his right arm and either leg moved, he kept his left arm and his back still. She was sorry for him, yet it made her feel a bit better about her own miserable condition.

"I feel foolish saying this, because I might be wrong, but I want you all to come out to the S Bar S with us."

"We're not going back to that place, ever," Paul said. The boy clenched his teeth, as hostile and stubborn as always.

"I know that's how you all feel, son."

"Don't call me *son*." Paul stepped back a bit to make the circle less closed.

Raising his right hand as if in surrender, Dare said, "My problem is, I need Ruthy to not help us today, and I can't think of a way to stop her."

Furrowing her brow, Glynna said, "Why don't you want Ruthy's help? She's the best worker on that whole ranch."

Dare smiled. "That's the honest truth, Mrs. . . . uh . . . ma'am." His smile shrank.

Glynna had asked him not to use the name Greer and it was rather familiar of him to call her Glynna.

"Anyway, the thing is . . ." A very faint blush appeared

on Dare's cheeks, which in no way went with anything she knew about this overactive, confident man. What could make him blush? "The thing is, I think Ruthy . . . that is Mrs. Stone . . ." Dare's eyes slid between all three of them again. "I expect that . . . just from my knowledge of doctoring . . . there might be a . . . a . . . that is . . . the Stone household may be . . . w-welcoming a young'un before long."

Glynna gasped. She might've blushed herself a bit. In truth, the same thing had crossed her mind when Ruthy had rejected a cup of coffee for no reason. Paul's belligerence faded. Janny even perked up and looked interested.

"Mrs. Stone is going to have a baby?" Janny smiled. One of the first genuine smiles Glynna had seen on her daughter's face since they'd come to live with Flint Greer.

"See, that's the trouble." Dare ran his hand deep into his unruly dark blond hair. "I don't think she's found out yet."

"What?" Glynna couldn't make sense out of that statement.

"I thought, from a few things I observed yesterday, that she might be with . . . with child." Dare blushed. The man looked like the conversation was causing him considerable embarrassment. "But I don't think she knows it yet."

Glynna couldn't really blame him. He worked with few women and now he spoke of his friend's wife in a most personal way.

Now that he'd gotten the personal part out, he began talking faster, as if he could leave it behind. "I know Ruthy well enough to be sure she'll be right beside us today, hoisting stones. I don't think she should. I don't feel quite right suggesting her condition to her before she's figured it out herself. But I don't know what to say to stop her from spending the day working like a man digging a tunnel for the railroad. I thought if you folks could come along, it would force her to take you into the house and act as a hostess—maybe she'd do it for me. Because I'm wounded. I was going to just go along and try that, but something tells me she'd just send me inside with orders to lie down, and then keep right on working. Then I thought maybe if your family came too, she'd almost have to stay with you. Paul, if you'd prefer, you can stay with the men and dig. I suspect I'll be doing little or nothing, but you could help if you've a mind to."

"Dr. Riker . . ." Glynna tried to use his formal name as was proper, but then she insisted he call her Glynna. She had to get going and name herself. "I think—"

"I know you don't like that house."

Glynna was pretty sure he was talking over her to prevent her from saying no. "It's not—"

"I can't say as I blame you." He cut her off again. "But this wouldn't be about you going home; this would be about you helping a friend."

She didn't really blame him for thinking she'd kick up a fuss about going. It'd taken most of a month to persuade her to go out yesterday, for the first time since Flint had died. "If you'll just—"

"I'm sure if you just think of Ruthy first, you could see your way clear to—"

"Dare!" Her jaw was clenched until it was hard to talk. "If I'll just think of Ruthy first?" Her voice rose with every word. "Did you really just say that to me?"

This time he seemed to hesitate. Too late. But at least he did it. "I didn't mean—"

"Oh, yes, you did. You meant I'm such a weakling and so fragile that I'd put my own delicate feelings ahead of the life and death of my friend's child."

From the look in his eyes, Glynna discerned that he had no idea how to respond to that, not without sticking his foot further into his mouth.

Into the silence, which Glynna was proud to say she'd scared him into, she said, "Of course we'll come. And we need to hurry because Ruthy is one to get an early start."

"You won't tell her, will you?"

That reminded Glynna that this had started with Dare asking her and her children if they could keep a secret. Glynna looked at her youngsters. "We won't tell her, will we?"

Paul said, "I can keep my mouth shut."

Janny chewed on her fingernail and didn't speak, which was its own kind of answer. Janny wouldn't say a word.

"Good. Let's get on our way, then. Do we take the wagon again?" Glynna looked to Dare, wondering if he could handle sitting on a horse for the ride to the ranch.

"Jonas and Vince are harnessing the team."

Arching a brow, Glynna said, "You were that sure I'd go?"

"No, not one bit sure. But I convinced them I was going, and they decided I'd fall off my horse before I got there. The wagon is for me, but you're more than welcome to ride in it. And just possibly save your friend's baby's life, in the event there is a baby." Dare smiled, teasing. A great smile.

Somehow, though his hair was shaggy and curly and barely finger-combed, and his mustache drooped and he never dressed up much, he was about the finest-looking man Glynna had ever seen. Of course her first husband, Reggie, had been a decent-looking man, as well. Too bad he had a mind as twisted as a Texas cyclone, the sneaking soul of a chicken-killing weasel, and all the honor of a thieving coyote—all things she'd noticed after they'd been married awhile.

And Flint, well, he'd been neat and clean when he'd stepped off the stagecoach in Little Rock. Not a good-looking man, but considering the treacherous place Glynna found herself in at the time, she'd hardly cared about his appearance. In fact, he'd looked like a knight in shining armor. Only later had she realized he was a devil in disguise.

"Oh, and I haven't told my suspicions to Jonas or Vince yet, either. So the secret is just between the four of us."

Glynna said, "We'll get our wraps on and be right out. Go sit down before you collapse."

Dare left, and she smiled, liking the idea of sharing a secret with him, for some reason. Then she turned to find her coat and saw Paul staring after Dare, frowning. . . . No, it was more than frowning. It was suppressed rage.

Glynna quickly wiped the smile off her face before her son could think she had the slightest liking for Dare Riker—the nice, handsome man who'd saved her life and set her free from purgatory.

"Ruthy! How are you?" Glynna as good as yelled at Ruthy, but she yelled in what she hoped was a perky, friendly way.

Truth was, she spied Ruthy reaching for a rock bigger than her head, and she'd called out to distract her friend from lifting the heavy stone.

Ruthy straightened and smiled. Her red hair was still neatly pulled back, and her dress was clean. Glynna hoped that meant Ruthy hadn't been hauling rocks for long.

Luke and several other men were working at the rock pile. Speaking too loudly himself, Luke said, "Ruthy, you should take Glynna into the house. It's too cold out here . . . uh, for the children."

By the way Luke spoke, and the way Ruthy glared and plunked her hands on her hips, Glynna suspected Luke had been objecting to Ruthy helping from the minute they'd started.

"It is a bit chilly, and we're not bundled up very well." Glynna turned to help Janny down from the back of the wagon and whispered, "Try and look cold."

Janny let a grin peek out, her second that day. Glynna prayed it was the second of many more to come. Wiping away the smile, Janny crossed her arms over her chest and did a serviceable job of shivering.

"It was colder than I thought it'd be on the ride out." Janny stuck her bottom lip out and it almost looked like her baby girl was fighting tears. "But I will stay out here with you if you want me to help carry stones, Mrs. Stone."

Paul, jumping down from the wagon behind Janny, muttered into Janny's ear, "Carry stones, Mrs. Stone."

Glynna saw the spark of humor in Janny's eyes and turned to face Ruthy in such a way as to block the sight of her supposedly distressed daughter—who looked to be on the verge of giggling.

"I'd be glad to stay and help," Paul announced and then walked toward the jumble and began heaving rocks out of the way. It struck Glynna that her son, though still not broad-shouldered, was as tall as some of these men and nearly as strong.

"Maybe after we warm up, we could come back." Glynna did her best to sound doubtful, which was no hardship. She would help pick up rocks if it was needed, of course. She wasn't afraid of hard work. But there were, with Jonas and Vince and Paul, and Luke's hired men, a large crowd of men to do all this heavy lifting. Glynna thought she would probably just get in their way.

"And I think Dare should come inside, too." Glynna waited to be overruled by the stubborn doctor, but he surprised her.

"I thought I'd have more strength, but I need to get off my feet for a fact." Dare walked toward the rubble, sounding like he meant every word.

Luke had made headway clearing a narrow path, but not even a horse could get through it yet, let alone a wagon. On foot they'd have to climb over a few of the big flat rocks.

Ruthy gave the pile of rocks an almost comically frustrated look as if she couldn't bear to leave such a mess. Then her good manners took over. "Yes, of course. Anyway, I need to get a good meal on for everyone." She raised her voice. "Luke, I'll make enough for the men, too."

"Nope," Dodger said, shaking his head. "I've left Tennessee behind in the bunkhouse this morning. His joints ache something fierce in the cold, but Old Tenn ain't got any pride if he can't help somehow. At least let him make the cowhands a meal. Reckon he's already started it anyhow. Just plan on your family and friends, Mrs. Stone."

Glynna recognized gray-haired Dodger Neville and gave him a smile. He'd helped save her, too.

Dodger touched the brim of his hat, then went back to heaving rocks.

Glynna directed Janny ahead of her. They followed Dare through the debris and headed for the house. Glynna kept waiting for Dare to find a way to go back and prove a mountain falling on his head couldn't keep him from work, but instead he went with them toward the house. He looked a little pale by the time they reached the two-story log-and-stone cabin.

Once inside, Ruthy said, "Come on into the kitchen. I heard about the cut on your back, Dare. You can straddle one of the kitchen chairs and not put any pressure on your stitches. I've got coffee left from breakfast. You can have a cup, and there are sugar cookies. We can visit while I get a noon meal started."

"Ruthy," Dare said, reaching out to stop her from leaving the room, and suddenly his weight shifted and Ruthy was holding him upright. "Is there somewhere I could lie down for just a few minutes?"

Glynna rushed to Dare's other side to help bear his weight. She looked at Ruthy across the broad expanse of Dare's chest, each of them with one of his arms around her neck.

"We've got a spare bedroom right this way." Ruthy guided them to the room Glynna had slept in alone. It was now unused, and Ruthy had done her best to give everything in it to Glynna just yesterday. But Glynna had enough bedsteads, and so she'd refused to take this one. Now she was glad of that.

Glynna, mindful of Ruthy's possible condition, tried to bear more than her share of Dare's weight.

Ruthy quickly stripped back the blankets, and the two women eased Dare to a sitting position.

"I'll just rest a few minutes," Dare said. His head drooped forward, and Glynna steadied him. Then he seemed to gather his wits and reached for his boots.

"What were you thinking coming out here, Dare Riker?" Ruthy said.

Glynna brushed his hands aside and pulled his boots off, reminded of the times she'd tended her first husband when he'd come home battered.

After dropping his second boot with a thud, Glynna looked up from where she knelt at his feet to smile. It was wasted on him because his eyes were already closed. Glynna and Ruthy helped him to lie facedown on the bed, and then Glynna pulled a blanket over him.

Janny had followed at a distance, and she now stood in the doorway.

"Should we leave him?" Glynna asked. She thought he'd fallen asleep too fast. "Is he unconscious?"

"No reason he'd pass out," Ruthy said. "He's just exhausted and wounded and needs more rest, the half-wit. Why'd he think he could come out here today?"

Glynna, feeling like she was betraying Dare, shook her head as if confused. "Men are just stubborn, I reckon."

"We'll look in on him from time to time." Ruthy guided Glynna away, and the three headed for the kitchen, closing Dare's door behind them.

"Let's get coffee," Ruthy said. "I'll do some quick work to start a meal and then we'll sit in the front room." She bustled toward the stove. "We're close enough to him in the kitchen that we might wake him with our chatter."

Glynna loved the idea of chatter. She and Janny ate a few delicious cookies while Ruthy worked with amazing speed and skill. Ruthy pulled the coffeepot close to the edge of the stove and lifted it to serve Glynna.

"Is the coffee all right?" Ruthy wrinkled her nose. "I might've let it boil too long."

Glynna's stomach had been turned by coffee when she was with child. "It smells fine to me." Taking the cup from Ruthy, Glynna took a sip. "It tastes fine, too."

"I'm going to have tea instead, I think. Janny, do you want a glass of milk?"

Once Ruthy got everything in order, they followed her to the front room, which held ugly memories for Glynna. As they settled into soft chairs and shared their drinks and talked, some of those memories faded a bit, replaced by this pleasant interlude. It was perilously close to normal.

CHAPTER 4

"You slept all morning?" Luke asked as he rose from the kitchen table. "Why'd you come if you were feeling so puny?"

"I underestimated how beat up I was, I guess. I felt pretty decent when I first woke up, but after the ride out here, I was all done in."

Glynna thought Dare looked much better after a long nap, and he'd done more than his share of eating, so he must be feeling better. She also knew he wasn't ready to discuss Ruthy's special condition.

After spending the morning with her, Glynna knew almost certainly Ruthy was expecting. Between the perfectly tasty coffee upsetting Ruthy's stomach, and her moving at about half the usual speed—which was still faster than anyone else—and right now Ruthy looking a little pale. But then she was fair-skinned, so it was hard to judge. All in all, though, Glynna felt sure that Dare had diagnosed Ruthy correctly.

Glynna hadn't known for a while when Paul was on the way. But none of that could be mentioned as the reason Dare had come.

"I'm feeling better now. I can help some," Ruthy said.

"Nope, all the stones a man can lift are gone now," Luke replied. "We're tying a team of horses to bigger ones and we're getting in each other's way. Even with the horses, a few of the rocks can't be moved. I'll send a man into town to get some dynamite. By the time he's back, we'll have only the huge boulders left. We'll do some blasting this afternoon, and that'll be about it." Luke stood to get back to work. "Ruthy, don't be surprised at the racket."

Jonas, Vince, and Paul rose to head out with him. Dare poured himself another cup of coffee. Glynna noticed the man was still barefoot and doubted he'd had any intention of heaving rocks with the men.

As Luke swung the back door open, thundering hoof-beats came from the trail to the south, the direction away from the avalanche.

Glynna and Ruthy rushed to peek out and see what was going on, Janny crowding in beside them. A pinto pony came galloping toward them. The horse had a rider slumped over its neck.

Luke charged out with the men on his heels. Jonas and Paul weren't armed, but the other two had their hands steady on their guns, ready to draw.

A crowd of armed cowhands came boiling out of the bunkhouse, Dodger in the lead.

The man, nearly lying on his horse's neck, was dressed in a deerskin shirt and fringed leggings. He had feathers hanging from two long black braids. His unsaddled horse wore a bridle with no bit.

An Indian.

As the horse tore into the ranch yard, it skidded to a stop and reared. Luke rushed forward but didn't get there in time to stop the rider from tumbling off and landing on the hard ground. A puff of dust kicked up, and the horse leaped over the unconscious man and charged off the way it'd come.

Luke dropped to his knees beside the man, then looked up sharply. "Get Dare."

Glynna whirled and raced back to the house. She hoped Dare was up to this.

"Dare, we need help!" Glynna shouted. "A doctor's help."

When she slammed the door open, Dare was already pulling his boots on. "What happened?"

"An Indian, outside. He's hurt. Luke needs you." And those words, *Luke needs you*, seemed to put starch in his backbone.

He strode from the room. "I brought my doctor bag. It's been left behind in the wagon on the far side of the gap."

He was outside so fast he got past Glynna, and she had to hurry to keep up with him.

"Vince!" Dare barked orders as he rushed toward the unconscious man. "Get my doctor bag out of the wagon. Don't go alone. Where there's one Indian, there can be a whole band of 'em."

Vince slapped Jonas's arm, and the two of them sprinted for the wagon.

Dropping to his knees beside the collapsed man, Dare knew what was wrong instantly. "Measles."

Almost by reflex, he disarmed the man. There was a

hatchet hanging from the left side of his belt and a knife tucked in a scabbard on the right side. Dare tossed them out of reach.

His gaze swept everyone gathered around. "Who's had measles? It's contagious. Anyone who hasn't had them should get back and stay as far away as possible."

Rolling the man over onto his back, Dare studied the red spots that covered his face, neck, and hands. Looking up, he saw that no one had backed away, except he didn't like what he saw in Luke's eyes.

"Have you had measles?" Dare asked.

Luke shook his head. "People get them all the time and they get over 'em fine."

"True enough. But not Indians. This might be deadly for an Indian. You'd likely survive it, but there's no sense spending time sick if you don't need to."

Luke nodded, then looked at Ruthy and got to his feet. "We should go inside."

"I've had measles," Ruthy said. She stepped up to Luke's side. "I had them twice as a child, as a matter of fact. I was told there are two different kinds, and I've had them both."

"Get Luke out of here, Ruthy. And have him wash his hands in hot water with lye soap." Dare looked between the two, and finally, with Ruthy almost dragging Luke, they headed back to the house.

Dodger turned from talking with his cowpokes. "We've all had measles. There's not a man here who's been spared. We can help however you need us, Doc."

"I've had them and so have both of my children." Glynna came and knelt across from Dare.

Luke stopped and spun around before he'd gone too far. "I remember the Kiowa boys I played with when I was young talking about a disease going through their tribe. It was before my friends were born, and before my family moved here. Pa said later that from the description, it sounded like cholera. Some said it nearly wiped out the whole Kiowa and Comanche nations. Measles aren't like that, are they? Not when so many here had them and survived."

"Measles aren't usually serious for whites, but they can devastate an Indian tribe."

"That makes no sense." Luke looked again at the man, who was now lying faceup. "Red Wolf?" He took a step toward the man, but then Ruthy grabbed his arm and held him back.

"You know him?" Dare asked.

"I think so," Luke said. "I recognize that scar on his arm." He then pulled his sleeve back to reveal a similar scar on the underside of his forearm. "We were blood brothers along with Gil Foster. We cut a little deep and ended up with matching scars. I haven't seen him since before the war, but this is Red Wolf, I'm sure of it." When Luke spoke the name a second time, the man's eyes fluttered open. "Red Wolf, is that you?"

"I h-heard you come home, Luke Stone. My . . . my tribe is dying of these red spots. I h-hope for help. My tribe, many are sick . . . some dead." Then the man's eyes fell shut again and he lapsed back into unconsciousness.

"Get out of here, Luke," Dare ordered. "You're no good to me if you're sick, too. We'll take care of Red Wolf and see what his people need."

Dare looked at Luke until finally Luke managed to tear his gaze from Red Wolf.

"There are other ways to help without getting too close," Dare added. "I've got a little willow bark in my bag, but I'm going to need more—what I've got in my office back in Broken Wheel and all they've got at the general store. I ordered more, and it might be in. I'll have to make a poultice, and there are a couple of books I'll need, and . . . well, I'll write it all down. Ruthy, get me a paper and ink, then get some water to boiling. I can make one poultice with supplies I have in my bag, enough for Red Wolf but not for a whole tribe. Luke, you can get to town in half the time if you ride instead of taking the wagon. But I'll need enough things that you should take a pack animal."

Ruthy turned and rushed for the house. Dare regretted making her run. Probably he should tell her about her condition before she set to work saving the whole Kiowa tribe.

"We'll need plenty of men if we're riding into an Indian village. Just because they're sick doesn't mean they're friendly." Dare shook his head, imagining the extent of what lay ahead. "Believe me, there are plenty of ways to help."

Vince came running through the narrow passage with Dare's bag and Jonas close behind him.

"Red Wolf is Kiowa." Luke looked with a furrowed brow at his unconscious friend. "We always got along, but I'd better ride to the village with you. I know about where they'd be camping because I saw some buffalo yesterday, and their village would be near the herd. But I haven't talked with them since they've moved into the area. I didn't know Red Wolf was among this band. Have I got time to get to Broken Wheel and back? If I don't, Vince should go, because I have to ride with you. I speak a little Kiowa, enough to explain what we're doing. It'd be different if Red Wolf was riding with us, but he's not going anywhere."

"I'll be a while working with Red Wolf," Dare said, "and we can't head to the village until you bring me my supplies. You should go. I can keep Vince busy here and he's already had measles. But you'll need help getting everything on my list."

With a hard jerk of his chin, Luke said, "Jonas, come with me. Let's get saddled up." He strode toward his corral.

Jonas headed after Luke without question.

When Luke was far enough away, Dodger said under his breath, "He's right that his family always dealt well with the Indians. Most folks in Broken Wheel trade with them."

"I've never seen an Indian in town." Dare dug through his satchel, looking for supplies.

"It's done quietly," Dodger went on. "Tug Andrews at the general store meets them in the countryside and trades with them. There's some of 'em speak passable English. But Greer wasn't smart about the native folks. He was afeared of 'em and ran 'em off. And he had enough gunmen that they couldn't stand up to him. Luke may find them not as friendly as they once were."

Glynna, kneeling beside Red Wolf, exchanged a glance with Dare.

Dare shrugged one shoulder. "Reckon we'll find out what we're up against soon enough."

Ruthy came out of the house carrying a large pail of

steaming water, using a towel to protect her hands from the hot metal handle.

"Paul, help her carry that," Glynna said to her son.

Dare should've known Ruthy would be carrying the heaviest bucket she could find. He only needed a few cups.

Paul moved fast and grabbed the pail out of Ruthy's hands so quick she didn't have time to fight him for it, which her glare said she'd have done. Ruthy didn't expect anyone to do a job she could do herself.

"I'm going to make a poultice." Dare looked up. "But he'll need a bed. Ruthy, can we bring him inside?"

Dare knew folks who would forbid an Indian from coming in their house. If Ruthy was such a woman, he'd make a bed in the barn for Red Wolf.

"I should have thought of that. You told me to heat up water, but I didn't need to bring it out here. Give me back the bucket, Paul. We'll move Red Wolf into the room Dare took his nap in."

A mild flush heated up Dare's cheeks. "I wouldn't exactly call it a nap."

Ruthy gave him such a withering look, he figured he'd offended her by even hinting she might not let Red Wolf inside. That made Dare like her more than ever.

"Paul, take the water back in. Ruthy . . ." Dare then reeled off a list of ingredients he needed for his poultice, which sent Ruthy scurrying back to the house. Not a single thing heavy in that list.

"I'll send out a scout to find the village," Dodger said. "We'll be able to make good time when Luke gets back." He snapped out a couple of orders, and the cowhands split up.

Dare saw the look in the men's eyes. They'd be riding along and they'd go armed. Dare wondered if he should put up with going on a doctor visit with an armed escort.

"Get a horse for me, too," Glynna called after Dodger.

Dare flinched when he heard Glynna's determined voice. "No, you're not coming. It could be dangerous."

"And me." Paul must've heard his mother just as he was about to go inside. Of course the boy wouldn't let his mother ride off without him.

Janny was still here. Dare braced himself for the little girl to also demand a horse.

"Sure, you'll go, Paul," Glynna said firmly. "We'll need every hand. Now get the water inside and help Ruthy gather the ingredients the doctor needs."

With a sullen jerk of his chin, Paul turned and went inside.

Dare turned to look at Glynna, so delicate, barely healed from Flint's mistreatment of her. Her face scraped up from yesterday's avalanche. Now the confounded woman wanted to ride into a village of possibly hostile Indians. He opened his mouth to forbid it.

"I'm going." She cut him off before he could say a word. "You've been talking about all the medicine you need and how much work it's going to be to treat the whole village. You need every hand."

"Not yours. You and Ruthy and your children are staying here."

"I'm going. Did I not just sew up your back yesterday?"

"What's that got to do with anything? No one's gonna need stitches in the Kiowa village."

"What it's got to do with anything is, I've done more than

59

sew up bullet wounds. I've nursed my children through the measles. I've tended fevers caused by festering wounds. I've even set a broken arm. In fact, the only doctor in these parts who's better than me is you, Dr. Riker."

Scowling, Dare said, "I've told you not to call me that. I've not had proper training, and that means I'm not a doctor."

"Well, fine then. I'm the *best* doctor in these parts. From here on out, call me Dr. Glynna. I'm going. You can come along and hold the horses."

Dare thought *hold your horses* was a real good idea—for Glynna. "You've got no place in an Indian village. You saw the weapons we took from Red Wolf. We're going where we're not even sure to be welcome, and we could very likely meet resistance that includes tomahawks and knives and even guns."

"Red Wolf is here. He must have told his village he was coming for help. Why in the world would we meet resistance? You know very well, we'll be welcomed with open arms."

Some of the hired men who hadn't wandered out of earshot started coughing, and they pivoted to head for the barn. Dodger said, "I'll just start saddling. You settle this."

"Red Wolf came here, yes, but there may be others in the village who aren't happy about what he did." Dare decided to talk slow. Maybe then the half-witted woman would be able to understand just what a terrible idea this was. "And they'll be upset if he doesn't come back. They might take their upset out on us."

"They won't hurt us. We'll explain about Red Wolf and tell them we have medicine. We'll be fine."

"We'll be dead."

"Then you'd better not go, either."

"I have to go. I can't sit here and do nothing while people are dying for lack of a doctor."

"Which you are *not*. You said so yourself." Glynna turned from Dare and said to Janny, "You go on in with Ruthy. You can help tend this sick man, but I'm going to help in the village."

Dare closed his eyes. "You're not going and neither is your boy."

"Paul is about as tall as you, and just as fast. And judging by how much time you're wasting arguing when you should be tending that man, I'd say he's smarter than you, too."

Dare wondered if he knew Glynna well enough to take her over his knee. He reckoned not, but the idea had merit, and he didn't toss it away entirely.

In the meantime, he decided to settle this up quick. "You are staying here at the S Bar S and that is that. I am laying down the law. You're not going and neither is your son." By the time he was done he was roaring. "And I don't want to hear another word about it."

Glynna made a point of riding just a pace ahead of Dare. Glancing at him—back just slightly. She'd had more than enough of men dictating to her. A fact she'd just demonstrated very clearly.

"I can't believe you're riding with us." Dare glowered at her, but it was just words.

There was no action he could take to stop her, short of tying her up. Thank heavens he hadn't thought of that.

"I should have tied you up and stuffed you into Luke's house."

Which meant he had thought of it.

"That's your pride talking." She actually said it politely, trying to soothe his manly feelings. "You'll be glad I came along. I can be a big help."

He spurred his horse to ride beside her. She resisted the urge to speed her own horse up. No sense starting a race.

"Ruthy could've used the help, you know. I'm surprised we managed to persuade her to stay behind."

"Well, someone had to stay with the sick man."

Dare snorted. "You mean the sick man who carried a knife and a tomahawk in his belt? He's never seen Ruthy before in his life and could be a might upset if he wakes up surrounded by strangers."

"Red Wolf was unconscious. Do you think I'd have left Janny there if I was a bit worried? You can use every hand. Admit it."

Dare rode closer to her. He took a look at Luke, who was well ahead of them, and his voice dropped to a whisper. "Ruthy has a baby on the way, which I still haven't informed her of. Neither one of you women nor your son has a place in this mess. I should've stopped Luke from coming, too."

"Someone who speaks Kiowa might be the difference between life and death."

"In this peaceful village that is waiting to welcome us with open arms?" Honestly, Dare's sarcasm was not welcome.

"Dodger said they've got some English speakers, but Luke was hopeful his Kiowa language would make a difference."

Dare quit nagging her and they rode on, almost companionably for a while—well, more like the battle lines were drawn, but at least the silence was welcome.

Then he turned to her. "So where'd you go to medical school?"

More sarcasm. "What is that supposed to mean?"

"You said you know how to sew up bullet wounds and set a broken arm. Nursing the children through the measles . . . I can see how you learned about that. But was it one of your young'uns who had the fever caused by festering wounds?"

With a humorless laugh, Glynna said, "Except for the measles, my training all came from doctoring my husband."

"Flint?" Dare's eyes narrowed, and he was really watching her now, too interested.

"No, Reggie. Paul Reginald Sevier—was named for his father and his grandfather before him. And Paul is named for the lot of them. We always called my husband Reggie." Glynna never talked about her first husband. She'd buried her past, right along with Reggie, and good riddance to them both. Why had she brought him up? She would've been better to blame the war for her doctoring skills—which was true, mostly.

"He was a clumsy man?" Dare sounded sarcastic again.

"As clumsy a man as ever lived." Deciding it was past time to change this dreadful subject, she said, "Well, you learned doctoring somehow, but you say you're not a doctor. Would you care to explain that?"

Dare jerked one shoulder. "I told you, I was in Andersonville Prison. I helped the doctor and ended up learning a lot, but I never went to school. Never did what I should've done to be a real doctor."

Glynna considered that. "You treated me when Flint knocked me down. I think you're a very good doctor." She smiled but suspected it was a sad sort of smile. "I'm glad you were there, whether you've had all the right schooling or not. Thank you for helping me when I was so rude."

Their gazes met, and the only sound was the pounding of the horses' hooves as they moved toward sickness and possible danger.

"You've got the prettiest golden eyes, Glynna."

The compliment ended the moment. She turned to face forward. "I've heard enough flattery to last a lifetime."

The bitterness almost echoed across the canyon, though they still spoke quietly. "If my looks are pleasing to men, then I'd as soon be a shriveled old crone. Men have made my life a misery."

"I don't know Reggie, but if he's anything like Flint, I'd say you're right."

"He was nothing like Flint, but there are many ways to be a useless excuse for a man, and I've had my share of variety."

Dare chuckled. "Maybe your luck will change."

"It certainly will. I'm through with men." That was a very good reason why she shouldn't be looking deeply into Dare Riker's blue eyes.

"You've got one man there's no getting shut of."

"No, I don't."

"Your son."

Startled, Glynna looked at Paul. "I don't think of him as a man."

"I promise you, he thinks of himself as one."

It didn't suit Glynna to let her son come along. But the Indians were probably too sick to be dangerous, and she knew Paul would never let her ride off alone. And for once, he seemed interested. He wasn't glaring and glowering at every word out of Dare's mouth. He was, in fact, riding up ahead between Luke and Jonas, not even looking back to see where his troublesome ma had gotten to.

Maybe being needed would help Paul find himself again.

And then Paul looked back and scowled. He dropped back beside Glynna on her left. That drew Luke's attention and he fell back to ride close on Dare's right.

"How's your back?" Luke asked Dare.

"I'm good."

Luke snorted but didn't say more. Jonas was soon on Luke's far side, then Vince. The two of them led the pack horses.

Glynna looked down the row of strong men, four of them riding abreast. She felt their brotherhood. She prayed that Paul would learn to trust and depend on these men, but he'd been made suspicious in a hard school.

"How far to the Kiowa camp?" Dare asked.

"Dodger said it's just over an hour's ride," Luke said. "They're close to a herd of buffalo I saw yesterday."

"Buffalo, really?" Paul sat up straight and looked interested. "Can we see them?"

"I've never seen one, either," Dare said. "I wouldn't mind a gander."

Luke smiled at Paul. "I'll make sure you see 'em, but we've got to go to the village first. When I saw the buffalo yesterday, I figured the tribe would be close to hand and I was planning to ride over and speak to them."

"Red Wolf won't hurt Ruthy and my sister, will he?" Paul gave Luke a worried look.

"He's not going to be dangerous," Dare answered in his soothing doctor voice. "The way his lungs sounded and how hot his fever was, he'll be a mighty lucky man to beat this disease." Dare added, "He came to you, Luke. He'd heard you were back and he came riding, sick as he was, for help. His people must know he was heading for the S Bar S, so there's a good chance we'll be welcomed."

Luke nodded. "Yep, and there were others I knew too, besides Red Wolf. I went hunting and scouting with him and some other Kiowa boys, and Gil Foster. My pa traded with him and was right civil, not friendly like I was with Red Wolf, but they respected each other, and the Kiowa left us alone. The Comanche were never as friendly, though we did some trading with them. With the Comanche, well, there were a few scares, but nothing bad ever came of it."

Luke gestured to a line of trees that grew near a narrow canyon entrance. "The stream comes up out of the ground just ahead. We'll have to ride single file down the middle of the water to get through that canyon, then we're close to the Kiowa village."

Luke's voice took on a tone of command. "Ride mighty careful, and watch for sentries."

They strung out, and the going was slow in the shallow, rushing water. Glynna had never seen anything as beautiful as the red stripes in the jagged rocks all around them. When she'd first seen them, riding home with Flint, she'd thought all her problems were solved. The Palo Duro canyon was rugged, but the red was pretty and she'd believed she'd finally found a home.

When the canyon opened up, the gusting of the chilly November wind bent the stunted mesquite. The stiff wind and the scent of junipers helped her turn her thoughts from memories of Flint.

A cottonwood shot up here and there, and grass—some of it short in thick clumps, some tall as a horse—filled in the rocky landscape. They rounded a mesa and spooked a herd of antelope, then minutes later circled another mesa and a wide valley opened up before them. Grazing in the valley was a huge herd of buffalo.

Glynna heard Paul gasp at the magnificent beasts. She was pretty sure she'd made a similar noise. They were riding single file, and her son was right in front of her, trailing Luke.

"Give those critters a wide berth." Luke veered away sharply from the animals. "They're mean if they take a mind to be."

Glynna couldn't take her eyes off the herd. A couple of the spring calves took notice of them, and one even trotted in their direction as if curious. But the adults all kept grazing, as if riders were an everyday sight. Glynna had heard of the buffalo hunters and she could well imagine how easy it would be to shoot the big animals.

"Tighten up." Luke's voice snapped Glynna back from thinking of the majestic buffalo to see Luke pulling his horse to a walk until they'd all come up beside him. "Look ahead."

Smoke.

The ground was so broken it looked like the smoke came out of the earth, but as they continued forward, there was a steep slope. As they neared it, a teepee appeared about a half mile away, smoke curling from its top. A moment later, a second teepee came into view, not quite as tall, followed by at least a dozen more.

A breath of wind blowing in their direction carried the wails of mournful song and the smell of death.

CHAPTER 5

"Let's get down there." Dare tightened his grip on the reins, but Luke stuck out a hand.

"Slow, Dare. I know you want to help, and maybe they're beyond protest, but there's a right way and a wrong way to approach an Indian camp. We're going in slow and easy."

As they reached the slope and started down, there was no guard who stepped forward, no one came out, armed, to challenge them. Instead, there were bodies, dozens of them, lying to the side of the village in tidy rows. Though they could hear the loud cries, not one living man, woman, or child was visible.

"This is a fraction of the normal size of this village, even counting the dead," Luke said, picking up speed as if he couldn't stop himself from hurrying despite his own warning. "I wonder where the rest of them are?"

Dare did his best not to spur his horse past Luke, to get there and then get to work. To help.

As they neared the village, Dare said, "Luke, stop! This is as far as you're going."

Luke stared at the village, hearing the rise and fall of

wailing sobs joined with the chilly breeze until the whole world seemed to grieve. They were about a hundred feet from the village. "I've got to go in with you."

Dare shook his head. "No, you're staying back. If one of them comes out and we need you, if we can't avoid it, then fine, you can help, but there's no sense in you exposing yourself to the sickness if you don't have to."

"I didn't ride all this way to stay back and watch."

"No, you didn't. You rode with us because you can speak some Kiowa and because you wouldn't stay behind. You can speak to anyone we find, but from a distance, if they don't speak English. Get started unpacking the horses. There's plenty to keep you busy."

The opening on one of the teepees flapped and a woman stepped out, her arms laden with what looked like a bundle, a blanket.

"Stay here." Dare gave Luke one more dark look. "I don't need to add any more patients." Dare began riding toward the village, the rest of their group right behind him.

The Indian woman turned. Her wailing stopped and she shouted guttural words. As Dare approached the camp, the woman sank to her knees as if to beg for mercy. She looked healthy. Her hair, liberally streaked with gray, told him she was an elder of the tribe. And that bundle, that unmoving bundle, the way she clutched it—Dare knew it was a child who hadn't survived the measles outbreak. How many more were there?

Dare pulled his horse to a halt and swung to the ground, his focus on the bundle so complete that he was only distantly aware of the other riders dismounting. He walked up to the woman slowly, his arms extended so she could see he carried no weapon. The same couldn't be said of all those with him.

"Help?" He hoped she knew this one word.

The woman's brow furrowed, but she didn't run, neither did she attack. Other teepees flapped open, and more people emerged. One adult man, the rest women. Seven people in all.

The man held a rifle and swept it up to point it at the group.

Dare froze. The man was healthy, his aim held true, and his eyes looked deadly.

"We're here to help." Dare saw the rifle swing to aim straight at his chest. "We mean no harm."

Could they even hope to ride out alive? The man pulled back the hammer on his rifle with a loud metallic click. Luke's men wouldn't stand still while they were shot. This could turn into a bloody shootout within seconds.

Raising his arms, Dare said, "Red Wolf came to us." He enunciated each word, not even sure they would recognize the words *Red Wolf*. Surely the man's name was spoken in his own language among his people.

Then the man spoke words that Dare couldn't understand.

"Help. We help," Dare repeated.

Slowly the man moved forward, wary. Dare saw two of the women take a step forward, each carrying a knife.

"I am a doctor."

There was no relenting of the suspicion. Dare knew they would have to ride away—if they were allowed to.

"Anemy? I am Luke Stone."

Dare heard Luke right behind him and wanted to growl. But what was the point? Luke was all the way in, and if he got sick, Dare would doctor him.

"Red Wolf find Luke?" The woman spoke in broken English, then sighed until Dare thought she'd collapse.

Luke walked straight for the woman, right into the middle of the circle of teepees and drawn weapons. "Yes. Red Wolf reached my ranch."

"He lives?"

"Yes." Luke nodded. "He rests there."

A furrow creased the woman's forehead, and Dare doubted that she was understanding more than a few of the words Luke spoke, but she said something in her own language to her people and they seemed to relax, at least a bit. The rifle lowered, an inch at a time, toward the ground, but none of the Kiowa took their eyes off the group from the S Bar S. The knives were still in hand.

"Luke help my people?"

"Yes," Luke said, turning to point at Dare. "My friend, medicine man."

"Kiowa medicine man, Wise Buffalo, died as sun rose. Red Wolf rode away to find you."

"We will help, Anemy."

The woman turned to face the handful of healthy Kiowa. Anemy spoke swiftly in words that reminded Dare distantly of the few native people he'd seen from time to time.

Though there was no sign of pleasure at her words, the group nodded. Each of them retreated back into their teepees except the gray-haired woman with the bundle. She walked toward the row of bodies and, once there, knelt with the bundle and resumed her wailing chant.

Anemy turned back, and Dare stepped in, wanting to talk directly with her. "I need boiling water."

The woman's brow furrowed in confusion and she shook her head.

Dare turned to Luke. "Help me."

Luke came closer. "*T'on.* That's the Kiowa word for water." Then he said to Anemy, "You are Red Wolf's woman. I am a friend to the Kiowa. Please talk with our medicine man." Luke rested a hand on Dare's shoulder. "I will stay close. He needs *t'on.*"

A halting exchange between Dare and Anemy, with Luke's help, began to produce what Dare needed. Anemy's broken English became a bit better, as if talking with Luke was bringing back a long-forgotten memory.

"How long since your village fell sick?" Dare asked her.

"Seven suns. The first child red sickness. This come before. Spreads and kills."

While Dare worked, he found out that every family except the one with the sick child had packed up and moved a distance away. They'd left the child's family behind, but they'd also separated from each other, agreeing to return if the sickness came to them. Putting distance between them and a contagious disease. A self-imposed quarantine? These people had almost as much medical knowledge as he did. There were many families in this Kiowa band, but only these ones had returned, and it had been long enough that Dare hoped no one else had been exposed. The healthy ones here in the village, like Anemy, had survived the last measles outbreak. They'd stayed behind to tend the sick and bury the dead.

But he did have some medicine they didn't, like a good supply of willow bark tea, though maybe there were plants in this region with the same ability to bring down fevers.

With good care and proper medicine, he hoped he could save some who would have died. He also hoped that Luke would react like white people often did. Unlike native people, measles was an unpleasant illness for whites, but rarely fatal. White folks usually survived just fine, yet they were likely to expose tribal people to the terrors of disease.

"Do you have hot water . . . uh, *t'on*? I need to get to work."

Anemy nodded. "I show."

⚬⚬⚬

In the light of a fire in the center of the teepee, Glynna knelt and gently slid her arm beneath the shoulders of a delirious boy just a bit younger than Janny.

"Take a sip," she urged. Glynna slowly lifted him, every muscle aching after hours spent tending the sick children. It was time for another dose of the fever-reducing medicine Dare had prepared.

This little one moaned and struggled weakly. There were four other children in the teepee, also sleeping in the early hours before dawn. All of them needed the tea, but Glynna hated to disturb their sleep, because when they were awake, they cried from the torment of the itching rash and the burning fever.

There was barely room enough to move between them. "Paul, hold his head still. Help me."

Dare had moved all the children together, then put Glynna and Paul in charge. Glynna wondered if his aim wasn't more about her safety than the importance of getting the children in one place. Some of the stricken adults had fought Dare's treatment. Only the fact that the healthy Kiowa had helped calm their family had prevented serious injuries.

The children fought too, but they hadn't the size or the strength to do much damage.

Kneeling across from Glynna, Paul steadied the child's head, and the boy's whimpers rose to near screams. The rash was worst on this child until it no longer looked like spots. His whole body was bright red where it showed around the white poultice. Glynna prayed as she urged him to swallow, wondering if she was causing him pain everywhere she touched.

Anemy, the woman Luke had recognized, stuck her head inside the teepee. The suspicion in her eyes was hard to endure. Glynna didn't blame the woman for letting the distressed child upset her.

"Can you help?" Glynna knew the woman was running herself ragged trying to keep an eye on the people who had invaded her village. She didn't trust them, but she let Dare take charge. Anemy was doing her best to translate, talking mainly with Luke but answering questions asked by Dare.

Would helping make Anemy less worried? Or was it one thing too many for the overburdened woman?

Nodding, Anemy picked her way between the children

to kneel at the boy's head. She crooned to him in her native language as she used both of her strong hands to keep him from turning away from the tea. Paul supported the child in a sitting position. Glynna tried to squeeze the boy's mouth to get it open. Anemy reached for the boy's nose and pinched it. The child gasped for air, and Glynna, exchanging a lightning-fast glance with Anemy, quickly poured the tea in. The boy sputtered and coughed, but the tea mostly went down.

Glynna smiled at Anemy. "Good idea."

Anemy said, "Who next?"

Working as a team and using Anemy's method, the three of them got the medicine administered just as Dare came in bearing a basin of pasty white liquid with a stack of cloths over his arm. "Time for a new poultice. Cover the rash as much as possible. It will ease the itching and help them rest more comfortably." He set down the basin.

"How are they doing?" Glynna regretted speaking the moment the words were out. Anemy's attention was so rigid, fearing more bad news.

"We've lost three more." Dare looked at Anemy.

Anemy didn't respond. Glynna didn't know if she understood Dare's words, but there was no doubt she caught his meaning.

"They were so sick. There was nothing . . ." Breaking off his words, Dare looked overcome with guilt. Swallowing, Dare went on, "I see signs of pneumonia and encephalitis in quite a few of your tribe. Those are deadly complications." Dare shook his head. "I'm sorry, Anemy, but there is little chance those will pull through."

"Pull through?" Anemy didn't seem to know what this meant.

"Pull through . . . uh, get well. Live." Dare sighed, looked the woman in the eyes. "They will not live."

"More Kiowa die." The woman, though young, showed lines of grief on her face. "Red Wolf should be with his people."

Glynna remembered Dare saying Red Wolf had pneumonia. He gave orders to Ruthy before he left, but Glynna knew pneumonia was a killer. Yet a young, healthy man, with good care and God's healing grace, had a chance.

"Red Wolf is resting at Luke's cabin," Glynna said.

As always, the mention of Luke's name had an almost miraculous effect in gaining Anemy's cooperation. Despite the risk to Luke, because he was now exposed to the measles, they'd have never been allowed to help the Kiowa if he wasn't here working beside them.

Dare left the poultice. Glynna, with Anemy's and Paul's help, tended the children through that night and the following day.

A wail went up through the village too often. Glynna knew it meant another had died. The children held on. Dare, on one of his visits, said their fevers had lessened. Of course, the sickest had succumbed before the group from the S Bar S had arrived.

Glynna only knew the day passed because of the fading light. She was still on her knees, replacing poultices, bathing fevered bodies, dosing willow bark.

Dare came into the teepee. "I'll watch the little ones. There's food. Go eat and get a few hours' sleep."

Glynna lifted her eyes from the little girl she tended. Only then, as if she felt the effort it took to focus on Dare, did she realize how near to collapsing she was. "I can keep working."

"The children are asleep right now. They won't struggle as I examine them and listen to see if their lungs are clear. This is a good chance for you to get yourself something to eat and then a little sleep. I promise I'll wake you if I need help."

"You need sleep, too," Glynna said. She wanted to say more, but she noticed Paul had fallen asleep where he sat. His head was slumped forward and his eyes were closed.

Glynna stood and stumbled. Dare caught her and prevented her from tumbling onto her patient.

"You're done in, Glynna. Take a break now. I need you rested." Dare didn't let her go.

Glynna realized she was leaning almost all her weight on him. In the dim light of the teepee fire she saw the strength in Dare. He'd been up for just as long as she had, and he'd been hurt in the avalanche.

"How's your back?" she whispered.

His blond brows arched in surprise. Then his mustache bent upward in a tight smile. "Believe it or not, I forgot about my back. I reckon that means it's okay."

It couldn't begin to be okay, but Glynna knew he'd never quit working, so she didn't bother to chide him. She just stood there, supported by him, another burden. Their locked gaze seemed so open, as if she could look into his soul and see his need to heal, his grief when he failed, and his strength to bear what he must.

"You're a fine doctor. I don't care what papers you've earned or not earned."

"No, Glynna, I—"

She rested her fingertips on his mouth to stop his protest. "We can argue about what you should be doing with your life another day. Save your energy for doctoring these good people."

The prickle of his mustache on her fingers reached well past her hand until she seemed to feel it all up her arm, into her heart. Her very tender, very untrusting heart.

Lifting her hand away, she stood on her own two feet. They were too close, and she was drawn to him like she'd never been to either of her husbands.

For one moment he leaned closer, and she thought he'd kiss her—and even hoped it.

A soft cry from one of the children had them straightening away from each other.

Dare jerked his head toward the teepee entrance. "Go. Take Paul and you two get something to eat. One of the women made stew. Make sure to savor it—you won't get too many chances to eat buffalo."

Glynna decided retreat was a wonderful idea. Besides, being near Dare right now was too confusing. "Wake me when it's your turn to get some sleep."

Dare's eyes flickered to her lips, then away.

She turned to awaken Paul and saw he was watching them. Paul sprang to his feet and with two long strides was face-to-face with Dare and swung a fist. Between exhaustion and surprise, the fist landed hard on Dare's chin. The unexpected attack nearly knocked Dare into the fire.

Glynna cried in horror and caught Paul's arm as he drew back for another strike. "Paul! Stop that right now!"

Dare stayed on his feet, rubbing his chin and staring at Paul.

"You keep your hands off my ma. Leave her alone. She doesn't need another man. She's got me."

"Paul—" Glynna began.

"No!" Paul wrenched his arm from her grasp and turned on her. For one terrible second she wondered if her son would now hit her. She saw Dare gather himself as if he would step in to protect her. It made Glynna sick to think of Dare and her son fighting. Dare would win, a tough man and fully grown. Another terrible failure for her son.

Paul didn't swing. "You told me there'd be no more men. Not without my blessing."

Glynna was shocked at how deep her son's fury went. She searched for her authority as his mother. "Paul, there's no reason to think—"

"You're a liar."

"No, I've told you no lies."

"I should've killed Flint for what he did to you. I should've killed my own pa. But I was too weak to do it." Paul turned to Dare. "I'm not anymore. You stay away from my mother or I'll kill you."

Paul looked as serious as the tomb as he stormed out of the teepee.

Glynna exchanged a helpless look with Dare, then hurried after her son. At the teepee entrance she turned back to see Dare, still rubbing his chin, looking at her, his eyes blazing . . . though she wasn't sure with what. Anger? Regret? A man's interest in her?

She needed to learn how to live without a man. She had to do that if she wanted to do right by her son. But Dare's eyes, burning with blue fire, seemed to want her to forget all she needed to do.

She turned away before she made another terrible mistake. She couldn't trust her future to another man, no matter how appealing he was. She pushed herself on out of the teepee to find food and sleep and *sense*.

Dare barely noticed time passing, barely noticed the daylight from the nighttime. He ate when he could, slept when he collapsed, doctored the living, and laid out the dead.

The howl of the wind woke him. He was sleeping by a fire, outside, in the center of a circle of teepees. The sun peeked over the horizon and lit up a wall of red rock on the west side of the canyon until the world seemed to catch fire overhead.

He lay in the dark depths of the canyon and listened for the wail of grief or a moan of pain. He heard neither. Shoving himself to his knees, he realized the entire village was asleep. That hadn't happened since he'd arrived.

The last patient had turned a corner in the night. Most likely no more would die. He tossed wood on the fire and stirred the embers to life. As the flames grew and crackled, he saw all his friends sleeping around the fire. Glynna— who'd avoided him like he was a rabid skunk since her reckless fool of a son had slugged him in the face—wasn't here. He remembered that she'd gone to sleep in a teepee with Anemy. There were places to sleep in abundance because so many of the Kiowa hadn't survived.

His relief at knowing the worst was over darkened, and the weight of his failure rested like stones on his shoulders. As if that avalanche the other day had buried him alive.

Could a more skilled doctor have saved more of these folks? Of course there was no other doctor. The choice was between him and nobody, but he still felt his lack every time he lost a patient. Driving both hands deep into his hair, he sat back on his heels and bowed his head.

Please, God, let it be over. Let it be true that no more of them die.

A drumbeat of hooves drew his attention, and he rose and stepped away from the fire to help his night vision and to make himself a harder target.

A rider raced for the camp. Luke and Vince vanished from their bedrolls so swiftly and silently that Dare barely knew they were ready for trouble. The crack of a cocking gun came from the direction Luke had gone.

"It's Red Wolf." Luke stepped back into the light, holstering his gun. "He made it."

Dare wondered how long it would be until Luke started running a fever. Usually it took a week or two after a person was exposed to the measles. He realized he had no idea how long they'd been here. When they got back to the S Bar S, he'd ask Ruthy. She seemed like the type to keep track.

Vince came back to the fire when he heard Red Wolf's name and sat down, rubbed his face, and let his shoulders sag with exhaustion.

Several teepee flaps opened. Dare saw Anemy step outside.

"Red Wolf!" She said her husband's name with a cry of pleasure.

Red Wolf charged straight into the campsite and leaped off his horse to drag Anemy into his arms.

The reunion was so affectionate, Dare looked away, feeling as if he were intruding on a private moment.

As sick as Red Wolf had been, he should've been laid up for a week. Had he healed fast, or had they been here in the camp that long?

Luke strode over to his Kiowa friend, who released Anemy and turned, smiling. The two men shook hands firmly, and Luke clapped Red Wolf on the back.

They were dressed differently, but Luke, with his Italian heritage and deep tan, was nearly as dark as Red Wolf. They could have been brothers.

Their pleasure at seeing each other again helped Dare to let go of his sense of failure. After a few moments, Red Wolf slid his arm around Anemy and held her close as she spoke of what had happened while her husband was away. Red Wolf's grief was there for all to see, even in the dim morning light. He pulled Anemy close, and she buried her face in his strong chest.

Glynna stuck her head out of the teepee Anemy had emerged from, drawing Red Wolf's eyes. At first she watched the reunion in front of her, then turned away, as if it was too painful to see two people so much in love. Glynna's gaze fell on Dare. Their eyes locked.

Had Glynna never been held with that kind of tenderness?

Paul had spoken of his father with as much anger as Flint Greer. Dare wanted to go to her, tell her it could be like this between a man and a woman. Then he remembered Paul's killing rage and the fist that had nearly knocked him on his backside. Being with Glynna would only hurt the boy, and that was the last thing Dare wanted.

Dare had to try to help the boy get rid of his anger before it destroyed him. But how? The kid was so angry, he couldn't say a civil word to Dare. It wouldn't be easy, and it had nothing to do with Dare's interest in Glynna, but the young man needed to be saved from his own fury.

He fought down the urge to teach Glynna the kindness a man could show. Maybe someday when her children had healed.

The day was spent tending the ailing Kiowa, but most of them were on their feet now, the rash fading, the coughs easing, the fevers all but gone.

Red Wolf was much more fluent in English than Anemy, and the day went smoothly, with no new grief.

"The disease is no longer contagious," Dare told Red Wolf.

Frowning, Red Wolf carefully repeated, "*Con tay juss?* What is this?"

"It means the red spots will no longer spread from those who are sick to those who are well. It means the rest of your people can come home now."

With a satisfied nod, Red Wolf asked the other healthy man in the village to search for the rest of their tribe and tell them the good news.

As the man hopped on his horse and galloped away, Red Wolf turned to Luke. "Our people will return in time for the moonrise. Many of our tribe are not happy with the whites. They blame them for the red sickness that killed so many. It is best you leave. But I thank you, Luke. And you, medicine man." Red Wolf solemnly nodded at Dare. "I know good and evil cannot be judged by the color of a man's skin."

"Will you be near my home for long?" Luke asked Red Wolf.

"Many years the herd goes no more south. The grass is deep. I believe this will be our winter hunting ground."

"Then come to my home again, and bring Anemy. I'd like my wife to meet her."

Red Wolf's deeply weathered face brightened. "We will come. Your wife is a fine woman. I owe her my life, and Anemy has told me how you worked to save our people. You can remain on Kiowa land for yet another year."

Luke laughed. "And you can stay on Stone land for another year, my friend."

Red Wolf joined in the laughter, and Dare knew this was an old joke between them.

Red Wolf turned to Dare. "My people say you saved many."

Dare thought of all he hadn't saved and wanted to protest, but held his tongue. Next time he was needed, he wanted Red Wolf to know he would help. The Kiowa traded often with the whites, so they came in contact with them regularly. Unfortunately, diseases, strange and deadly to the Indian people, would come again.

"I was glad I could help," Dare told him. He then thought of Luke and the measles he was certain to catch. Turning his thoughts from the suffering of the Kiowa, and the image of Luke sharing in that suffering, Dare said, "Let's head home."

Riding away as the sun lowered in the sky, Glynna came up beside Dare. She looked toward him, and he saw surprise on her face. She hadn't meant to ride so close to him. She reined her horse back to put space between them, but then Paul rode up to where Glynna had been, and the anger in his expression almost made Dare rest his hand on his six-shooter.

Dare had seen other young men with anger like this. He'd fought beside them in the war. The young ones, once they'd lived through a few brutal skirmishes, often grew a ruthless streak that would put an older man to shame.

Living with Flint Greer might count as a brutal skirmish.

Paul wasn't riding armed, and it was hard to believe a kid like him would actually kill. Then again, he'd said it himself that he should have killed his ma's no-good husbands when he'd had the chance.

"Paul," Dare said, "I'm sorry I've upset you. But you can't let this rage you're carrying around eat at you."

"You just keep your hands off my ma and I won't be angry anymore," Paul seethed.

"Is that true?"

Paul furrowed his brow. "I just said it, didn't I?"

"I don't mean to say you're lying. I mean to say that I think the anger is something you're carrying around with you all the time. You've focused it on me, but it's always there, boiling and stewing. Why don't you ride out hunting with Vince and me? It'll help you realize there are more kinds of men than the two who've been so hard on your family. Most men will protect a woman and children. You know I'd never put my hands on any of you in anger, don't you?"

Paul stared straight forward, but his jaw wasn't quite as rigid as it had been. "I reckon hunting would be fun. I did some hunting back in Arkansas."

"With Luke in the area raising beef, hunting isn't as important, but I still like the taste of antelope now and then. You can ride out with us."

"I'll think about it." A look of interest pushed aside Paul's usual scowl. "But that doesn't change nuthin' about you staying away from my ma." The scowl returned with a vengeance. Paul reined his horse aside and dropped back to ride next to Glynna as if he'd taken all of Dare's company he could stand.

It was a better talk than any they'd had before. Dare had worked beside a lot of young men during the war, and maybe that experience would come in handy now.

Even with that bit of hope, Dare could feel the kid at his back. Dare sure hoped the young'un never took to carrying a weapon.

CHAPTER 6

Glynna Greer had a weapon of her own—aimed straight at the bellies of every man in Broken Wheel. Dare found out right along with the rest of the town why Glynna's children didn't want her to open a diner.

She couldn't cook worth a hoot.

His foot hit the bottom step on his way up to the board sidewalk that led to the diner just as black smoke billowed out its front door, followed by a herd of cowboys running out, coughing, and covering their mouths.

The diner had only been open a few minutes.

Well away from the building, Tug Andrews, who owned the general store, yelled, "Let us know when the smoke clears, Mrs. Greer. We'll wait."

Glynna stepped out of her restaurant, coughing, looking awful with her scabbed-up face. It had been two weeks since the avalanche, most of that time spent with the Kiowa tribe.

Looking at her now, Dare thought she probably should've waited another week. Although her face was so sooty, it covered most of the injuries, so it didn't much matter.

Especially since, soot and scabs notwithstanding, with

her golden hair and matching golden eyes, her customers all looked at her like she was the prettiest thing they'd ever seen.

Which she sure enough was.

"I let the potatoes boil dry. I'm so sorry," Glynna said. She folded her hands at her waist and smiled at the men. With that smile alone she gave them all a meal to tempt the most persnickety appetite. Dare doubted whether all that soot came from just burning potatoes, but then he wouldn't know. He'd never burned potatoes. He made a point of taking them off the stove before they began puffing out black smoke.

Her eyes went from the men to him, and her sweet, apologetic smile trembled a bit as if she fought tears. "I'm having trouble with the stove, I'm afraid. The top seems to have overheated."

"Anyone could have trouble with a new stove, Mrs. Greer." Duffy Schuster spoke from the waiting crowd. Duffy owned the only saloon in town and was a man with rough edges to spare. But right now he was acting like a Southern gentleman, at least when he wasn't spitting tobacco.

Another said, "Don't trouble yourself about it, Mrs. Greer. We'll be glad to wait."

"Could you all please call me Glynna?"

"We could never treat you with such disrespect, ma'am."

Dare smoothed his mustache to cover a smile. He wasn't sure who some of these men were. Most of them weren't from around here. Did that mean men had come from a distance just to eat a meal? But looking at Glynna explained everything. She was a terrible mess and still she was pretty enough to make a man's heart leap in his chest. All these men had shown up to get a look at her, and that inclined Dare less toward smiling.

"I don't know how many of you knew my late husband, Flint, but I can't abide having his name attached to mine." There was the softness of an Arkansas accent in her voice and a quiver of regret. She glanced over her shoulder. "My children have my first husband's name, so I will go by that. Call me Mrs. S-Sevier."

From the way she stumbled over her name, he knew she didn't like that name, either. Two rattlesnake husbands. Mighty bad luck for such a sweet, pretty woman.

Paul stepped out from behind her, his blue eyes shining out of a blackened face. He took a second to glower at Dare, who was so used to that look it didn't even bother him. Much.

"I got the tater pot out back, Ma. The smoke's thinning. You can all come back in now and eat a meal." He added under his breath, "Such as it is."

The boy turned and went back inside. Through the open door, Dare saw Paul go to his sooty-faced little sister and mutter, "Ma running a diner is a poor excuse for an idea."

Dare had noticed the children weren't encouraging to their mother in her plans. It made him mad. The poor woman could use their support. Only now he wondered . . . they might have their reasons.

Glynna smiled at her adoring customers, waved her hand to beckon them forward. "Come on back in," she said. "I hope you'll enjoy what there is left of dinner." She turned and went inside.

Dare was a bit slow to follow her, and he was nearly trampled in the stampede of men thundering past him.

He took one step toward the door just as someone clapped him on the back. On the side he hadn't just had stitches cut out of, so that was good. He turned to see Vince on his way to eat, it would seem.

"She finally got it opened, huh?" Vince had helped out by providing most of the food she was cooking. He'd "found" flour and sugar and potatoes in his storage cellar. He should've hung on to the potatoes.

"Hold up!" They both turned and saw Luke riding into town. Their friend swung down and hitched his horse, then came up to meet them. "I need to talk some details about my property with Mrs. Greer."

"Mrs. *Sevier*," Dare said.

"What? Mrs. Sev Yay?" Luke tilted his head as if maybe his ears had failed him.

"She just told every man in town to call her Mrs. Sevier. Says she doesn't want to go by Greer—her first husband's name, the father of her children."

"That's gonna take some gettin' used to." Luke shook his head. "She wouldn't take nuthin' for the land and cattle. She abandoned it all. She says the land Greer stole is mine, free and clear."

"Which is only right," Vince, the lawyer, said as if he knew what he was talking about.

"The land, sure, and some of the cattle, but Greer stole land and cattle from other men, not just my pa. I have no claim on that. And Greer owned a stretch of land before he took to his thieving. That land belongs to Glynna. I'm not taking it."

Luke held up a fistful of letters. "I'm writing to everyone

I can find who lost their land to Greer, telling them it's theirs for the taking. I figure these folks have a claim on a portion of the cattle raised on their land, too. I hope some of them come back. I found cash money stashed in Greer's bedroom—I'll starve before I take a penny of it."

"He made at least some of it working your land," Vince said.

"Don't matter. I don't want it."

The three of them walked into the busy diner while Luke talked. They were lucky to find three seats at the end of one of four long tables.

"What stinks?" Luke pulled his hat off, his eyes wide.

Dare slugged him. "Shut up. Glynna had some trouble with the stove. Give her a chance."

Paul came out of the kitchen carrying four plates. Each with a blackened . . . thing on it. Dare hoped he wasn't trying to serve the burnt potatoes.

He wasn't. It proved to be the roast.

The little girl named Janet poured coffee from a pot that was too heavy for her. The men helped as best they could. When Janet got to Dare, she'd lightened the pot enough that it wasn't such a chore.

Dare smiled. "Thanks, Janny."

The girl smiled back so shyly it put a little hitch in Dare's heartbeat.

A choking sound from the other end of the table drew Dare's attention as Sledge Murphy spit his coffee back into his cup. The twisted expression on the blacksmith's face said more than words could about Glynna's coffee.

Janet shook her head and whispered to Dare, "Ma

probably shouldn't've taken up a career as a cook." She slipped back into the kitchen as if running to hide.

Scowling, Sledge turned toward the kitchen, drew in a breath to shout something just as Glynna came out, twisting her hands together in front of her, smiling. Her face washed, her golden skin was a match for her hair and tawny eyes. But she was still bruised, pretty yet fragile.

Dare got ready to punch any man who said one word of complaint.

"Thank you so much for coming here today, gentlemen." Glynna's voice was soft, womanly. She spoke quietly, and everyone in the room leaned forward a bit to catch every word. "I know my husband was hard on this town. You've all been hurt by him at one time or another. That you came here today to my diner . . . well, I'm honored." Her eyes flashed golden and for a few seconds they brimmed with tears, but then she squared her shoulders and lifted her chin.

Her hair was in a knot on top of her head, with little blond curls escaping and hanging over her temples and ears and neck. Dare knew where all those curls hung because he looked mighty close for far too long. She was a vision so beautiful, her skin and hair and eyes all of a rich golden color, delicate. That she had a few bruises and scabs on her face made her look like she'd come through a battle, weary but unbroken.

She was the bravest little thing Dare had ever seen.

"I'm afraid I'm not giving you the best meal today," Glynna said. "It's not good enough for all you fine men who have no reason to support me after all you've suffered at my family's hands. I'll understand if you don't want to pay. This meal can be my gift and my apology to you all. Tomorrow will be better, I promise. I'll have a better handle on my new stove by then."

"The meal is fine, Mrs. Survey. Of course we'll pay you for it." The choking blacksmith took another swig of his coffee and couldn't quite control a shudder.

Nods of agreement from the men of their willingness to pay made Glynna's beautiful eyes well up again. But she fought back the tears. A vision of true beauty and courage.

Her son came in with four more plates, serving everyone some substance that appeared to be lumps of coal. Dare noticed the boy roll his eyes as he dodged around his ma and plunked more food down on tables.

Glynna drew in a shaky breath, blinked at them all just as everyone with a meal went to eating. "God bless you all for coming. I'll help get your meals to you now."

She turned and rushed back into the kitchen just as Paul slapped a plate down in front of Dare. Which made him quit staring at the spot Glynna had just vanished from, though the shape of her seemed to be burned into his mind like he had stared at the sun for too long.

Dare looked at Paul, who was glaring back at him. A jolt of annoyance almost made Dare say something to the kid. Then the smell of the roast beef distracted him.

"How long has your ma been cooking, boy?" Luke asked, poking at the beef on the plate in front of him. Luke had a woman cooking for him, so he had something to compare this meal to.

"*Cooking* is a word that has never meant the same thing to my ma that it means to others. She seems to have a powerful fear of rawness." Paul returned to the kitchen just as Glynna came back with two plates.

Luke was sneaky, but Dare definitely saw him take the meat and shove it into his pocket.

Vince muttered, "A perfectly good cow died for this." He started sawing on his own meat.

That meal was a show. Every man there watched Glynna move as if he were entranced. She wasn't flaunting herself; she was just so pretty it was impossible to look away. She continued to serve them and pour more coffee. It was a roomful of ruffians. Broken Wheel, a miserable little town in Indian Territory, was a place for outcasts. Dare wanted to exclude himself and his friends from that, but he wasn't sure he should.

Among these coarse men, no one was other than polite and proper. More notable, no one said a word of complaint. In fact, their thanks were generous and delivered at length. They ate so slowly that Dare knew it couldn't be blamed on the food—which a man had to eat slowly if he wanted to retain possession of his teeth. No, they just wanted to be in Glynna's presence for as long as possible.

Finally, with the longest noon break ever taken in Broken Wheel over, the crowd thinned out.

Dare noted that the cost of two bits for the meal had been paid by everyone. Of course, each man chose his moment and then paid Glynna personally; no one just left money on the table. She graced them each with a smile and a few words, a few seconds of her time and attention. That alone was worth the money, regardless of the food's quality. She also gave them the good news that she was going to be open for breakfast and lunch starting tomorrow.

God have mercy on them all.

Glynna's pockets were heavy with coins. Her restaurant, at least on day one, was a rousing success. Dare knew good and well every one of those varmints would be back tomorrow. Twice.

He sure would be.

He might eat before he got here, but he'd come. And he'd wear a coat with big pockets. He sure hoped she didn't serve stew. Although, considering today's meal, maybe her stew would be hard enough that it wouldn't make much of a mess in his pocket.

When at long last the diner was nearly empty of patrons, Glynna came out and looked at Dare, Luke, and Vince—the last ones remaining.

"It went well, don't you think?" She apologized for the food again. "Do any of you want more coffee?"

Luke had his back to the kitchen, so Glynna couldn't see his face when he closed his eyes in what looked like pain. "No, thank you, Mrs. . . . uh, what's your new name again?"

"Sevier."

"Sev Yay, got it. I'll try and remember. Mrs. Sev Yay, can you sit down for a few minutes?"

"Just call me Glynna, for heaven's sake." Glynna sat beside Luke at the end of the bench, straight across from Dare. Vince was on Dare's left, across from Luke.

"I've got a few things to work out with you about your land."

"I told you, I won't take a cent from you."

"You told me, all right, about fifteen times. I don't like it, but I understand how you feel. But that leaves me in charge of a bunch of land that's no more mine than it was Greer's. I'm not takin' nuthin' from that polecat." Luke pulled a stack of letters from his pocket. The chunk of . . . food rolled out and bounced on the floor with a loud *crack*. It reminded Dare of the avalanche just because that was the last rock he'd seen rolling until now. Vince caught the thing on the bounce and stuffed it in his own pocket. Glynna didn't seem to notice.

"I'm writing to everyone who lost land because of your husband." Luke ignored Vince, or maybe he was trying to keep Glynna's attention. He laid the letters on the table in front of her. "I've found who I can, and I thank you for your help with names and such. There were men in town who knew more names and where those folks ended up. I'm going to give back every bit of land that isn't mine. That leaves us with a stretch of land that belonged to Greer before he started with his stealing. What I can find tells me he owned it legally, so that makes it yours."

"I won't take it."

Luke sighed. "So you've said, ma'am, but it's still yours. It has to be dealt with, and no one but you can do it. Even if you want to give it away, it has to be done right and proper."

Glynna got a stubborn look on her pretty face. Luke didn't argue with her. He just looked at her, calmly but without backing down.

Finally she wilted. "What do you advise me to do, Luke?"

Dare wondered if Luke had learned that trick since he'd gotten married. Dare memorized the exact expression on Luke's face, planning to use it in his future dealings with the woman.

CHAPTER 7

Glynna began what could only be described as an all-out assault on the bellies of Broken Wheel. Because it had been Dare's idea, that might be something he would have to answer for at the Pearly Gates. On the other hand, it was going to be great for the doctoring business.

Yet despite the terrible food, no man in town would ever think of missing a meal. Glynna was just too pretty. All she had to do was come out of that kitchen with her golden eyes, grace each and every man with one of her sweet smiles, and the men figured they'd gotten their money's worth. Besides, none of them could cook worth a hoot, either. The difference being most of them had more sense than to try.

Every morning and noon, Dare went to the diner for a meal. He liked a moment of Glynna's attention as much as the next man. He was greeted by a crowd of men and billows of smoke. He had to hunt for a place to sit.

The diner was a true success, if you didn't count the food, and so far none of the men did. There was an endless parade in and out of Dare's office each afternoon. Mostly due to bellyaches. So Glynna was helping make Dare's business more successful, too.

These men kept him up late with indigestion complaints as well as glowing compliments about Glynna's pretty face and sweet manner. After a hard day of treating their bellyaches, Dare fell into bed, exhausted. He was asleep in an instant, dreaming about halos of golden hair, bouncing roast beef, and thick black smoke wafting toward him like a rain cloud, which then rained silver coins down on his head like an avalanche.

A loud crack jerked Dare awake. He smelled smoke, and considering his twisted-up dreams, it took him a while to realize he wasn't smelling dinner.

The smoke filled his lungs and started choking him, and he came fully awake to realize his house was on fire. He jumped out of bed and felt the heat coming up through the floor. Yanking on his britches, he snagged his boots and shirt but didn't take the time to put them on as he rushed to his bedroom door. He grabbed for the knob.

It was burning hot, and he snatched his hand back with a shout of pain. He knew, even in the pitch-dark, that his bedroom was filling with smoke. The cracking sound was something giving way, maybe the floor in the hallway. Then he saw a flicker of orange cutting through the smoke. Backing away from the door, he rushed to the bedroom window and flung it open. Flames shot up. This is where the light had come from—fire outside as well as in.

His window was right above a small roof sheltering the front door, and that roof was engulfed in flames. The crackle turned to a roar as if the fire were a living beast, consuming his house to fill its belly.

The floor he was standing on grew hot enough that, while he tried to think of a way out, he tugged his boots on, then his shirt so he could keep his hands free. By the time he was finished he was hacking, the smoke making his chest burn from within. He had to escape before the whole house collapsed under his feet.

One more glance out the window told him that way was out of the question. There was only one other. He went back to the door, grabbed the tail of his shirt to protect his hand, and twisted the knob.

Flames slammed the door open and exploded into his room. He staggered back and fell flat. A white-hot blaze shot over his head, straight for the window. Clawing his way backward, he saw he'd made a trail of fresh air to feed the fire.

On his back now, he felt the boards hot beneath him, the fire already eating into the wood from below. As the floor heaved and the fire howled, Dare remembered the war—the battlefields and those days he'd thought he knew what hell would be like. Here he was with another devilish example.

He knew the floor wouldn't last much longer. Praying for protection, the first burst of flames eased, and in the evil red light he saw, straight above him, the trapdoor to the attic.

The attic with its pull-down steps was right over his head.

Dare had rarely even poked his head up there. Going higher in this house seemed like a blamed fool idea.

Another loud crack told Dare something big had just

collapsed. The floor beneath him shuddered as if it had taken a hard blow.

He scrambled to his feet in the choking smoke. A rope hung down from overhead, and he reached up and yanked down the steps to the attic. Before leaving the room, he grabbed his doctor bag from where it sat near the door. Then he was up the stairs like a shot.

Remembering how the fire had rushed for the open window, he tugged the ladder closed to slow down the raging monster. He choked and fought for every breath. The fire was corralled for the moment, but the attic was also filling with smoke. Instantly Dare dropped to his knees, where the smoke wasn't quite as thick. He knew there was a window on each end of the attic. A glance at the nearest window showed flames flickering outside it. No way out on that side. He hitched the strap of his bag around his neck and crawled toward the far window, staying low to keep his head out of the smoke. He knocked boxes and furniture aside to clear a path forward.

His house was the last one on this side of town. Looking through the window before he opened it, he saw a long way to jump, but there was no fire to be seen anywhere.

He tugged on the window and it rose an inch, then jammed. He didn't have time for a struggle. A glance for something to smash the glass revealed a plank of wood close to hand. He picked it up and swung hard. The glass broke, but there was a wooden frame dividing the window into four small panes. He clubbed the window until the frame shattered and fell away and there were no jagged shards of glass left on the edges. Then he crawled out to sit on the sill. Three full stories high. He'd likely break his legs jumping, possibly even die. The roaring from the floor below told him he had no choice.

He turned to hang from the sill and cut a few feet off the fall. Facing into the attic, he heard a loud *whoosh* as the fire blasted up to where the attic steps were. The sill Dare sat on lurched, and he felt the building sway.

"Catch the rope!" The shout came from below.

Dare twisted to look down and saw Vince.

"Tie it off inside and slide down!" Vince with a lasso and a plan. God bless him.

"Ready?" The fire roared like a hungry panther, but Vince roared louder and swung the rope in a loop over his head.

Dare shifted to face outward. "Throw it!"

As always, Vince was skilled at anything he tried. The rope would've settled over Dare's shoulders if he hadn't grabbed it.

"Grab my bag." Dare tossed his precious doctor bag to Vince, who snagged it without trouble.

Climbing back into the attic, Dare quickly tied the rope off on a beam still holding up the roof. Another blast of fire exploded into the attic. The stored boxes and furniture were now catching fire.

The fire was racing straight for him, devouring everything, fed by the cool night air pouring in through the broken window.

Dare grabbed hold of the rope and went back through the window, sliding downward. Flames shot out the window just as his head dropped below the window level. Skin scraped off his hands as he scrambled, hand over hand, down Vince's lariat.

Flames crackled and howled above him as if they were angry he'd gotten away alive.

The rope couldn't last more than a few seconds with the fire chewing it to bits. He was still ten feet off the ground when it snapped.

Plunging, he landed with a heavy thud on his feet and fell flat on his back. The burning end of the rope landed on top of him. Cinders rained down, and his shirt caught fire. The whole side of the house fell straight for him.

Vince grabbed his arm and dragged him until Dare got his own feet working again. A blow to Dare's back almost knocked him down.

He looked sideways to see Vince slapping him as they moved.

"You're on fire!" Vince kept whacking until Dare's clothes were no longer burning. He glanced back. "The whole wall is coming down. Keep moving!" They doubled their pace.

A great *crack* drew Dare's eyes around to see the wall falling, coming toward them in a rush, refusing to let him escape.

With a deafening crash the wall slammed down just inches behind them. The concussion knocked them to the ground. Which saved them, as burning debris blasted over their heads.

Rolling and slapping at flames, Dare felt Vince fighting the fire on Dare's body and his own. Dare was almost too addled to help. Finally he could think, and he checked both of them. No flames on either of them.

They staggered to their feet and then turned back to see Dare's house completely engulfed in flames, the roof crashing in. But the important thing was that he'd made it out. He was okay.

Vince breathed hard. He was mostly recovered from Flint Greer shooting him a few weeks ago, but he wore out fast.

"My books," Dare said. He took one step toward his house. One futile step.

Vince gripped his arm and turned him away from the fire and landed the doctor bag Vince still carried right in Dare's belly. "You're alive. You can buy more books."

"I don't know how to be a doctor without them." Dare thought of all the volumes he had, destroyed now by the fire. He'd spent every cent he could spare on his books, studying like mad to learn enough to treat his patients correctly.

Jonas ran up, appearing out of the smoke and falling cinders. "Are you all right?"

His red hair caught the light of the flames until it looked like his head was ablaze.

"He got out," Vince replied, walking in the direction Jonas had come.

Dare's horse whinnied frantically. "I've gotta get my horse out of the corral."

There was a small stable near the house that had caught on fire and was even now going up in flames. The horse was on the far side of the corral behind the stable. Glowing red cinders rained down like brimstone in a wide arc all around the house, falling too close to the spooked horse.

"I'll do it," Vince said, "then I'm going to the other side. Good thing you're far enough from the woods and the town and there's no wind tonight. The fire shouldn't spread much, but we still need to keep watch."

Dare nodded, then tossed his bag behind him, well away from the flames.

Jonas turned to stand beside Dare. "What caused it?"

His question stopped Vince in his tracks. "I'd like to know that, too. Did you leave a fire in the fireplace or the kitchen stove?"

"No. I let them both die out, but I guess there was a spark."

"I got here pretty fast," Vince said. "The fire was all over the front door, burning straight up to the window of your bedroom. I ran around back and kicked the door open, and the flames were in the stairway. The kitchen with the stove, and your office with the only fireplace, were the last to catch fire."

Both men looked at Dare, who raised his hands as if in surrender. "I can't explain it."

"A lantern left on?" Jonas asked. "A candle burning?"

"Not by the front door. I don't have a lantern there or in the stairway, and I rarely burn candles." In the curling, snarling inferno Dare could almost see the devil dancing. He tried to look away and study the danger, the woods, the other town buildings. The horse in his corral was a ghostly shape, the black night made even darker by the contrast to the blinding firelight.

He saw his horse move, then saw a second horse. Dare narrowed his eyes. There weren't two horses in there. Was that a horse or a man? Who was out and about in the night but wouldn't show himself? Who chose the darkness over the light?

Dare took half a step toward the corral.

"A cigar maybe?" Vince usually smiled over most anything, but he was dead serious now.

His question drew Dare's eyes away from studying black shapes on a black night. There was nothing there, he decided, just shadows. "I don't smoke, never."

"Maybe a patient had a smoke?" In the flickering fire, Vince looked thoughtful.

"Nope." Dare had a clear memory of everyone he'd seen today. It had been busy, thanks to Glynna's cooking.

"Not even when you were out of the room?" Jonas asked.

"I'd have noticed the smell," Dare said flatly.

"I'll move your horse and then watch the fire from the other side," Vince said. "We'll talk about this later. Jonas, go watch that side." Vince jabbed a finger toward the back of the house nearest the woods. "Sparks are flying upward and can carry a long way. Be mindful of any that float into the woods. Dare, you take this side of the house and keep an eye out. This town hasn't got enough men to form a bucket brigade. We don't even have enough buckets, so there'll be no putting it out. But we can keep it from spreading. I hope."

Jonas left Dare and Vince alone. Standing there by the blazing, crackling fire, Vince said quietly, "I don't like it, Dare. I think someone set this fire on purpose."

Dare thought of that shape he saw near his corral. But had he really seen anything, or was it just shadows cast by the fire? "Who?" he asked.

Shaking his head, Vince strode toward the corral.

Sudden movement shifted Dare's attention just as Glynna came running toward him. Right behind her were Paul and Janet. They all looked like they'd dressed on the run. Buttons half closed and not lined up right. Shoes untied.

"Dare! You're all right." Glynna came at him, and for just a second their eyes met. Gold met blue. Her fear and relief were shocking to Dare for all they revealed. He thought for one moment she might throw herself into his arms. He was more than certain she intended to do exactly that. And he intended to catch her and hold on.

Then she stopped and clutched her hands together as if holding herself back physically. Her children came up beside her. Janet, scared and quiet. Paul, sullen and angry.

In other words, the same as always.

Dare saw the young man and thought something gleamed in the boy's eyes. Maybe the flickering of the fire cast something that wasn't there. But the youngster looked almost . . . satisfied. The boy didn't like him, didn't like any man who looked too long at his ma, and Dare didn't rightly blame him. Dare then noticed the youngster, unlike his ma and sister, was fully dressed.

A crash drew all of them around to face the fire as the second floor of the house collapsed. An updraft blew what was left of the roof apart, flinging flames in all directions. Jonas shouted just as Vince ran out of the corral, leading Dare's horse.

"Get back to the diner, but don't go inside," Dare ordered. "This fire could spread and the whole town could catch." Grabbing Glynna's arm and herding the children in front of him, he ran around the front of his house, giving the blaze a wide berth.

When he got around it, he saw that the fire hadn't caught anywhere further. Somehow the fire stayed contained, even as the rest of the house caved in.

A crowd was gathering, all of them prepared to fight the fire if it spread in order to save their own houses and businesses. Dare didn't much like his house burning down to nothing to be looked at like some kind of show, but he understood.

He thought again of his books.

The feeling he'd been fighting about doctoring grew as his house and all his doctoring books turned to ash.

That was when he got an idea that he should've thought of a long time ago. He considered it for all of ten seconds before he decided it was an idea with merit. Striding away from a fire that was staying put, he found Glynna standing in front of her diner, both children sitting on the steps, watching the show. Paul's eyes left the fire and burned right at Dare.

Dare made a point of staying well away from Glynna and speaking loudly enough that the kid could hear every word. "When Luke told you to deal with Greer's land, you said you didn't want any part of it."

"That's right. I won't profit off my marriage to that man." Glynna jerked her head in a sideways nod at the diner. "Besides, I'm doing real well with my restaurant. I can support myself and my children without touching Flint's ill-gotten gains."

"I want to buy it. Let's come up with an honest amount,

what it's really worth." Maybe it would be enough money to get her to stop serving up burnt offerings to the hapless, charmed men of Broken Wheel twice a day, six days a week.

They were all like moths to Glynna's flaming meals. She'd been cooking up a storm, almost literally, for two weeks now. And Dare had treated more upset stomachs in that time than in all the months he'd been here.

The men all saw the connection, they just couldn't help going back for more.

Dare hadn't missed a meal yet, either.

"You can have it. I'm glad that's settled. I've never really known where it is, but my understanding is that Flint had an old shack there. And that land is closer to town, I think, than Luke and Ruthy's place. You could live there and ride in to treat your patients without much trouble."

"I'm done with doctoring." Dare turned to face the fire. It was almost cheerful watching his life burn to the ground. He'd struggled with a lot of guilt since he'd failed so miserably with Glynna, not recognizing Flint's mistreatment of her. He'd learned a lot of doctoring in the war, but he'd never gone to medical school. In fact he'd had precious little schooling at all. And he'd taken foolish pride in not wasting years studying.

Until his training had failed him.

"This town needs a doctor." Glynna clearly wasn't seeing the good in his new decision.

"They sure enough do. I hope one moves to town right soon."

Glynna plunked her fists on her hips. "That's not what I mean. There are four empty houses in this town right now. They've been abandoned. Some even have furniture in them. So you could move right in. That's what I did with the diner. You can be back in the doctoring business tomorrow."

"Just sell me your land. I'm going into ranching."

"No, I refuse to profit from my marriage to that varmint, and besides, I think you're making a mistake. Do you know anything about cattle? Did you grow up on a ranch yourself?"

Dare was silent for a long time. Finally, though he hated to admit it, he said, "My pa was a wheelwright. That's useful for a rancher."

"Only if your cows have wheels."

Dare, disgusted, said, "We'll talk about this later. You can all go back to bed. The fire's dying. It's not going to spread."

They didn't move. Which irritated him. "I'm glad watching my whole life burn down is fun for this town."

Every man, woman, and child in Broken Wheel was out watching the blaze. Of course "every woman" was Glynna. And "every child" was Janet. Paul didn't count. He was taller than his ma. Dare sure hoped the youngsters learned to cook soon. Someone in this family had to before everyone in town had a stomach in full rebellion.

No reason Paul couldn't learn. Dare had been working with his pa for years at Paul's age.

Which was why he had next to no schooling.

Which was why he'd never had a chance to go to medical school and get the training he needed.

Which was why he was a fraud and a liar and a failure.

Which was why he was going to buy Glynna's land and become a rancher.

He wondered what all a rancher did besides watch their cattle get fat, sell them and count the money. Luke seemed to keep busy, but Dare had never watched him real close. Maybe the man slept until noon and barely stuck his nose out the door.

But there had to be more to it than that.

"Good night, Dr. Riker." Glynna herded her children into the diner.

CHAPTER 8

Glynna looked back to see Dare striding toward the crowd in the street watching the fire. Just as the children got inside, she heard a strange scraping noise from around the side of her building.

She stopped and listened. What was that?

It was long past midnight. It wasn't too frigid outside, but neither was it a night someone would stand around in unless a building was burning down. Glancing back at the fire, she saw all the townsfolk still standing there, still watching.

If someone was out there, why wasn't he gawking at the fire like everyone else?

A tiny whine came after the scrape.

What was that?

Her diner was the last connected building on this short stretch of what amounted to Main Street in Broken Wheel. Glynna hesitated. A dangerous animal wouldn't wander into town, would it? Maybe if it was injured or rabid. One cautious step at a time, she went to the end of the board-walk and peered around the corner to see. . . .

"Lana?"

Lana Bullard. She'd vanished after her husband, Simon, died in the same shootout where Flint had been killed.

Flint hadn't liked Glynna associating with anyone, and Lana had shown no inclination to associate. Flint made sure Glynna heard of Lana's disreputable past, and Glynna, more out of fear of Flint than any snobbery toward Lana's past, had stayed away from the woman.

Lana was the only other woman around back then. Ruthy hadn't lived here then. Ruthy had come to town with Luke because he'd found her stranded in the wilderness after being swept away from her wagon train by floodwaters.

Luke had come home to regain his ranch, and as part of that, the Regulators had saved Glynna from Flint. To flush Flint out of the well-defended ranch, they'd had Glynna hide and made it look like she'd run off.

Flint came charging into Broken Wheel with his men to drag her back home, and he'd been faced down by Dare, Luke, Vince, and Jonas, as well as their Texas Ranger friend Big John. Flint and his foreman Simon had died. The other gunslingers Flint employed went to jail. Luke married Ruthy and moved back home to his ranch. Glynna, meanwhile, moved into the abandoned diner with plans to start a business.

And Lana was never seen again. Until now.

Now here she was, crouched down in the shadow of the diner, trembling with cold. Only the light cast by the flames made her identifiable. Where had she been all this time?

"Are you all right?" Glynna asked her.

Slowly Lana stood, using the building for support. Glynna hurried to slip an arm around Lana's waist. She'd been a stout woman, but now she was so thin, Glynna was scared for her.

"Let me help you."

Paul appeared on the board-walk. "What's going on?"

Her son. So angry and suspicious and, under that, scared. Glynna wondered if he'd been changed forever. If he was safe long enough, could he rediscover the sweet boy he'd been?

"It's Lana Bullard, Paul. Looks like she needs care—something to eat and a warm place to stay." Glynna thought of the town doctor, the obvious person to send for. But Lana might only need a hot meal and a warm bed, and that was all. She'd leave Dare alone for now.

Paul hurried down to help support Lana.

"I'm just tired is all." Lana's voice broke. "A meal and a bed sound like heaven."

Glynna, with a lot of help from Paul, got Lana up the single step to the board-walk and then inside. They helped her to a chair, and she nearly collapsed onto it.

"Paul, get a piece of bread and some milk."

Paul dashed off to the kitchen. Janet stood, half hidden by the door that led up to their attic room.

Glynna touched Lana's forehead. No fever. She was deeply chilled, though. Her fingers were like ice. Her face was deeply lined and filthy.

"Stir the fire in the kitchen stove, Janny, then add some kindling and push the old coffee forward so it'll heat." Glynna asked too much from her children, she knew. But she was afraid that if she quit supporting Lana, the woman would topple over.

"Whiskey," Lana said. "I just need a drink and I'll feel better. And I ache. Have you got any laudanum?"

That told Glynna more than she wanted to know about Lana Bullard. "I don't have either and can't get any." She wouldn't get any if she could, but that was news Glynna would pass on later.

Lana folded in on herself, and only Glynna's quick reaction kept the woman from slumping to the floor. Paul was back with bread and milk. In the kitchen, the thud of wood being dropped into the stove told Glynna that Janet was hard at work stoking the fire.

Paul set the food down.

"Eat something, Lana." Glynna tugged on Lana's shoulders to get her to sit up straight enough to see the food.

Paul turned the lantern up, and Glynna got her first good look at the poor woman. She'd only seen her a few times before, and that was from a distance.

Her dark hair was graying and greasy and snarled so badly that Glynna wondered if they could get a comb through it, and Lana's skin was as pale as ash. She reached grimy hands for the bread, a curve of dirt under each nail. Glynna was tempted to stop her and make her wash before she ate, but she wasn't sure Lana had the strength.

"Paul, get a basin with warm water. The wells on the stove should be warm by now."

While Paul did as he was told, Janet came in and began thrusting small logs into the potbellied stove in the dining room to heat it up. Janny had thought of it on her own.

The fire crackled. They could be generous with wood because the diner was thriving, and beyond making money, the men kept showing up with wood already chopped and split. Glynna had a winter's supply already with more coming every day.

Lana took a bite of bread and grunted. "What is this?"

"Bread," Glynna answered. "It must've dried out some."

"Honest?" Lana looked up and for the first time seemed to really see Glynna. Lana's face was deeply lined. Her skin hung nearly in folds on her emaciated face. Glynna wondered how much work it was going to be to get Lana to take a bath. Fortunately, because of the weight loss, she'd fit into one of Glynna's dresses, and then Glynna could burn the rags Lana now wore.

"Yes, I'm sorry. I baked it this morning."

Lana took a sip of milk, shuddered, then drank the rest of it down fast, like she was taking a dose of foul-tasting medicine.

"Janet, go upstairs and get my green calico dress, please."

Janet vanished as if happy for an excuse to run away.

Paul came in carrying a small washbasin. He had towels draped over his arm and a bar of soap clutched between two fingers. Her son knew exactly what was called for.

"I got the biggest tin tub and put it by the fire in the kitchen. I filled it with hot water for bathing. I filled an empty coffeepot with more warm water on the stove to use for hair washing. I also refilled the water wells. More oughta be warm soon."

"Thank you." With pride, Glynna realized her boy was thinking faster than she was.

"If I weren't starving, I'd never be able to swallow this bread." Lana took another bite. "I can bake better bread than this in my sleep."

Miffed at the woman, Glynna said, "Would you like some more milk? That's all we've got that hasn't been prepared by my hand."

Glynna didn't bother to offer the woman any roast beef. That had dried out some, too.

"Bring the milk. I hate it, but it weren't burned past eatin' at least."

Janet was back with the dress for the ungrateful wretch.

Paul returned with more milk.

"Go on to bed now, children," Glynna said. "I'll help Lana wash up."

Both of them left eagerly. As a rule, they didn't like their ma being out of their sight. But this was Lana Bullard, a woman. Usually their ma was surrounded by men.

It was a night to remember, no matter how badly Glynna would have liked to forget it. Lana cooperated in nothing. Glynna got her to stand in the tub and endure a bath mainly because the woman was too weak to protest.

She put on the very modest calico dress only because Glynna burned her other one. Glynna did end up cutting Lana's hair to shoulder length and did a poor job of it, but there was no other way to bring order to the rat's nest on Lana's head.

Finally, in the wee hours before dawn, Lana Bullard had her hair washed and combed. Her dress was on and her belly was full, though mostly of milk.

"Let's go upstairs now. You'll have to sleep on the floor,

though. I have a blanket for you but nothing else at the moment."

"Do you mind if I sleep down here?" Lana had a shifty tone, and Glynna fully expected to wake up in the morning to find the woman gone. Which suited Glynna fine. If a starving woman's first request was for whiskey, then she had no place here in Glynna's home. There was no money lying around and no whiskey on the premises. Lana was welcome to anything else she decided to steal.

"I'll bring a blanket down for you," Glynna said, then went up the stairs and straight back down with the blanket. "I'll see you in the morning."

"Good night, Mrs. Greer."

Glynna decided to wait until the morning to correct Lana about the name—if the woman was still here.

The next morning, when he ducked out of the buffeting wind and into Glynna's diner, Dare almost tripped over his own feet.

It smelled like heaven. The place was packed, even for Glynna, who always did a bustling business.

Men were actually swallowing the coffee with not a single shudder.

Then Dare saw the eggs. They were yellow; he'd expected something a bit darker. One plate had the eggs with the yolks all together, surrounded by the whites. Since when did Glynna know how to do that? Maybe she'd finally learned how to use the stove.

Glynna stepped out of the kitchen carrying a coffeepot, and men everywhere extended their cups.

Dare found a seat at the corner of one of the tables. Vince was here, but there was no open seat near him. Dare had slept on the floor at Vince's house last night and awakened to find Vince gone.

Jonas was at another table, and he glanced up at Dare, waved, then went back to reading something.

Glynna smiled at Dare and came to him with her pot and a tin cup.

Paul came out of the kitchen carrying plates piled with fried potatoes, bacon, and eggs. Not a one of those things was black. On each of Paul's four plates sat a golden biscuit. It looked like the crown on top of a royal feast. Dare's mouth watered. The boy was busy waiting tables; so was Glynna. Was it possible Janet had learned to cook?

Dare got his plate and tore into the hearty meal. A few of the lingering men had moved on—and of course he did some lingering of his own. A chair beside Dare opened up. Vince walked over and sat beside him.

"What!" Jonas rose so suddenly he tipped over the bench, which was now empty except for him. He stared wide-eyed at the paper in his hands. He ran one hand deep into his red curls without tearing his eyes away from the letter.

"Bad news?" Dare knew Jonas had family back East—a little sister and maybe an aunt.

"It's . . . it's . . ." Jonas fell silent as he read it again. "It's impossible."

"Did someone die?" Vince went to Jonas and, with a firm hand, guided Jonas over to Dare's table. He had to apply some force, but he got Jonas to sit down.

Jonas's mouth opened and closed like a landed catfish.

Finally, because he always thought he knew best, Vince snatched the letter out of Jonas's white-knuckled grip. It was only one page. A second page or two or three was left behind at the spot where Jonas had been eating. It had to be from Jonas's baby sister. The girl was famous for her long letters. This page was clearly about something that was not good news.

Vince gave a bark of laughter and shoved the paper back at Jonas. "Your little sister is coming to live with you?"

It was bad . . . for Jonas. Dare didn't figure it would bother him overly. It wasn't *his* sister. Of course, this land could be hard on women. Glynna's husband had almost killed her. Ruthy had been nearly drowned and involved in a land war. Lana Bullard was crazy. The Kiowa woman Anemy had watched half her village die.

Nope, no place for a woman. Dare said, "Tell her she can't come."

Dare felt like he knew Tina Cahill at least some, and any problem of Jonas's was a problem for all the Regulators.

"She's already left," Jonas replied, nearly choking on the words. "I hardly know her."

"Sure you do." Vince clapped Jonas on the back, clearly enjoying the parson's distress. "She wrote you constantly during the war. We all got to know her. Those letters coming to Andersonville were like a ray of sunlight."

"A ray of sunlight?" Jonas turned to Vince, his teeth bared. Speaking through a clenched jaw, he said, "She's got no business coming here to Texas without asking. And we live in a desert—we don't need any more stinking sunlight."

121

Vince raised both hands like he was surrendering, but of course Vince never surrendered. "She'll be all right." Vince's voice broke on a laugh, quickly squelched. "We'll help you guard her from the no-account cowboys who want to marry her, the cougars that'll aim to eat her, the avalanches that'll try to bury her, and the Indians who might want to scalp her or maybe just carry her off. It'll be fun."

Jonas clenched a fist, while Vince, no longer pretending not to laugh, prepared himself in case he had to run.

"You didn't mention lunatic women," Dare added, having fun for the first time in a while. "And don't forget rattlesnakes and fires and stray bullets and . . ."

The fight went out of Jonas, and he leaned forward until his forehead clunked on the table. Dare was glad Vince had moved him, or his face would've landed right in his plate of food.

Jonas, speaking past the wood, mumbled, "I don't know how to care for a child."

"Christina can't still be a child," Dare said. He'd read Jonas's letters from his sister. The girl was a letter-writing fool, and they'd all read them over and over in Andersonville until they felt they knew her. She *had* been a ray of sunlight. Dare wondered if those letters hadn't saved his sanity. Jonas hadn't seen the girl since he'd left home at least a decade ago; only her letters had kept them connected. But she was a pill. A pesky, prissy little reformer. She often told stories of how she was fighting to change the world, or her little corner of it anyway. Broken Wheel was going to have to look out.

"Yep," Jonas said, "and Aunt Iphigenia remarried, and

apparently there's been trouble between Tina and Iphigenia's new husband."

Dare expected the new uncle had been on the receiving end of Tina's wagging finger once too often.

"Aunt Iphigenia found a freighter who travels with his wife. They'll give Christina a ride to Broken Wheel. She's already on her way. Aunt Iphigenia paid her fare. It sounds like my penny-pinching, cheeseparing aunt was eager to do it."

Dare and Vince exchanged a look, then both of them started laughing.

Vince scrubbed both hands over his face. "Good luck, my friend. It sounds like you're going to need it."

Jonas lifted his bowed head, scowling at them. "I left home when she was a toddler. I went home now and then, but I haven't seen her since she was . . ." Jonas fell silent, and Dare saw him moving his fingers like he was counting. "She couldn't have been more than ten years old, maybe nine. And then I only saw her for a couple of days. Aunt Iphigenia didn't approve of me, so I mostly stayed away."

"Well, you ran wild for a few years," Vince reminded the parson. "Your aunt had a point."

"How am I supposed to take care of a little girl?"

"How old is she now?" Vince asked.

Jonas shrugged. "I'd say eighteen or nineteen."

Dare laughed. "She isn't a child anymore. I had two sisters married and already mothers at the age of nineteen."

"She was always a chubby little thing."

"Chubby?" Vince said.

Jonas scowled at him. "Okay, she was a tub of lard. She

had skimpy bits of flyaway white hair always snarled up. More than her share of skinned knees. She had a black eye once when I was there. Aunt Iphigenia told me Tina was apt to get sent home from school for scolding the other children, and she wasn't afraid of a fistfight if she thought someone had it coming. I had to play big brother and protect her a few times. It was usually her own fault that she got in trouble." Jonas's red brows lowered. "And from her letters I'd say she's still not a careful young woman. She's coming to a town full of men, and she's going to start right in reforming all of them."

Smiling, Dare recognized the big-brother attitude and couldn't say he blamed him. "You can probably take worrying about no-account cowboys showing interest in her off your list. There isn't a man in all of Texas who'd put up with a fat, bald woman scolding him. So we can stop worrying about that, whatever her age. That only leaves cougars and avalanches and Indians and lunatics and fires and—"

"She'll want to reform both of you, too." Jonas glared at Dare's smile.

Vince's smile shrank away.

Dare had no interest in having a woman haranguing him. "When she gets here, tell her to stay on the wagon. We can all chip in to pay the man to haul her away. She'll have to learn to get along with her new uncle."

Vince and Dare being upset seemed to cheer Jonas up considerably, which didn't seem very Christian of him. He changed the subject. "I found you another house, Dare. There's a decent one right behind the diner. It's right next door to the parsonage. No one's got a claim on it."

"I'm through being a doctor. That house burning down was a message straight from God."

A loud clatter of fast-moving wheels sounded outside and a man shouted, "Whoa!"

Dare turned to see a covered wagon skidding to a stop right outside the diner window. A cloud of dust swallowed the man sitting high on the wagon seat.

"I need a doctor!" The man, who had ebony skin, leaped to the ground from the dangerously high seat. "Somebody help me! My son, Elias, I think he's dying!"

Dare was outside in the blustery November wind before he gave serious thought to moving. He sprinted for the back of the wagon, meeting the man as he turned, holding a young boy in his arms. "He's running a high fever."

"I'm a doctor." Dare took the child, burning hot.

Vince was at Dare's side. "Bring him to the law office."

Dare saw a woman and two more boys, younger than this one, climbing out of the wagon.

"We have to get him out of the cold. Follow me." Dare hurried after Vince, who had his desk cleared by the time Dare got inside. It was the only flat surface in the room.

Stretching the child out, Dare looked up at Vince. "Get me cold water. We've got to get this fever down."

"I'm on it, Doc."

Dare thought he heard sarcasm in Vince's voice and undue emphasis on the word *Doc*, but he was too busy to pay it any attention.

CHAPTER 9

"His fever broke." Dare straightened from the child's side and staggered.

Vince caught him and did his best not to smile. Dare could not stop being a doctor.

"How long has it been?" Dare rolled his shoulders and twisted his neck back and forth to ease the aching.

"I don't know." It'd been the longest day of Vince's life, helping Gil Foster chase after his harum-scarum sons. "Hours . . ."

The sun had set, and this whole thing had started during breakfast.

Elias had roused a few times, mostly shaken out of his unnatural sleep by fits of painful coughing.

"Will my son be all right, Doctor?"

Vince heard the almost worshipful note in Melanie Foster's voice. Dare had that effect on women. Mrs. Foster was a pretty lady with shining black skin, wearing faded yellow calico. Melanie had worked like a mule skinner, refilling Dare's basin with cold water, heating water so the boy could breathe moist air under a tent. Fetching and carrying, following orders as fast as Dare could give them, which was real fast. The woman had done anything and everything she could to help. She stood now wringing her hands as if to stop working was to let her son die. Her husband, Gil Foster, and the other children had been in and out. Tending the two active younger sons, one just a toddler, was keeping Gil, an old friend of Luke's, mighty busy.

Jonas had helped Vince chase after the young'uns, but he'd needed to split his time inside praying with the mother, leaving Vince and the boys' pa to tend them alone for the most part. Glynna and her children had helped too, but they'd had a crowd in for the noon meal and weren't available most of the time. Those little terrors were more than a two-man job.

Glynna had offered her rooms above the diner for naps, and Gil had grimly informed her that his sons had given up napping at about a year old.

"Your son has pneumonia," Dare said.

As if to prove that, the boy inhaled and his chest rattled. Then he exhaled with a groan.

"He's going to need care for a while, but usually, if I can get the fever to break, the patient makes it." Dare rubbed the back of his neck.

The woman let out such a huge sigh that Vince thought she might just deflate all the way to a puddle on the floor. She did sink, and Vince took one step to catch her, but through pure luck there was a chair behind her and she sat down hard.

"Thank you, Doctor." Melanie could barely choke out

the words. "Thank you so much. God bless y-you." Her voice broke and a sob tore from her throat.

Dare looked at Vince helplessly.

Vince shrugged. He hated crying. "Don't look at me. You're the doctor."

The distraught mother buried her face in her hands and wept until she bent in half. Vince wondered if he oughta go pat her on the back, or maybe fetch her husband. Then Vince might get stuck chasing after those wild boys who were rampaging all over town—which would be better than watching a woman sob.

Dare dropped his voice to a whisper. "I'm just going to let her cry for a bit. I think she needs to."

"That's a stupid thing to say," Vince whispered back. He could've probably spoken right out, as weeping was a noisy business. "No one *needs* to cry."

"I think maybe they do."

"They don't and that's that. I'm not listening to hogwash about needing to cry from a man too lazy to go to doctoring school."

Finally the crying quieted and the woman regained control of herself. Shuddering as she straightened, her eyes glowed with gratitude. "You saved my son, Dr. Riker. He would have died without you."

Vince looked at the tent Dare had erected around the boy, the steaming kettles to make the air humid. Dare had coaxed medicine down the boy's throat, which he'd been lucky to find in the general store, Dare's own medicine supply having burned. There had been warm liquids that the boy had resisted swallowing, including beef broth that

Vince had fetched from the diner with a sense of wonder that it wasn't crispy, a chest plaster that Vince remembered his nursemaid used to make, and constant bathing with cool cloths.

Dare had indeed saved this boy.

Frowning, Dare said, "Ma'am, it's important that I tell you I'm not a doctor. I worked with a doctor in the war, but I've had no schooling for this."

"You are in every way a doctor, sir." Melanie dabbed at her eyes with a kerchief she pulled from her sleeve, and then her eyes glinted as if she would fight anyone to the death who challenged her on that. Except the only one challenging her was Dare himself, and she wasn't about to kill him.

"No, I can't let you think that. I've got some healing skills, but to present myself as a doctor is wrong."

And since Dare had been presenting himself as a doctor ever since he'd come to town, Vince hoped it wasn't all the way wrong. Did they arrest people for impersonating a doctor?

How about a lawyer?

His eyes went to his copies of Blackstone's *Commentaries on the Laws of England*. Reading them, and a whole lot of other books, was all he had in the way of schooling. He'd never exactly been asked to do any lawyering of a complicated nature, so it'd been sufficient. Probably illegal but sufficient. Especially sufficient in a miserable little town in the middle of Indian Territory.

"Should we send for the doctor, then?" Melanie asked. "Why didn't we call him in earlier?"

Silence fell over the room. The woman, and Vince too, wondered what Dare would say to that.

"There isn't a doctor in town, ma'am," Dare said.

"Are you saying you wish you'd let my son die rather than present this masquerade of being a doctor?" She sounded genuinely offended, and Vince couldn't blame her.

"I'm just trying to be honest with you. I don't hold with lying, and to let you go on thinking I'm a real doctor is a low-down lie."

The woman, her eyes red and swollen from tears, smiled. "You are what the good Lord gave me today when my son needed help, and you'll always be Dr. Riker to me. God bless you."

Vince thought the tears were starting up again and prepared to put on his high boots to escape the flood. Instead, the woman squared her shoulders and lifted her chin in a show of good sense. "I believe I mentioned that my husband, Gil, and I are here in response to a letter sent to us by Luke Stone. Do either of you know him?"

"We do indeed, ma'am," Vince said. He welcomed the change of subject to—he hoped—one less likely to bring on another bout of soggy caterwauling. "He's a friend of ours. He got his ranch back from Flint Greer, and he's trying to restore the land Greer stole from others."

Scowling, Melanie said, "That Flint Greer was an awful man. My husband left to fight for the North, and before he got back, his father died and his mother went back East. His mother said Greer killed Gil's pa, but there was no way to prove it. There was no home for Gil to return to. We were married and living a hardscrabble life when Luke's letter came. We decided we should come home to Texas."

"Well, I'm Luke's lawyer. He's spoken fondly of your husband and the time they spent running the hills as children. I have a list of who all he contacted. I know your house is still standing on your property. You can go on out to it right now and settle in." Vince really wished she'd go. Her eyes were still a little watery.

"I need to stay with my boy."

Of course she does, Vince thought.

She sniffled in a threatening manner . . . well, at least Vince felt threatened. He hadn't considered it, but for certain she needed to stay in town with her ailing boy. It was at that moment he realized he was going to get thrown out of his own house with its one small bedroom upstairs.

That didn't suit him, especially when there was a much better idea close at hand.

"I'll go tell your husband to head on out to your place for the night." Vince didn't bother to mention his other errand to any of these home invaders.

"Thank you." The woman's eyes filled with tears. Probably tears of gratitude, yet that didn't make it any easier to take.

Dare woke up when Vince came in on a blast of cold air. It was full daylight, and Dare didn't even remember going to sleep.

It'd taken some wrangling, but he'd convinced Mrs. Foster to go upstairs and lie down. Vince hadn't been there to ask. Dare hoped he didn't mind. Then Dare had watched over his patient until the youngster fell into a natural sleep. His breath still rattled in his chest and the danger hadn't entirely passed, but the fever had left the boy, a good sign.

Dare had sat down next to his patient, thinking to just rest his eyes for a few minutes. Now here he was, how many hours later, waking up.

"Is Mrs. Foster bedded down upstairs?" Vince pulled his coat off and hung it up.

"Yep, she was asleep on her feet and I finally persuaded her to rest." Dare considered things through a daze of exhaustion. "Where'd you spend the night?"

"I've been working as hard as you. Maybe harder." Vince arched a brow to let Dare know Vince had caught him sleeping. "I haven't gotten a minute of sleep."

"Doing what?" Dare rubbed his aching head, wishing for coffee. That really good coffee they'd had at the diner yesterday. That'd make his brain start functioning again.

"It's a long list, and I don't have time to run through it all. For now, I set up that house behind the diner as a new doctor's office."

"I told you, I'm through being a doctor. I'm gonna buy Flint Greer's old place—as soon as I can get Glynna to take money for it—and then I'm gonna become a rancher."

Vince flashed a smile at Dare that, for some reason, set Dare's teeth on edge. Vince had always been a hard one to manage.

"Don't be a doctor, then. But I set up an empty house for you to live in when and if you decide to help out the ailing folks in Broken Wheel." Vince jerked his head at the boy, who was swathed in a white sheet rigged like a tent. "You're never gonna be able to say no to someone in need, and Greer's old place is a ways from town. You can't do any doctoring from out there—if you ever decide to do any, that is."

Dare scrubbed his face with both hands. He needed to be a lot wider awake to win an argument with the Invincible Vince Yates.

"How cold is it out there?" Dare asked, changing the subject. "Can we move the boy safely?" He'd felt a blast of cool air when Vince came in, but he'd barely noticed it, what with being asleep and all.

"If we wrap the boy up tight, we can move him just fine." Vince seemed overeager to get his house back, and Dare couldn't blame the man for that. "There were a few things left behind in your new house—not much, but enough to get you started again. I've been cleaning and making it livable. I even moved a bed into one room on the main floor that will make a good doctor's office."

It wasn't much fun having someone take over managing his affairs. It made things easier, though. Dare's stomach growled. "I need coffee. And breakfast. I haven't eaten since yesterday morning."

"Sure, you did," Vince countered. "I brought meals in twice for you and Mrs. Foster."

Wrinkling his brow, Dare reflected back on yesterday. He did have a vague recollection, come to think of it. "Beefsteak and biscuits?"

"That was supper. Glynna has added an evening meal to her diner. The noon meal was a roast beef sandwich you swallowed almost whole while you worked on the boy."

Dare shook his head, then looked around the room. Little Elias was resting quietly on top of Vince's desk. There were things piled everywhere—sheets and medicine bottles, basins and kettles—whatever Dare had needed, Vince or Mrs. Foster had somehow found. Now Elias needed a real bed, and Dare needed more space. It sounded like Vince had found that, too.

He hated waking Mrs. Foster, though. The woman had been near the end of her rope. Then a footstep creaked overhead.

"Call upstairs and tell Mrs. Foster we're moving her boy." Dare ordered Vince to do it, just to get in his share of being bossy. "I'll get Elias wrapped up so no wind blows on him, especially his face. I don't want to set off any more coughing fits if I can help it."

It was almost noon when they finally had the house set up and Elias resting comfortably again.

"You got all this medicine at the general store?" Dare looked at the lineup of bottles. There was a lot missing, but a surprising number of the things he needed were now at hand.

"I did," Vince replied. "The freight wagon that brought Jonas's letter had a big order for you."

It occurred to Dare that Vince didn't seem to have much lawyering work, yet he always seemed to have plenty of money. How did he manage that?

"I also sent a man on a fast horse to Dalls Pass with a list."

Dare knew the slightly bigger town would have more of what he needed, and Vince had been familiar with the medicine and supplies Dare used.

"Whatever they don't have is being ordered over the telegraph, so it can come in a matter of days."

"Did you include carbolic acid?" Dare thought that one medicine had saved more lives than all his other medicines combined.

"Yep. And I remembered a few of the books you had and told them to check for those, too."

Dare clenched his jaw. He couldn't afford to replace all his books, and he knew from the look in Vince's eyes that his friend was paying for everything, which Dare couldn't allow. "I'm paying you back."

Vince shook his head. "How about instead you let me pay you for your doctoring help when I got shot in the head a while back?" There it was, the reminder that Dare had saved Vince's life.

"Or let me pay you for that time you saved my life back in Andersonville," Dare said. Vince had been there to drag a man off Dare, who'd just shoved a knife into his ribs. Dare didn't figure Vince owed him a thing, but he decided to shut up about paying for the books, since he couldn't afford to do it anyway.

The boy lying on the bed, covered and tented, began one of his coughing fits, and Dare had to leave his wrangling with Vince for later. Mrs. Foster came in carrying another basin of steaming water, heavy with herbs Dare needed to help open the boy's air passages.

Returning his attention to the fragile little boy, Dare didn't think much more about Vince Yates and all he'd sacrificed to help get his friend's doctoring business back on its feet.

CHAPTER 10

"I need a lunch tray to take to Dr. Riker." Glynna finally had time now that the noon rush was over.

Lana, leaning over a cutting board, straightened to meet Glynna's eyes. "Dr. Riker?"

Something flashed in Lana's eyes that Glynna couldn't define. With a peeled potato in one hand and a butcher knife in the other, Lana clutched the knife so hard her knuckles turned white and the tip of the blade trembled.

For one pure, clean second, Glynna felt a wave of fear unlike any she'd ever known. And that was saying something, considering her year of marriage to Flint.

"Will the noon special suit the doctor?" Lana's words held nothing to upset anyone, and yet Glynna couldn't deny that she was upset.

Lana set the potato down on the wooden surface and sliced through it with the knife. The knife severed the crisp spud with a single downward stroke. Lana kept the knives razor sharp with a strop that was hanging on the wall. Glynna hadn't noticed the strop and wouldn't have known how to use it if she had, but Lana was teaching her.

The knife hit the wood with more force than seemed necessary. Lana's hands moved so fast, they were nearly a blur. The knife flashed, glinting in the light, reducing the potato to shreds with an expertise Glynna wouldn't have believed if she hadn't seen it herself.

Glynna had noticed from the first that the woman was a natural with food. And chopping up a potato to fry in a skillet was among her finest talents.

"Y-yes, the noon special will be fine," Glynna answered.

Suddenly Lana's hands stopped, frozen as surely as if they were made of ice. Lana looked into the distance, past Glynna's shoulder. Glynna glanced around, expecting to see that someone had come into the kitchen behind her. A chill rushed down her spine as if that someone were dangerous.

No one was there.

Lana's eyes remained focused. She seemed to be listening for something . . . or to someone. Then an instant later she was back at work, throwing a small mountain of potatoes in a hot cast-iron skillet. The sizzle and the rush of steam made Glynna's mouth water, distracting her from Lana's odd behavior. Glynna had been run off her feet and hadn't eaten since before sunrise.

"Do I need to send enough to feed Mrs. Foster, too?" Lana asked.

Disturbed by the strange shift of Lana's attention, Glynna swallowed, wetting her dry throat. "Why, yes. I hadn't thought of that. It's a wonderful idea. Of course we need to make Mrs. Foster a plate. Thank you for suggesting it, Lana."

"I reckon your main interest is in the doctor, ain't it?" Lana's eyes rounded on her then, causing Glynna to almost step back. Again, for no reason. The woman hadn't raised her voice. She hadn't so much as frowned.

"I'm interested in helping, that's all," Glynna said matter-of-factly.

Lana focused on the knife in her hand. She lifted the strop and whipped the knife back and forth with a smooth swish. Glynna couldn't work the strop and knife half as fast and she tried to study the motion. But Lana's hands moved too fast for Glynna to be sure of anything except the gleaming edge of the knife as it was being honed to razor sharpness.

Lana snorted in a way that wasn't suitable for a lady or an employee. Lana had come from a hard life, working as a saloon girl with all the terrible aspects of that career.

Glynna did feel she needed to speak to Lana about her inappropriate comment, as if Glynna harbored some sort of interest in the doctor. Such a thing couldn't be repeated in the presence of her children.

"There's nothing between Dare Riker and me, Lana." Glynna then thought of the moment they'd shared in the Indian camp and suspected that might qualify as *something*.

The knife must've been sharpened to suit Lana because she quit the rapid-fire movements and finally laid the knife aside. Lana felt a surge of relief to see that knife out of Lana's hand, and she realized how ridiculous that was. Lana had a troubled background, but she worked hard and was a talented cook. Glynna had no reason to think ill of the woman, and it spoke poorly of Glynna's Christian faith that she judged Lana based on her past. Truly, Glynna was benefiting greatly from Lana's gifts.

"My plan is to never inflict another man on my children. I've proven to be a poor hand at picking husbands."

"Greer was a decent sort, by my book."

"He used his fists on me. There was nothing decent about him."

"A man loses his temper from time to time. No sense squawking about it. If'n you don't like it, you pick your moment and teach him a lesson right back."

Glynna shuddered. What would Flint have done to her if she'd ever dared to hit him? It didn't bear thinking about, but it told Glynna a lot about what poor Lana had suffered at the hands of men.

The door to the diner opened and voices sounded. "I'd better go see who it is," Glynna said. "I can run that food over when it's ready. I'll tell Paul to serve the newcomers. He went up to his room for a break a few minutes ago."

Glynna knew Paul wouldn't like her going over to Dare's new office, and that sparked a bit of rebellion, the idea of being dictated to by her own child. "No, I don't need to bother him. I'll go see how many meals they need and then you can serve them. The dining room's empty now. I'll lock it up so you can finish with the meals and be done for the day."

Lana nodded as Glynna hurried into the dining room. Maybe she'd be back before Paul noticed she'd been in the presence of a dreaded man.

"How's he doing?" Glynna brought in a tray heavy with food.

Mrs. Foster gave her a weary smile. "God bless you for bringing in our meals."

"Your husband and sons are eating right now. They came in the diner just as I was leaving, and Luke and Ruthy Stone are with them. They want to meet you if you can get away. I told them I'd ask."

Melanie Foster didn't suggest her unruly sons come to Dare's house. "Gil has spoken so often of Luke; they were great friends as children. I want to meet them, but I need to stay with Elias."

"Go on over and join them." Glynna tilted her head toward the door. "I ordered a meal for you over there. It's time you take a break."

"I can't." Exhaustion and worry had drawn lines in the woman's face. Her husband and sons had been in and out many times in the last week, though the active little boys meant that the visits be cut short. Gil would bring them in, check on his oldest son, talk with his wife about how they were settling into the house, then herd his boys back out before they broke anything.

"He's much improved, ma'am." Dare straightened from where he was lifting the tent away from the boy. "I don't think we need this anymore." Elias blinked his sleepy eyes at Dare. "You've been raring to get out of bed this morning, haven't you, son?"

Glynna hadn't seen the boy awake before.

Elias smiled and nodded his head firmly. "I don't like lying around."

"That's a good sign." Dare swiped one large, gentle hand over the boy's tightly kinked black curls. "But before you get up, I think a bit more sleep might add to your strength."

Glynna smiled at Mrs. Foster. "Your son's going to be fine. I'll fetch and carry for the doctor while you get off your feet for a few minutes. Go see the rest of your family now. Luke and Ruthy Stone are eager to meet you."

Mrs. Foster turned and the worry lines eased as she looked down at Elias. "Yes, I do believe he is better. But I should stay."

The boy's eyelids were heavy as he shook his head. "Go on and see Pa. I'm going to sleep a little while, then I wanna go out 'n play. I can, can't I, Ma?"

"Just as soon as you feel up to it."

Elias's eyes closed, and he relaxed into sleep. Mrs. Foster looked at Dare.

He nodded and said quietly, "You heard him, go on. You're only a few steps away. I'll call if I need you."

"Thank you, Doctor." She drew in a deep breath and smiled as she hurried out.

"Come and eat, Dare. Get off *your* feet for a while." Glynna carried the tray to a table near the front window. There was a kitchen with a proper table in the back of the house, but Glynna suspected Dare wouldn't leave his patient, even with the youngster sleeping.

Dare sank into a chair. Glynna quickly lifted a red gingham napkin off a plateful of chicken and noodle gravy that had been poured generously over two biscuits and a mile-high stack of hash browns. Dare grabbed a fork off the tray with such enthusiasm, Glynna couldn't help but smile.

"Sit down," Dare said, "and join me."

Glynna had brought food for two, hoping Melanie would go see her husband, but was prepared to feed her if she didn't. They ate companionably for a while. Finally, Dare seemed to quiet the worst of his hunger and he relaxed and lifted his coffee cup.

Glynna began gathering the plates.

"No, wait, don't rush off. Talk to me for a few minutes, if you have time. I haven't been outside this house for days, and I'd love to hear a different voice."

"What do you want to talk about?" Glynna settled in across from him.

"Vince said another covered wagon came into town with a family who'd been driven off by Greer."

Glynna controlled a flinch at her late husband's name. "It was two brothers. No women and children. And we got letters from two more who are heading back." Glynna told Dare any other news she could think of while he sipped his coffee.

"When did you learn to . . . uh . . . ?" Dare looked up from his plate and his cheeks went a bit pink.

"When did I stop burning things to a cinder and start cooking good food?" Glynna asked with mock severity. "Is that what you were going to ask, Dare Riker?"

"No, the food's always been . . . uh . . . good. Now it's just . . . well, different." Dare started talking faster with every word. "A different kind of good."

Glynna had a mental picture of him trying to dig himself out of a hole.

"Lots of different ways to make a roast or make chicken

stew. Not saying one's right and one's wrong. You're a fine—"

"I hired a cook." She interrupted before he had to tell any more kindhearted lies.

Dare was silent, probably because he didn't want to say what a smart idea that was. "Who'd you hire?"

"Lana Bullard."

"Lana Bullard?" His fork clattered against his empty plate and bounced onto the floor. "You hired Lana Bullard?"

As if on cue, across a stretch of bare dirt, the back door of the diner swung open and Lana Bullard stepped outside and threw a pan of dishwater onto the ground.

"Yep, that's her," Dare said, eyeing the woman through the window. "She's lost a lot of weight. I don't know if I'd've recognized her if you hadn't just said her name."

Glynna watched Lana straighten, rub the back of her neck, then go back inside. "She works really hard and she's a right good cook."

"But she's . . . crazy."

Glynna frowned. "No, she's not." Glynna's mind flashed to that moment when Lana had frightened her, but she shook off that foolishness. "She keeps the kitchen neat as a pin, and she's teaching me and both my children how to cook properly, although it seems like she takes everything off the fire too soon. I worry about things being too raw." With a shrug, Glynna added, "Paul has picked up so many tricks from her that he's already a better cook than I am."

Looking from the diner to Glynna and back, Dare leaned close.

Glynna was surprised how much that didn't bother her.

Whispering, Dare said, "She's a lunatic. She thought she was going to have a baby, and she came in to see me, in a mouth-foaming panic, twice a week from the day I arrived to this town. She treated me like every word I spoke came straight from the mouth of God."

"Well, people often love their doctors."

"That hasn't been my experience."

"Well, you mostly treat men, and at least in Andersonville they mostly all died, right? That could be why you haven't seen much devotion. Melanie Foster seems quite fond of you."

"When I finally convinced Lana she wasn't expecting a baby, she accused me of killing her son."

Glynna sat up straighter. "What?"

"And since there wasn't any baby, it couldn't very well have been a son, now, could it?"

Silence reigned for a long moment as Glynna looked at Dare's concerned expression. Finally she said weakly, "Her fried potatoes are just delicious."

Glynna didn't want to hear anything that might make her lose her cook.

Dare forged on. "It took me some time, but I finally realized she was past the age of bearing a child and she'd mistaken that for being in the family way."

"How could you tell that?"

Dare gave her such a dark look, she regretted the question. "I'm not gonna talk with you about a woman's time of life, Glynna."

That was probably for the best.

"When I told her there'd be no baby, she ran off. And the next time I saw Bullard, he told me he'd come to town to kill me for what I'd done to his son."

"The poor woman was distraught."

Dare rolled his eyes at Glynna. "She wasn't distraught; she was mad as a barking moon bat."

"I'm sure you're overstating things. Any woman who believed a child was on the way might be forgiven for a moment of anger or odd behavior."

"What about the part where she treated me like she worshiped me and kept screaming at Bullard to share his whiskey?"

Glynna fell silent, then looked at the diner. A moment stretched to several. Finally, Glynna said, "That woman can fry potatoes like nobody's business."

"*That woman* near to wiped out the laudanum supply at the general store. Tug Andrews had to reorder. And she drained Duffy's Tavern of his whiskey, and when he told her it was all gone, she got so upset he had to bar her from the premises."

"Duffy doesn't bar anyone. His standards are so low, I'm surprised to hear he has any."

"Lana was mighty surprised, too. She was so surprised, Duffy ended up with a black eye and split lip."

"She mentioned whiskey once, the night she came. She's never spoken of it again. I've seen no sign that she's popping a cork on the sly, either."

"Probably because Duffy's mad that he let a woman punch him, and he won't sell her any."

"Well, for whatever reason, I've never seen her consuming liquor. I know she sleeps in Asa's boardinghouse, gets up before sunrise every morning, and is hard at work by the time I get downstairs. Her eyes aren't red, and her speech isn't slurred. She never acts dizzy or complains of a headache or a sick stomach in the morning, nor have I caught her having herself a nip to stave off the symptoms left by excessive drinking from the night before."

Dare gave a humorless laugh. "Where'd you learn so much about how a drunk acts?"

Glynna stiffened as she remembered just how she'd learned. She didn't intend to speak of it. To change the subject, she asked, "So how much longer will you need to keep the boy here?"

She stood from the table and walked over to Elias, still sleeping. As she adjusted his blankets that didn't need adjusting, she waited for Dare to answer. At last in the silence he stood from the table and came to her side. "Glynna, do you want to tell me who the drunk was in your life?"

Slowly, an inch at a time, she lifted her gaze to meet Dare's. "You . . . you know I came out West to marry Flint, right? I was a mail-order bride."

"That's what I heard." Dare took her hand, busy tinkering with the blanket, and gently but firmly pulled her around to face him. "Were you leaving something behind that involved a drunkard?"

Inhaling slowly, she said, "Among other weaknesses, my first husband, the children's father, was overly fond of . . . of hard drink."

Glynna became very busy inspecting the toes of her shoes.

149

"Among other weaknesses?" Dare's hand tightened on hers, and he drew her back to the table and sat across from her. "What others?"

Glynna shook her head. "Too many to count. My children aren't just hostile because of Flint. They started learning at a very young age that a man could bring a world of trouble."

"They'll be all right, Glynna."

"Paul is so angry. Janny is so quiet, and she's scared of her own shadow."

"It's fear for Paul, too. Men see fear as weakness, so when he's scared he bulls up and turns sullen. Give them time and safety. They'll heal."

She wanted to believe it so badly. To keep busy, she gathered the plates. Her hand trembled on Dare's tin coffee cup and tipped it over. A thin trail of coffee spilled straight for Dare's lap. Glynna leaped to her feet. Dare jumped up from his seat as Glynna grabbed the cloth she'd used to cover the tray and slapped it on the spilled coffee. As Glynna moved forward and Dare moved sideways, the two collided.

Dare was six feet and then some of rock-solid male, and when she hit him, he didn't budge. Her arm, reaching for the spill, and his reaching to steady her became an embrace. Looking up to apologize, their faces were inches apart. Dare's blue eyes seemed to beckon her to somewhere safe. He leaned down slowly, his eyes open, asking. But she was too entranced to turn away—which was his answer.

He kissed her.

One of his strong, healing hands rested on her cheek. It

reminded her of the times Flint had struck her, and Dare's touch replaced that memory with something sweet and decent. He pulled back and met her eyes with his own. "Glynna, I think we need to—"

A violent cough jarred them apart. Glynna stumbled back, away from Dare. She glanced at the coughing boy and saw he was wide awake, watching his doctor kiss a woman. If he mentioned this to his mother, the gossip would spread all over town.

Blushing, Glynna dodged around Dare and quickly finished stacking the dirty dishes.

"Glynna, stop. Leave the dishes." Dare's quiet voice almost lured her into trusting him. But misplaced trust had nearly destroyed her in the past. It had cost her a home, a husband, her father's love, her community's respect. Mostly it had cost her any sense of honor and integrity. If Dare knew of her past, the kissing would surely stop, and so it was better not to even start.

Stacking the plates onto her tray with the loudest clatter she could manage, she drowned out whatever Dare was saying.

Suddenly a hand landed on her shoulder.

"No!" Whirling around, she moved toward the door. "Just stay away. Please—"

"Glynna, we can't share a kiss and then pretend it didn't happen. Or pretend that it won't happen again."

She was turning to leave with the tray of dishes when Dare stopped her again, this time more forcefully. The tray tipped, and the dishes threatened to crash to the floor. Wrenching free of his hold, she dropped the tray back down on the table, then ran for the door. But as she reached for the knob, the door slammed open and nearly struck her.

"Ma, what's taking you so long?" With suspicion in his eyes, Paul looked at her, then at Dare. Heaven only knew what he was imagining. Glynna didn't take the time to ask.

"Pick up the tray, please, Paul. I need to get back." Then she rushed out of the room, leaving Paul and Dare to deal with each other.

She knew all too well what Paul thought of her spending even a second enjoying the attention of a man.

To encourage Dare might destroy her son's last chance to grow up straight and strong and decent. Her son had to come before everything else.

Paul stalked to the table. Dare stepped back enough so the kid wouldn't be tempted to throw a fist.

The dishes had scattered around, and Dare had a few seconds while Paul stacked them again. How could he reach this young man? Despite what had passed between him and Glynna, and no matter how this thing ended up between them, Paul needed help. He needed a man to be a good example to him. He needed some kind of outlet for all the anger he carried around.

"Paul, hold on a minute."

"What was going on in here with Ma? She looked upset."

Dare didn't want to lie, but he sure didn't want to tell the truth. Instead he tried to divert the kid's attention. "Elias will be going home soon, so I can finally keep that promise I made about taking you hunting. We talked about it on the ride home from the Kiowa village, remember? You and I could go. Maybe Vince and Jonas too, if they want to come along. If we got ourselves an antelope, you could serve the meat in the diner."

That might justify taking a few hours away from the diner in the youngster's head. The boy worked hard for his family.

Paul looked at Elias. "The boy's going to make it?"

"He sure is. He's still coughing some, but he's sleeping a lot now, and the rest is healing him." The sick child had lapsed back to sleep after his coughing fit had interrupted Dare's kiss with Glynna. The interruption was a good thing, too. Kissing her was a blamed fool idea when Paul wanted to tear his head off. Dare needed to clear things up with Paul before he got any closer to the boy's ma. Glynna was right about that. Unless Glynna just didn't want Dare around and she was using her children as an excuse . . .

Dare knocked that idea aside before he started fretting about it, and it showed on his face. It didn't matter anyhow, because whatever happened between Glynna and him, that didn't change the fact that the boy needed help.

Since Paul was showing interest in Dare's treatment of Elias, Dare decided to see if the kid would let down his guard for a bit to talk doctoring.

"The youngster's temperature is normal. I got it down that first day he came in, but it went up a few more times, which happens sometimes with pneumonia. But it's been down a couple of days now, and his lungs are clear."

Paul looked at Dare with a frown that didn't cover a

shadow of grudging interest. "I've seen Ma test our temperature by feeling if our foreheads are hot, but how can you tell if his lungs are clear?"

Maybe this was a better thing to talk about with the boy than hunting. Dare went to the bedside table and picked up his stethoscope. "I use this." Dare stuck the earpieces in place and rested the little trumpet end on Elias's chest. Speaking softly so as not to disturb the boy, Dare explained, "It's a medical instrument called a stethoscope, and it makes everything louder. I press it against Elias's chest, and if the lungs are clear, the sound is smooth and steady. If they're congested, as they are when someone has pneumonia, there's a rattling sound. You can't miss it."

Dare offered the tool to Paul. "Try it. You'll hear what normal lungs sound like. Then if you ever hear infected lungs, you'll know the difference."

"I'm not trained to listen to anyone's lungs." Paul's scowl wasn't as deep as usual, and there was a spark in his eyes.

Dare smiled. "I probably wouldn't let you perform an operation, but you can't hurt Elias with this. And you know, Jesus sent the disciples out to practice medicine without a license, and heaven knows I do it, so why shouldn't you?"

A smile flitted across Paul's face, quickly suppressed. He took the stethoscope, imitated Dare by putting the little plugs in his ears, then listened to Elias's chest.

"What's the thumping sound?" Paul's face grew solemn with concentration.

"It's his heart beating."

Paul straightened from the boy. "Really? It's banging like a drum."

Dare nodded. "The stethoscope lets me hear all kinds of things going on inside someone's body. And I can hear that Elias's lungs have healed. He'll go home soon." Dare smoothed the boy's hair off his forehead, glad the little one was healing up enough to want to get out of bed. "He could probably go right now, but I wanted him to stay a few more days and rest up, just to be sure. Once he goes home, he'll be running outside in the cold if he can escape from his ma, and I'd like to put that off until he can regain his strength."

Paul pulled the earpieces free and handed the stethoscope back to Dare. "Thanks. I've never heard tell before of a tool that'll let you hear inside someone's body."

"Would you be interested in helping me with my doctoring?" Dare wanted to say, *"Now that your ma's not cooking anymore,"* but he refrained. "Mostly it's pretty quiet, not a lot of sick folks around these parts. But I could use help now and then. Some doctoring is a two-man job."

"You've been doctoring night and day for weeks."

"The Indian village was unusual, and having a boy this sick doesn't happen very often. Once I get Elias on his way, I reckon I'll go back to doing mostly nothing."

Until he quit and went to ranching.

Paul looked straight at Dare for a long spell and finally said, quietly, "I see the way you look at my ma. No man is ever going to put her in the way of harm again. You say you're a decent man, but my pa was decent, at first. Then times got hard and he turned on all of us. Greer seemed good, but that didn't last long. I don't think you can know how you'd act if times got hard. So nothing you say could ease my worry."

"Paul, you've heard how Vince, Jonas, Luke and I met in Andersonville Prison, right?"

He nodded. "I know a bit about it. A prison camp for Yankees during the War Between the States."

"It was as mean a place as there's ever been on earth. I've been stabbed and starved. I've lived with fear and I've had a hand in bringing bad men to justice and seeing them hung. I've stood over bedsides while men died in agony. So don't think I don't know how I'd act if times got hard. I've faced some real hard times, son, and I came through them without taking to a path of evil."

"You shot Greer." Paul said it like an accusation.

Dare knew that no one had wanted Greer dead more than this boy. "Yes, I did. He was doing his best to kill my Regulator friends and me after we helped get you and your ma and Janny out of his house. He was bent on getting you all back, and he wasn't going to stop until someone stopped him. If there'd been a choice, I'd have let Greer live. Killing a man leaves a scar on your soul that never goes away. I hope and pray you never have to bear that scar, Paul."

"Are you going to stay away from my ma or not?"

Dare wasn't about to make a promise he couldn't keep, and he wasn't going to make the mistake Glynna made of giving this boy the power to make a decision as important as whether or not Glynna let a man into her life. Dare thought of their kiss but shook the vision away. There was no room in his life for kissing, not while he wasn't sure what his future might hold.

"I will promise you that I'll never treat your ma with unkindness or disrespect. And I will promise that I'll listen to you and do my best to earn your trust. But you need to promise me you won't take your anger out on me for things other men did. Maybe we can make a start on your letting go of your anger by working here with me when I've got a patient. You think about it, and while you're thinking, let's go hunting once Elias has gone home."

By the frown on his face, Dare knew Paul wasn't satisfied with their talk, but his eyes did light up at the thought of hunting.

Then it flickered through Dare's mind that teaching this kid to handle a gun might be a real poor idea.

CHAPTER 11

Dare and Vince rode side by side out to Luke's cabin, and then the three of them would drive a herd to Gil Foster's.

Dare had asked Paul to come along, but the boy wasn't interested. Just as well. Dare wasn't going hunting or doctoring today; he was helping with some ranch work, hopefully to figure out what it was cowboys did all day.

He thought he might end up embarrassing himself, and the fewer witnesses the better. He'd left Melanie to watch Elias and asked Paul to be on hand if any more help was needed. Glynna was going to stay with them as much as possible, too. Every day Dare could keep Elias in bed helped, though it wouldn't be for much longer. The young'un was healed enough to be restless.

Jonas didn't come. He was busy driving himself crazy getting his house ready for his chubby, bald sister to move in.

Dare didn't envy him the task or the sister.

Vince and Dare met up with Luke and fell in with him behind a herd of twenty cows, most with a calf running alongside and a couple of bulls thrown in. Luke had picked young cows with calves, born after the spring roundup, still unbranded, so Gil could slap his own brand on them right away. Luke insisted that a chunk of the cattle Flint Greer had built up had come out of the Foster herd Greer had stolen, and it was only right that the Fosters get them back.

The cattle were placid, and driving them was proving to be simple. Dare thought he could handle ranching just fine. True, he wasn't learning any new cowboy skills, but he was enjoying the ride.

Several of Luke's cowpokes rode along, keeping the herd bunched. Luke, Vince, and Dare rode drag.

It was a crisp morning, the sun still low in the eastern sky. As the sun rose, it lit up the red in the canyon walls as they wound their way along.

"I've never seen the like of these red-striped stones," Dare said. It was a raw, harsh kind of beauty. The ground was rugged. The canyon walls were torn away to show layer upon layer of red, all different shades. Palo Duro wasn't a welcoming, fertile land like Indiana. The grass was clumped and widely scattered, not lush pasture broken by rows of tall corn like Dare had known back home. But Luke's cattle were fat and contented.

They moved along at a fast walk. Luke held a coil of rope in his left hand and waved it occasionally at a lagging cow. There was no trail. Luke was following an old memory. The canyon floor was broken and rocky, so they moved along slow and easy. No sense harassing the cows or risking their horses with a mad rush.

"Luke, I've made my decision. I'm going to be a rancher." Dare didn't see anything here he couldn't handle, although he knew they were going to brand these calves later and he had no idea how to go about that task. "I've a mind to buy Greer's old land and change professions."

"Do you have any money?" Luke asked.

"No."

"Because you need money to buy the land."

"Glynna offered to give him the land." Vince jumped in, always talking.

"She did?" Luke frowned. "I don't know if that's right, taking land from a widow and her fatherless children."

"I'm not taking her land," Dare said in disgust. "What kind of coyote do you think I am? I can pay her—eventually."

"Okay, fine. Then you'll need cattle and horses. It costs a lot to get a ranch up and running . . . unless, wait!" Luke sounded excited.

Dare thought maybe he could get this ranching concern going, after all. "What?"

"You can go out into the hills and round up some wild longhorns. But they can be killers—you've gotta watch the horns. Backbreaking work, yet there are cattle aplenty running wild. That's how my pa started his herd. I could loan you a few men and horses until you got a herd together."

"I'd pay your men while they worked for me."

"With no money?" Luke arched a brow.

"I'll pay you over time, like I'm gonna do with Glynna."

"And maybe we could find a herd of wild mustangs and get yourself some horses that way. Rounding up wild horses is tricky. Then you've got to break them. I've ridden out by Greer's place. He's got a ramshackle cabin that probably won't stop the snow and cold wind through the winter.

And there are no outbuildings or corrals. You know how to patch holes in a cabin or raise a barn?"

Dare pretty much just knew how to be a doctor. In his youth he'd been a decent wheelwright too, with his pa's help. Now that he thought about it, he probably was fooling himself about the wheelwright skills. "I asked you to teach me, didn't I?"

"You don't have any hay for the winter, but there might still be some tall grass, winter-cured, on Greer's place. You know how to mow hay and stack it?"

"I can learn." Dare thought maybe his voice, always deep and a little gravelly, qualified now as a growl.

"You know, cattle and horses get sick, too."

Dare perked up. "I might kind of enjoy doctoring them."

"Probably the best thing would be if you came out to my place and worked for me as a cowpoke," Luke offered. "That'd be a good training ground. We'll see what kind of rancher you'd make."

"I'm a little old to be starting out as a cowpuncher."

Vince flashed a smile. "You're a little old for a lot of things, Dare, my friend."

Dare had a surprising desire to wipe that smile off Vince's face with a fist. Vince seemed to know that, because he smiled even wider.

They didn't call him Invincible Vince for nothing, so Dare knew better than to take a swing. All the same, Dare enjoyed imagining it.

"Come on out." Luke pulled his hat off, smoothed back his overly long brown hair with a swipe of one hand, then anchored his hair again with the hat.

Movement from the south drew Dare's attention.

"Here comes Red Wolf. I told him we'd be riding over to Gil's, but I wasn't sure he'd come along. Gil and Red Wolf and I had us a time running wild in these canyons." Luke smiled at the memory. "Look at that man ride."

Dare watched Luke's Kiowa friend ride his horse, no saddle, the only bridle woven strips of cured hide. The horse stretched out, galloping across the rugged terrain as Red Wolf leaned forward, his spine straight as a lance. Man and horse moved together with such grace it was like they were one.

A moment later, Red Wolf came even with them and slowed to match their pace, riding on Luke's right while Dare and Vince were on his left. "You say our friend Gil has returned?"

"Yep." Luke reached across the space between his horse and Red Wolf's and grasped his friend's forearm. Dare noticed they clasped each other's arm over their scars, and he wondered if it wasn't a secret handshake of sorts.

"He's moved back into the cabin he grew up in. He's come into the country with a wife and three sons. The oldest of them had pneumonia, just like you had, and Dare's been doctoring him." Luke told Red Wolf about the sick boy.

Red Wolf turned to Dare. "Your healing has helped another family, medicine man."

Dare nodded his head. He couldn't reach far enough to shake the man's hand, but he felt as though there was a friendship between them.

"Maybe we oughta make Dare and Vince blood brothers like you, Gil, and me." Luke raised his scarred forearm.

"That's a nasty cut." Dare frowned at the ugly wound. "You're lucky you didn't sever a radial artery in your wrist and bleed to death or get an infection and die."

"Yep, you're a natural as a rancher." Luke and Vince laughed.

"No sense pretending to be a medicine man, Dare," Vince added.

Red Wolf looked confused and might have asked what they were talking about, but then a cow made a break for home. Luke herded her back into line with such ease that Dare had serious doubts about his ability to ranch.

They rode four abreast, trailing after the cattle until they reached the Foster holding.

"Bunch the cattle on that grass and hold them there. Holler when they've settled in, and we'll get to the branding." Luke's foreman, Dodger, took over while Dare and his friends swung down by the front door of the Foster cabin and lashed their reins to a hitching post—all but Red Wolf, who left his horse standing as if the horse stayed with him because it wanted to.

It was a one-story house, whereas Luke's house had an upstairs, but it was longer than Luke's. It looked more than big enough for a family of five. A fine-looking home, built with logs and the red stones that littered the neighboring canyon. A stand of cottonwoods was nearby, which had provided the logs for the house, and yet there were plenty of them left standing.

Gil opened the door, and the shrill laughter of his wild sons echoed out of the house. "Red Wolf!" Gil jogged across the wide porch and down three steps.

Red Wolf met Gil as he reached the ground. The two men shook hands in the same way Luke and Red Wolf had, then they laughed and Gil slapped the Kiowa man on the back. Luke joined in the good-natured talk, and Dare could see the boy in Luke, see more of the fires that had forged him into a strong soldier and a capable rancher.

After a few minutes, the Foster boys came charging out of the cabin, and Gil, a man with a lot of practice, snagged them both and held them wriggling in his arms. "These are two of my three sons, Red Wolf. Come on in. My boys will climb on your horses and go riding off if we don't pen them up."

"I can pen up the horses," Dare offered, though they looked fine standing tied to Gil's hitching post.

"No, I mean pen up my *boys*."

They all laughed.

"Let's go in." Gil hoisted the boys, one under each arm, as he went up onto his porch.

Dare watched Luke enjoy his friends, and the antics of Gil's boys reminded him of how fine a thing it was to see a child in full health.

They turned to the branding, and between the bawling cattle, the red-hot irons, the stench of burning cowhide, and two little boys who seemed determined to cast themselves into the fire or get hit by thrashing hooves, Dare wasn't sure what was even happening.

They were ready to leave when Dare saw Luke absent-mindedly scratching his neck. Dare saw a red spot, then a closer look revealed another and another.

Measles.

"We'd better head out now," Dare said. "By the way, Gil, have you and your boys ever had the measles?"

"Yep, sure have." Gil's brow furrowed, curious about the unexpected question. "We've all had them. Why?"

"Luke, you need to stop scratching."

"Why's that?"

"Have you had a fever?" Dare was struck by how differently he felt about Luke coming down with this than Red Wolf. There was a good chance Luke would be well in a few days with few, if any, complications. Why would such a thing be true? Some doctor, somewhere, needed to do some research on that.

"I feel fine." Luke gave Dare a man-to-man look that said nothing could lay him low.

Dare had a feeling Luke was going to spend the next few days learning different. "We need to get you home."

Dare decided he'd stay until he was sure Luke was going to get through this. It struck Dare that about the only thing that could make his life more hectic was if a cyclone blew into Broken Wheel.

CHAPTER 12

Tina Cahill blew into Broken Wheel tired, filthy, and scared. What if Jonas didn't want her?

Fighting down all her fears, she jumped off the back of the bumpy wagon just as a tumbleweed rolled across the street right in front of her. For days she'd ridden through the most barren wilderness, riding in a full wagon with the couple up on the bench seat mostly ignoring her.

She missed the lush green of Ohio. She missed the only home she'd ever known. She even missed stern Aunt Iphigenia . . . a little.

She missed her church work and even managing her home to Aunt Iphigenia's exacting standards. The woman had taken cleanliness being next to godliness to the Commandment level.

Then, after all her years of hard work and dedication, she'd been cast out as surely as if she'd been Satan leading a rebellion in heaven. The man Aunt Iphigenia had married was nearly sixty years old, overly fat, and none too fond of bathing. None of that was the problem. It was the loathsome way her brand-new uncle Auggie had looked at her with hungry, wet, pink-as-a-pig eyes.

He liked to touch her when he walked past, lay a hand on her back—low on her back—and brush his body against hers when there was plenty of room to avoid it. The touches had grown bolder, the eyes hungrier. Aunt Iphigenia had noticed and accused Tina of flaunting herself. Then she'd cast her out.

Her aunt's betrayal, picking the wretched new husband over Tina, was disgusting, but Tina had been only too happy to leave. She'd had a letter from Jonas, so she knew he was here in Broken Wheel, Texas. She'd written him a letter and left before Jonas could get it and tell her not to come—a plan Aunt Iphigenia had wholeheartedly endorsed. Both of them were worried he'd tell her to stay away. Now here she was, unwanted and uninvited, to make her home with her brother, whom she hadn't seen in years.

At last.

Squaring her shoulders, she turned to instruct the driver and his wife how to best handle her trunks.

Motion drew her attention to a dark-haired man wearing a tidy black vest, walking across the street. She could see him over the backs of the horses, but he only had eyes for the wagon and its eight Missouri mules.

"Tina?"

She turned and saw a man coming down the board-walk toward her. "Jonas?" From the red hair she knew this had to be her big brother. He was nearly ten years older than her, and she hadn't seen him since she was a child. She wouldn't have recognized the broad-shouldered man as her scrawny brother if not for his hair.

Aunt Iphigenia hadn't approved of Jonas back then, and she'd run him off quickly when he'd stop by for a visit. But Tina had always loved him.

Uncertain of her welcome, she managed a wobbly smile. "The red hair is a dead giveaway that you're Jonas."

During the war, Jonas had turned to the good Lord and begun writing letters home. They'd been kind and full of his new faith. Tina had always adored him, even when Aunt Iphigenia had railed at what a scoundrel he was. When he'd become a man of God, Tina's love for her big brother had deepened. She'd poured all her dreams of family and love out to him in long letters. She'd never directly asked, but she'd hoped he could tell she wanted him to come for her and save her from the dragon that was raising her. She'd been devastated when he'd set out to preach the gospel in the West without even seeing her.

"Tina? My baby sister?" Jonas's good-natured shout sounded just as the dark-haired man reached the meager excuse for a board-walk.

"I'm not a baby anymore." Her heart was warmed by Jonas's hearty welcome.

The approaching man's eyes went to her, then widened. His mouth dropped open. He walked right into the steps up to the board-walk, tripped, and landed flat on his face. With a sniff of disdain, Tina realized the man had no doubt found his breakfast in a whiskey bottle.

"You sure aren't." Jonas reached out both hands and she clasped them, glad for someone to hold on to. Behind

Jonas a second man with overly long, dirty blond hair stepped out of two swinging doors. Smells wafted out of the building he'd emerged from. A saloon. Hmph!

The man turned, drawn perhaps by Jonas's voice. The man looked at her and walked smack into a post holding up the board-walk roof. He staggered under the impact and fell backward through the still-swinging doors.

Another drunkard. This town needed to shut down that saloon, and she'd be glad to help organize the effort to get it closed.

"You've grown into a beautiful woman." With a delighted laugh Jonas slid his arms around her waist, hoisted her into the air, and swung her in a circle.

"Jonas!" Laughing, she slapped at his shoulders. "Put me down."

But it felt wonderful to have someone in the world who was her very own family. She wrapped her arms around his neck and nearly strangled her big brother with a hug. "It's so nice to see you."

On one of the swinging turns, Tina saw that the dark-haired man who'd fallen had stood back up. He had a faint flush on his cheeks, no doubt embarrassed to be caught intoxicated in the morning. On the next rotation she saw him flash a brilliant, if somewhat sheepish, smile. Jonas stopped twirling her so her gaze could lock on the man's. His smile faded. He began walking toward her again—slow, steady, relentless. He was in Tina's estimation the most handsome man she'd ever seen.

Intoxication notwithstanding.

"It's wonderful to see you, pretty one." Jonas hugged

her tighter and drew her attention from the dark-haired man.

Jonas's voice held such kindness. Aunt Iphigenia was of a stern nature, and she'd been inclined to lecture any and all—most especially Tina—with fiery details of the afterlife for the unrepentant. Jonas's gentle flattery was like water in the desert, and the loving embrace was too wonderful. Unexpected and unbidden, she burst into tears.

"Don't cry, baby girl."

She'd never been a baby girl. From her earliest memory she'd been an adult, living on sufferance.

"You're home." He let her slide back to the ground.

She'd never truly had a home. Her parents had passed away very early on, and she'd lived with coldhearted Iphigenia from childhood.

"I'll take care of you."

She'd done a lot more caretaking in her life than having any care taken of her. Jonas's strong arms and the idea that he was a man who'd welcomed her home and expected to bear her burdens made her cry harder. It was completely unlike her.

She was a while obeying his urging not to cry, but she finally did. When the storm eased, he stepped back as if he regretted letting her go, then offered her a white handkerchief.

She mopped her face with it and then looked up, sniffling. "I apologize for my outburst."

Her voice broke. She fell silent as she tried to regain control of herself. The handsome man who'd fallen had stopped, still at a distance. He now stared at her in horror.

When their eyes met this time, Mr. Handsome Drunkard turned and walked briskly away.

Aunt Iphigenia had always scorned a drinker. She said consuming alcohol was like putting a thief in your mouth to steal your brains.

This man moved gracefully for a sot.

He was probably running due to shame for being inebriated in public in midmorning.

She then discarded that notion, for everyone knew drunkards had no shame.

"I'm telling you she was the most beautiful woman I've ever seen," Vince told Dare, although this wasn't news.

Dare had heard the same thing from everyone he'd spoken to since yesterday morning when he'd decided Luke was going to heal just fine from the measles. "Jonas said she was chubby."

"Well, she's slimmed down considerable." Vince scowled. Which wasn't like him. Vince usually had a ready smile.

No one seemed much interested in the wagon that had brought in a good load of doctoring supplies. All anyone could talk about was the woman who'd moved into the parsonage. There was even talk about a few sinners repenting just so they could attend services and catch a glimpse of the "golden-haired angel."

Duffy Schuster had come in to see Dare with big goose eggs on the front and back of his head and called her that. Vince had a small bruise on one cheek too, but he didn't ask for doctoring advice and Dare didn't offer any.

Dare wondered if God ever got plumb tired of the people He'd created.

Glynna stepped out of the kitchen with her heavy coffeepot, and five men stood like they had springs in their backsides and offered to carry the pot for her. Dare didn't stand by sheer force of will. Glynna might just slam the burning pot into his head. She hadn't forgiven him for mauling her the other day. And he hadn't stopped wanting to do it again, confound it.

"There's no prettier woman in this town than Glynna, so Jonas's sister can't be the prettiest," Dare said.

Vince quit his nonstop yammering about the new woman in town to arch a brow at Dare. A challenge.

Dare didn't know how to decide which woman was prettier, short of a beauty contest, and he didn't see Glynna cooperating—nor Tina Cahill, for that matter.

"Then she started crying like her head was a storm cloud. She just poured. I'm surprised Jonas didn't get hit by a thunderbolt coming straight out of her soggy eyeballs."

"You always have had a problem with women crying."

"No, I haven't. A woman gets hurt bad enough, I understand if she cries. Why, I wanted to cry myself when I got shot in the head." Vince rubbed two fingers over the scar, hidden by his hair, on the left side of his skull. "I didn't, of course, but I'd expect a puny little woman to go ahead and weep. But she wasn't shot, and there wasn't a sign of a broken bone sticking out of her anywhere. She had no cause to carry on like that."

"Could we stop talking about women for a few minutes and decide what I need to do to buy Flint Greer's ranch from Glynna? I need to get started with my new career. I think you should buy it, then sell it to me. She doesn't like me, and she won't cooperate."

"I don't call it not cooperating if she offers to give it to you."

"I can't just take it. I might as well stick up a stagecoach as steal that ranch from Glynna."

"You treated her wounds when she was hurt, helped kill her no-account husband, saved her from an avalanche, and you come to her diner every day even though there's a lunatic right in the kitchen with sharp knives and a grudge aimed straight at you. And Glynna's determined not to gain from Greer's land. She refuses to, and stupid as it is, I admire it. I'd just say take the land, but then that's stupid too, considering you're a doctor and not a rancher."

"I'm done talking about my former career. If I want a new job, that's my own business."

"It's your business until you get gored by a longhorn because you tried to put a bandage on some scrape on the bull's backside."

"I need to figure out a way to get Glynna to like me again—then she'll let me buy her land."

"Why wouldn't Glynna like you?"

"I dunno." In truth, Dare knew very well. "She just doesn't. And she won't sell to me."

"She won't sell to anyone. Don't act like you're special." As the two debated Dare's future, the diner began to empty of all the cowhands who rode in from the small ranches that dotted the countryside. No matter how much this town full of men liked looking at Glynna Greer Sev Yay, or whatever her name was today, they all eventually had to go back to work—except for the fake doctor and the fake lawyer. If there was work for them, someone would come running.

"I think she's especially stubborn when it comes to me." That kiss might explain exactly why.

"Why is that?"

Dare thought more about the kiss and forgot what he'd been saying.

"Dare!" Vince brought him back to the present.

"What?"

Rolling his eyes heavenward, Vince said, "Why would she be more stubborn with you than anyone else?"

"She, uh . . . she says she won't sell the ranch, but who besides me has made her an offer?"

"Well, then just take it. That'd be a cheap way to get started ranching. Even you probably couldn't go broke with a free ranch."

"I'm not taking her ranch for free. Do I look like a man who's gonna steal from a widow and her fatherless children?"

"What you look like is a man who's spent years being a phony doctor. That's not robbery, but it's not all that honorable either. You need to find an honest career or make peace with being a swindler."

"Like you have?" Dare asked.

"Yep."

They'd gotten off the main topic. Again. "Maybe she'll sell to you," Dare continued, "and then you can sell to me. Don't tell her what you've got planned."

175

"I'm not helping you buy a ranch. That's a plan hatched by a half-wit. You know nothing about ranching. If you don't want to be a doctor, then start repairing wheels. You learned how to do that from your pa. And didn't the blacksmith run off after the fight with Greer and Bullard? Take over his business, why don't you."

"That's Sledge Murphy. He came back."

"Then just repair wheels."

"I thought about being a wheelwright, though it's been a long time and I learned when I was mighty young. But even if I could do it, I'd starve. Every man in this town rides a horse—that's why Sledge can make a living. There aren't five wagons within a hundred miles of here, and the men who have one, like Luke, know how to repair their own wheels."

"All the better reason to be a doctor."

Dare drew in a breath, then let it out slowly.

"Look, if you feel so guilty about lying, then go back East and go to doctor college. How long could it take? A year or two maybe?"

"I checked. I have to go to regular school first."

"You have to graduate from college before they'll let you study to be a doctor? That's mighty picky."

"No, I don't mean go to college; I mean *regular* school. I have to go to high school and grammar school. Then I have to tangle with going to college."

Vince frowned. "How long will that take?"

With a shrug Dare said, "I'm not sure, but since I only went a few years, I might have to start back in . . . maybe fourth grade and go all the way through."

Flinching, Vince said, "You'd never fit in those little desks."

"Plus it'd be pure embarrassing to be three feet taller than every kid in my class."

"And the teacher," Vince added.

Dare nodded. "So doctor college is out. I need to change careers. I'm going to be a rancher. What I don't know—"

"And that'd be everything," Vince cut in.

"—Luke can teach me. I'll be fine. All I need to do is buy that ranch and get a few cows."

"That's so far from all you need to do, it's laughable." Vince proved that was true because he started to laugh.

The door to the diner opened. Jonas stepped in, and right beside him stood his sister, Tina Cahill.

Vince's laugh changed to coughing, until Dare worried the man might choke to death. Too bad there wasn't a doctor around to save him.

Every man in the place fell into a dead silence. Even Vince's coughing finally faded and Dare could look to see who'd come in.

Tina Cahill had arrived. Her eyes flashed like the vivid blue at the heart of a flame. Her hair was so golden blond that the sun seemed to shine out of the top of her head. She had lashes so long they tangled as she blinked at all the male attention. Then, as if it wasn't bad enough, she smiled.

That smile . . .

This was one amazingly lovely woman. No sign of Jonas's fat, bald sister anywhere.

She had a ridiculously fussy blue dress on, layers of flounces and ruffles over skirts and underskirts and maybe petticoats and bustles and corsets and hoops—something was definitely going on under that dress. Dare didn't think it was appropriate for him to wonder what.

Tina had a silken shawl draped over her arms to stave off the November weather, but surely all those skirts were as warm as a buffalo blanket. She wore a little hat that was garnished in ribbons and lace and other adornments. The hat alone was more elaborate than anything Dare had ever seen.

Of course, he'd never seen much besides gingham and calico and wool and cowhide, so that didn't mean a whole lot.

Everything about Tina Cahill was bright and lively and enchanting.

"She's the prettiest woman in the world." Vince spoke so quietly, Dare could barely hear him.

Vince wasn't the only man to whisper some sentiment, no doubt of a similar nature. There were five men left in the diner, and the stunned silence was suddenly broken with a buzz fit for a beehive.

There was no denying Tina was a beautiful woman. Not as pretty as Glynna, in Dare's opinion, but a beauty nonetheless. And since Tina was almost the same as a little sister—Jonas being like a brother to him—Dare immediately felt protective of her. The woman was going to get too much attention from all the wrong men. Well, *all* the men, the wrong ones included.

Confound it, why couldn't she have been fat and bald?

Jonas scowled at the men while Tina looked around, smiling, as if begging each and every man to say something that might get him punched by a preacher.

Dare decided to head off the fistfight. "Come sit with us, Jonas." He rose from his seat. The diner wasn't a big building, and Dare walked to meet Tina in about two steps. "Welcome to Broken Wheel, Miss Cahill. I was out doctoring when you arrived." He reached out his hands to Tina, and she took them, grinning back at him. "Jonas, your little sister looks nothing like you." Leaning closer to her, Dare whispered loud enough for everyone to hear. "Lucky you."

Jonas looked between Dare and his sister for a few seconds, then lost his scowl. "She takes after our ma. It's said I'm a throwback to my pa's mother's folks, the very Irish Donovans."

"Come sit down with Vince and me. There are flapjacks for breakfast." Dare let go of Tina's hands and gestured toward the nearly empty table. Jonas had probably deliberately waited for the breakfast crowd to thin out.

Good thinking.

"Tina already cooked for me. She's a dab hand in the kitchen. But I wanted her to meet you and suspected I'd find you here. She needs to make Mrs. Sevier's acquaintance, too."

Dare kept forgetting that was Glynna's name these days.

"You must be Dare Riker, the town doctor," Tina said.

Dare opened his mouth to correct her just as Vince slapped Dare on the back hard enough to make him bite his tongue.

"That's right." Vince came up beside him. "Good morning, Miss Cahill."

The scowl that had eased on Jonas's face when Dare

179

had greeted Tina now returned. Vince was probably a bit too good-looking for any brother to want near his sister.

If Jonas had been standing anywhere else but slightly behind Tina and could see his sister's face, he wouldn't have scowled. Tina turned her lovely little nose up just the barest fraction of an inch at Vince, then gave him a curt nod and, without speaking, went to sit at the table.

Vince looked dumbfounded. Dare was a little confused himself. Women usually responded well to Vince.

Jonas cheered right up.

Tina said, "I'd like to begin, as I mean to go on in this town, so there's no sense wasting time. We need to get that saloon closed, and I'd like every man here to help me."

A reformer.

Jonas had mentioned that.

The remaining men slunk out of the diner, no doubt on their way to the saloon to stock up, just in case. Dare sighed and sank into a chair across from Tina.

Jonas took a seat beside Tina and glared at every man in the place as they left.

He'd assigned himself the role of guardian as well as big brother, and they were all going to have to figure out how to handle his little sister correctly or face the parson's wrath.

CHAPTER 13

"She has hoops and a bustle?" Ruthy looked down at her calico skirt.

Glynna knew just how Ruthy felt. "Yes, and a corset and petticoats, too." With a sigh, Glynna added, "I used to have a bustle and petticoats, back in Arkansas before the war. By the time that was over, I had little left but a day dress and a Sunday best, and those were threadbare."

Ruthy shook her head. "I've never owned a spare dress in my life, until I came to Broken Wheel. Now I have what I found in the upstairs of Dare's house, which is plenty." She caught the skirts of her green dress, looked down, frowning, and said wistfully, "I can't imagine tending the house in a corset and hoops, though, so even if I had them, I wouldn't wear them. Not often anyway."

Ruthy looked at Glynna a little sheepishly. "I might put them on for church."

"There's Jonas, coming out of his house. Let's go over and we can walk back with Tina. She's really pretty. Young too." Glynna glanced at Ruthy and smiled. "About your age, I'd say, so only I feel old."

Ruthy laughed and linked arms with Glynna as they walked toward the small house Jonas lived in right next to the church. His sister followed him. Her eyes went immediately to Glynna and Ruthy.

"Good morning, Jonas." Glynna felt no envy for the woman's elaborate clothing or her stunning looks. Those things mainly served to attract men, and Glynna certainly didn't want to do that. "Tina, we'd love you to sit by us in church."

Tina smiled bright enough to shame the sun. "Thank you, I'd be delighted to."

Glynna quickly introduced Ruthy to Tina, then the three of them trailed after Jonas, who seemed distracted—thinking about his sermon, no doubt.

The Foster family was just descending from their wagon, and Ruthy called out to Melanie while Luke helped Gil lift the children down from the wagon.

"Come and sit with us, Melanie," Ruthy said as they drew near the Fosters.

Her toddler screamed and twisted in his father's arms until Gil almost dropped him.

"I think we'd better stay to the back row." Melanie gave her sons, who were running in circles, a look of affectionate exasperation. "You might want to sit a few rows away if you have any wish to hear what Parson Cahill has to say."

They all laughed as Glynna introduced Tina.

What with shuffling about so Luke sat next to Ruthy, and Glynna's children carefully keeping her separated from any man—Dare in particular, thank the good Lord—Tina ended up on the end of a short pew with one remaining space. Vince sat down in it just as Jonas walked to the crudely built podium from which he spoke.

Jonas looked at his sister, then at Vince, and frowned deeply. Then he seemed to gather himself and focus again on the service.

It was a lovely sermon, though Glynna had a tiny suspicion that the parson would have preferred to talk about sins of the flesh and eternal damnation.

"I'm surprised to see you up and about so early, Mr. Yates." Tina stood at the conclusion of the service. She probably shouldn't have spoken to him in any regard, but she certainly shouldn't have mentioned her memory of Vince falling in the street, overcome with demon rum in the morning.

Well, the man was here in church, so perhaps he had good days and bad. She'd definitely pray for him.

Vince turned to speak, sharing a bright smile. Before he uttered a word, Jonas came to her side, nearly skidding to a stop. "Come and stand with me to greet the parishioners, Tina."

He caught her arm in a no-nonsense grip and hustled her past Vince.

That suited Tina just fine. The small church was packed. It was all male except for Glynna, Ruthy, Glynna's daughter, Janny, Melanie Foster, and Tina. Not one single man failed to shake her hand, and they each hung on a bit too long. Jonas did a bit too much growling, in Tina's opinion, for a parson.

She'd pray for him, too.

When Glynna reached Tina, she said, "I've got a nice meal cooking in the diner. We're closed, of course, but my cook put a large roast on and added a few fixings before I shooed her off for the day. The Foster family is coming, too. The diner is the only place large enough to hold us all."

"There's another woman in town?" Tina thought she'd met them all.

"Yes. Lana Bullard. I asked her to church, but she's not a believer. She takes her Sundays off, though, and seems content with time alone in the boardinghouse where she lives. I'm hoping we can eventually persuade her to make her peace with God. She's had a very hard life."

Dr. Riker, bringing up the rear, muttered something, and Tina thought she heard the word *lunatic*. Vince shook his head and gave Dr. Riker a small shove.

"Can you come?"

Tina wanted to, but it seemed wrong to impose, especially on such short notice. She looked uncertainly at Jonas. "I hadn't begun preparations for a noon meal, but I have something I could—"

"No, Sunday dinner with my friends would be wonderful." Jonas smiled. "Thank you, Glynna."

Tina wondered for the hundredth time why she hadn't come to live with her kindhearted brother from the moment her parents had died. Her life would have been much easier.

∞

Dare saw the look in Vince's eyes and knew his life was about to get a whole lot harder.

"Dare, we got ourselves a problem." Vince leaned against one of the posts holding up the roof at the front of the diner, arms folded, ankles crossed, like a man without a worry in the world. Vince was always standing guard. He couldn't quit. He just made it look real relaxed.

"What problem? We've been talking all through the meal. Why wait till now to bring this up?"

Jonas and Luke were sitting on the board-walk. Dare was pacing on the dirt street in front of them, though not overly. He just needed to walk off his meal, so he moved. Sitting still had never suited him.

"I didn't want to say anything in front of the women and children." Vince's tone caught their attention, but then Vince had a way of doing that. He looked over his shoulder at the firmly closed door of the diner.

"Well, they're busy now." Luke sat up straight, frowning. Dare got the impression Luke knew what was coming.

The Fosters had headed on home after the meal so the children could nap. Paul had stayed with the women. He wasn't much interested in becoming friends, but Dare kept hoping that would change in time.

"I've been thinking this right along, but with the measles outbreak and you being away from town, then the Foster young'un being sick and Luke being sick, then Tina coming to town, well, there just hasn't been a chance to tell you."

Dare wasn't sure how much time Tina coming to town had taken Vince. She mostly stayed in Jonas's house.

"But there's been time to tell Luke?" That rankled Dare for some reason—them worrying about him and not saying anything.

"And Jonas."

Jonas gave Dare a lazy salute as if making fun of him for being annoyed. "Yep, we discussed it between us. Not much you could've done when you were so busy."

"I'm listening." Dare crossed his arms tight and quit moving to face Vince.

"The fire at your house wasn't an accident."

Vince's announcement brought a long stretch of silence to the four men.

Finally Dare said, "We talked about that at the time."

Vince nodded. "I've looked around your house since then."

A sound at the diner window turned Dare around to see Paul looking out. He didn't want the kid to overhear. "Let's walk over there."

All four men strode toward Dare's burned-down hulk of a house.

"Look at the kitchen. Those walls are still standing." Vince headed for that side first. "The cookstove almost looks like it blocked the fire, and that wouldn't be true if the stove was the source of it."

Dare walked ahead, faster than the others. Then he stopped to stare at that kitchen wall. "And the stovepipe . . . look at it."

The round metal poked out through the blackened wall. "A spark might get out around the pipe and start a fire, but then this wall would've burned first, and it didn't."

Luke jabbed a finger at the stones still intact in the midst of the burnt ruins. "Your fireplace might've caused it. It's more in the middle of the house."

Shaking his head, Vince kept moving, circling toward the front door. "I happened to look out my bedroom window and saw flames reflected in the window of the general store. I came running fast. I was here before the whole house was engulfed. This door was blazing. The fire had spread by then, but this was at the center of it."

"Right below the window I'd've climbed out," Dare said.

"And look how completely burned it is right here, practically down to fine ash."

It twisted Dare's stomach to look at the destruction—one of only two means he'd had to escape—except whoever struck the match didn't know about the attic access in his bedroom ceiling.

"The fire was white-hot outside my bedroom. I tried to get out that way first. The chimney could've started that, although I was real sure the fire had died all the way down. But that doesn't explain the front door."

"Then I ran around back, thinking I could get in and get upstairs and the stairway was burning, but there was unburned space between the stairs and the front door."

Dare didn't ask Vince if he was sure. Vince would've said so if he wasn't. "My front door is real close to the stairway. If there was unburned wood between them, the fire had to start in two places, and it hadn't been burning that long or they'd have turned into one big fire."

"Which says to me," Vince said, crossing his arms as he studied the building, "that someone used kerosene to get both fires big and hot real fast."

"So I couldn't get out," Dare added quietly.

Dare, Vince, Luke, and Jonas stood there staring as the

cool wind scattered blackened ash and whipped the scent of burnt wood in the air.

"Who did it?" Dare asked.

Vince shrugged.

"You've been checking everything else out—how about figuring the answer to that?"

"I've got a few ideas, but I don't know if I believe any of 'em."

"Let's hear it." Dare didn't like thinking someone wanted him dead. He'd helped a lot of folks in this town. It didn't seem real neighborly.

"Lana Bullard comes to mind," Vince said after a long pause.

A chill raced down Dare's spine as he remembered how strange she'd acted when she thought her baby had died.

Rubbing his hand over his mustache, Dare said, "Might be her. But a lot of men in this town would be mighty angry with me if I got her arrested and she couldn't cook anymore."

"What about Paul, Glynna's boy?" Vince's question was met with such utter silence, Dare wondered if maybe he'd gone deaf. "Have you noticed he's wearing a six-gun these days?"

Dare thought of the hate in the boy's eyes. He thought of how devastated Glynna would be if it was true. "He's so young . . ."

Vince scowled. "That gun he's wearing shoots the same whether he's fifteen or fifty."

"We saw some mighty mean kids in Andersonville," Luke reminded them all. "Plenty of 'em eager to throw in with the Raiders."

"A boy living with a brute could learn to hate any man who looked at his ma too long. And, Dare, I've seen you take some long looks at Glynna." Jonas was quiet about it, but his voice rang with conviction.

"Sounds like you know something about it, Jonas," Dare said.

"I do." Jonas glanced at the house. "Tina doesn't know this, and I trust none of you to tell her, but we didn't have the same pa. Her name isn't really Cahill. That's my pa's name, but she was too young to realize that when Ma and her father died. I suspect that's part of why we look so different. My pa died when I was about ten years old. Ma remarried. Then both Ma and her new husband died when Tina was still real young. But he had plenty of time to knock Ma and me around, and I had plenty of time to work up a grudge. I ran away from home three times. The third time I didn't come back. I was riding the outlaw trail when I was fourteen, the year my ma died. Tina was three.

"I heard Ma was dead and figured her husband had murdered her. I was so twisted up inside, I rode for home planning to kill him. All I could think was I should've done it sooner—" Jonas stopped abruptly, shook his head, and said, "Her husband had shot her and been hung for it long before I came home. Tina was already settled with Aunt Iphigenia. She was my pa's sister and no relation to Tina at all, but Aunt Iphigenia was the only family around and she did her duty. Made sure everyone knew what a sacrifice it was, too. Iphigenia was an upright woman. Too rigid, but a sight more decent than me. Iphigenia knew what I was, and she told me not to come back. I rode off to my

189

gang and stopped in from time to time despite my aunt's objections. Then I got dragged into the War Between the States. I found God in a muddy trench during one of those endless battles."

With a humorless laugh, Jonas said, "The war saved my life. Doesn't seem fair when it killed so many. A young'un can be mighty mean, and an abusive pa can drive a boy to terrible things. I don't see that in Paul, though. He hadn't put up with Greer that long."

"He said he wished he'd killed his own father," Dare said. "He said that right after he punched me and threatened to kill me for standing too close to Glynna."

"Standing too close?" Luke asked.

"Yes, nothing more," Dare snapped. Not that time. Later there'd been more. "That's what he punched me for. I probably deserved it."

Vince chuckled and slapped Dare on the back—on the side that'd been sewn up. It didn't hurt anymore. But it did make him wonder. He'd come close to death more than once lately. "There's no way an avalanche could be brought down deliberately, is there?" Dare asked.

All his friends exchanged looks. Finally, Luke said, "Sure it could. Paul was out there at the ranch. Did he have a chance to do it?"

Dare tried to remember. "I think he did go outside for quite a spell. Never thought about it, except I wondered if the house bothered him, reminded him of Greer."

"How would he do it?"

Luke shrugged. "Loosen the boulders, prop 'em up with sticks, and then kick the braces away."

"He was at the bottom of the canyon with us."

"There could be ropes hanging down to yank." Jonas narrowed his eyes. "I wasn't looking for anything like that. A rope I think I'd've noticed, but a dangling root might not have looked like it was put there on purpose, and the wagon was close enough to the sides of that narrow canyon that he could've reached a root and yanked it."

"If we think the avalanche was man-made, then how about Lana Bullard?" Luke said. "She's a lot more familiar with that area than Paul. I checked her house once right after Bullard died. She was gone, but I never looked again. She could've come back. Her cabin isn't visible from my place. She'd've had a lot of time to set that avalanche up. She knew we were friends, Dare. She had to reckon you'd be out to visit sometime. She could have been working on it for weeks."

"You said you have several ideas, Vince. Several is more than two." Dare frowned. "Nice to know you can think up a long list of folks who want me dead."

"You had a supply of morphine. There are men around who got addicted during the war and they might want to take your supply."

"Steal the drugs maybe, but why kill me?" Dare thought of a few men who'd come in with unexplained aches and pains, wanting laudanum mainly, but a couple of them had asked for morphine specifically. He'd refused them and talked with them about living without the drug. They'd never seemed dangerous before, but maybe he'd misjudged how desperate they were.

"To cover their tracks?" Vince suggested. "If it's someone

here in Broken Wheel, they'd probably have to quit the country if they stole and got caught. But a fire destroying a house would barely raise an eyebrow. Things like that happen. And no one is likely to notice bottles of morphine gone out of a burned-out building."

"Is that it?" Dare glowered at Vince. "Anyone else who might try and kill me?"

"Well—" Vince began.

"No." Dare cut him off. "Enough. We've got suspects aplenty and no way to find proof on any of them." Dare had very few ideas. All he could honestly think of was to keep a sharp lookout. "It seems like if it's Lana, she'd've tried again by now. So what do we do, post a guard?"

"We have been." Vince's managing ways, behind Dare's back, were irritating.

"What?"

"Jonas and I took shifts watching the whole time Elias Foster was sick at your place. And we intend to keep doing it."

"They didn't tell me until the day we went out to Gil's," Luke said a little sheepishly. "Then I got sick and I reckon I pressured you harder than I might've otherwise to stay out at my house. My men have stood guard there every night. Vince told Red Wolf and me at the same time. He's planning to come tonight and take a turn himself."

"Red Wolf's coming into town?" Dare couldn't believe it.

"He'll stay in the woods outside of town, but he figures he owes you. And Red Wolf doesn't like anyone killing his medicine man."

Vince might be too busy running things to care if Dare was upset, but Luke and Jonas realized it.

"You've posted a watch on my house all this time and never told me?"

"You were with that boy night and day." Vince crossed his arms, stubborn as always. "What good would it have done to tell you about a suspicion we had, when you couldn't get away hardly to eat, let alone take a turn on sentry duty?"

Dare decided fighting was a waste of time right now. He went back to the suspect list. "The only reason for Lana to do it is if she's plumb loco. Which she is." Dare had seen her eyes. Madness.

Nodding, Vince went on, "So she might've set off that avalanche and then been stopped when you went out to the Kiowa village. The fire hit almost as soon as you got back. We decided not to give her a chance to burn your new house down. But we've seen no sign of her trying anything."

"And if it was Paul . . . and we believe the avalanche was an accident," Luke said, sounding skeptical, "then he might've had a moment of fury and done such a thing but not be likely to do it again."

"And if it's someone after the morphine," Vince said, "then you just got a new shipment in. There was no sense attacking you when you had nothing to steal. Plus, a morphine thief might've found a supply from somewhere else to tide him over for a while."

Dare was opening his mouth to respond to that when Ruthy dashed out of the diner, shouting.

"Dare, come quick! Janny cut herself. It's bad!"

Dare was running before he had time to think.

But as he sprinted toward his next patient, his brain

started working. He was tired of there always being sick and injured people everywhere he turned. Of course, that was one of the hazards of being a doctor, and Lord knew he didn't mind helping them.

That wasn't the point. He was sick of being a liar. But how was he ever supposed to become a rancher if people kept needing him to doctor them?

He was fed up with the people in this town getting sick. They'd better get healthy and stay healthy so Dare could get on with starting his new career.

CHAPTER 14

There was blood everywhere. An artery severed maybe? The hand was so coated he couldn't see for sure.

Dare rushed to the little girl, pushing himself between Glynna and Tina, who were trying to stop the bleeding with a dish towel. He swept her into his arms. "I'm taking her to my house. It's quicker than bringing all the medical supplies over here."

He was already running by the time he reached the back door of the diner. Entering his house, he put her down on the bed he used for an examining table and grabbed a clean cloth.

Glynna was a step behind him. Vince next. No one else came.

"I told them to stay out." Vince read Dare's mind. "They're ready to help if you need it, though."

Dare dabbed at the blood on Janny's wrist. There was a deep slash, but the blood had no pulse. Shuddering with relief, he said, "She hasn't cut an artery."

But the little girl had come close.

Glynna let a tiny moan of fear escape as if she hadn't

even considered that. "It happened so fast. Janny was drying dishes and she picked up a butcher knife. It slipped."

"Get me hot water, Vince. Glynna, my doctor bag is by the front door." Dare gave a few more orders as he explored the wound. He looked at Janny's tear-soaked eyes. The little one was crying silently. He hated that she was so quiet.

"We'll take care of you, honey." A closer look at the wound told Dare the cut was deep on her palm and fingers besides her wrist. Praying for God to guide his hands, he said to the child, "It's okay to say it hurts."

She gave him a nod but remained silent.

The basin of hot water appeared at his side. Everything he'd demanded was delivered faster than he could get ready for it. "We're going to need to sew this up."

Whimpering, Janny tugged at his tight grip.

"Hold still, please." Dare fought to remain calm as he saw the artery blue and pulsing, the skin cut open to within a hairsbreadth. One false move on Dare's part might damage the vital artery and there might be no way to save the little girl's life short of amputating her hand. He wanted to beg the little one to stay very still until this mean cut was closed. But begging wasn't the way a doctor behaved. A doctor took charge. He gave orders. That was the way to comfort a patient and he knew it, but he was having trouble not babying the sweet child.

The muscle was damaged, and Dare couldn't sew that up and her skin both. It would leave stitches inside her, which would later become infected. He'd fix the muscle and let the skin close on its own. It'd be an ugly scar. Janny might blame him for that, but the muscle was a lot more important than the skin.

Thoughts of the war and the brutality of amputation made Dare sick to his stomach. He turned his thoughts to what needed to be done right now. "Get the sutures ready."

Glynna already stood across from him with his doctor bag open. She had what he wanted in front of him so fast it was startling. The needle was threaded.

"Vince, soak the needle and thread in whiskey. There's some in the cupboard there. Get a small bowl and let it soak while I work on the wound, then hold the needle to a flame." Dare's stomach clenched as he drew the skin gently closed on her flayed wrist. "You have to hold very still, Janny."

The door slammed open. Paul charged in. "I saw blood all over the kitchen."

A frightened cry from Janny was the first loud noise she'd made.

Paul rushed to the bedside, jostling Dare's grip on Janny's wrist.

"No, Paul. Stop. Be careful."

Janny's crying rose to a wail. She tugged against Dare's grip.

"Paul, watch out." Glynna's frightened voice upset Janny even more. The child threw herself toward Glynna, who grappled to keep her still while Dare kept an iron grip on her wrist.

The boy was white with fear. Dare couldn't blame the kid, but there was no time to calm him down.

Looking hard at Vince, Dare said, "Get him out and keep him out. Then I need you back. Get Jonas and Luke to hold him."

"No! Let me stay!" Paul clawed at Dare as Vince got hold of the boy.

Janny squealed and jerked her hand. The move was so rough that Dare was afraid she'd deepened her cut by that last fraction of an inch.

Vince dragged the shouting boy away. The door slammed shut, muffling the sound of the boy's protests. Janny's wrenching sobs shook her body, and she struggled against Dare's hold.

"You've got to stay still, honey." Glynna dropped to the bed and took Janny's right hand while Dare controlled her damaged left.

"No!" Janny rolled toward Glynna. "Stop! I don't want him to stab me with a needle. Get him away, Mama!"

Glynna wrestled Janny back. Dare grabbed the little girl's arm at the elbow, desperate to keep her from further injury. Her thrashing set the blood flowing faster.

"Let me go!" Janny's cries grew louder, her resistance more desperate.

He didn't dare let the little one fight any longer.

Vince came charging back in.

Tina Cahill was hard on his heels. "Let me help."

Dare said, "Vince, laudanum."

"No, I don't want her drugged." Glynna had been calm, but she reacted strongly to his ordering of laudanum.

"Mama, stop him. No!" Janny screamed. Her whole body heaved against Dare's grip.

"Hold her legs, Tina," Dare said. "We've got to keep her still."

Tina rushed to obey Dare. She looked sick to hold down the frantic little girl, but she didn't hesitate for a second.

"Please," Glynna begged, "let me try to calm her down without laudanum. Give me a chance to—"

"Help me," Dare snapped. He looked Glynna square in the eye. "You do what I say when I say it or I'll have Vince throw you out just like he did your son. I need her calm or she might—" Dare couldn't say Janny might lose her hand. He couldn't terrify the girl any more than she already was.

"Might what?" Glynna had her hands full, holding Janny on her back.

"Help me or get out." Dare's tone was ice-cold. Glynna's shocked expression said his words and the lethal tone chilled her to the bone, but it also cut through her panic.

A shudder went through Glynna as she visibly fought her fear. She cut off the questions and resistance to the laudanum and gave one hard nod of her chin.

Vince was there with the bottle and a cup in hand, too. "How much?"

Dare told him. Vince poured.

"I'll give it to her," Glynna offered with a nearly mad calm, taking the tin cup.

With Dare and Tina helping, Glynna kept Janny still just by holding on to her right hand.

Janny howled and turned her head away from the medicine.

"Janet Melissa Sevier!" Glynna's voice had the sound

199

only a ma who'd been at the job for a long time could muster. "You lie still and you take this medicine."

Janny stopped thrashing. Tears still streamed and the broken sobs tore from her throat, but the fight went out of her.

Dare looked up at Glynna, sickened to see this little one so scared.

"No, Ma. That's the medicine that made Pa so crazy. I remember it. I don't want it. I don't want to hurt anyone."

Those words cut Dare as deep as that butcher knife.

"You take this medicine right now, young lady!" Glynna released the child's hand, then slid an arm behind her trembling shoulders, sat her up very carefully, and held the cup to her lips. Dare realized he was holding his breath, worried that Janny would fight being dosed. But that magical mother voice was stronger than Janny's fear, helping to break the girl out of her panic.

Janny took a sip and shuddered.

"Drink it all, honey. Every last drop. Swallow it quick." Another version of the voice, this time comforting and loving but demanding obedience.

Janny finished the medicine.

Glynna set the cup aside and brushed Janny's disheveled hair off her face. Leaning down, Glynna kissed her daughter on the forehead and murmured soothing words.

Into the silence Dare decided he had a chance to speak, even more a chance to be heard. "I'm not going to hurt you, Janny. I'm going to fix your cut. I'm going to make you better."

Dare prayed fervently, *Please, God, guide my hands.*

Heal this child. Protect her. Calm Paul. Give Glynna peace.

He kept talking, using a soothing voice he'd learned had a good effect on patients. He focused on Janny. He'd never be able to stitch up the cut if she wouldn't hold absolutely still. He needed to get to work on the wound, yet he forced himself to wait until the laudanum had taken full effect.

As the minutes ticked by, Dare wondered if he'd given enough of the drug. Too much was dangerous, and someone as small as Janny might be at risk with a stronger dose.

Finally her eyes began to glaze over. The starch slowly went out of her limbs.

Dare looked at the laid-open wrist. The pulse in her artery was a thick blue river that visibly slowed and told him the laudanum was working.

Her eyes became heavy-lidded, then inched shut. Dare slowly relaxed his grip.

"Janny, can you hear me?"

The little girl didn't respond.

With a sigh of relief, Dare nodded. "She's asleep."

The tension left Glynna as if she'd taken the drug herself.

"Now I need the sutures." Dare blew out a long breath as he regained the detached doctoring tone.

Glynna's shoulders squared. She had a doctoring mind-set, too. But Dare suspected that was because she'd had too much practice getting through bad times. And as a single woman in the West, there were more bad times ahead. It was a hard life.

Vince had been busy getting the thread and needle to soak in whiskey. Dare gave his friend a quick look of gratitude.

"No surprise Mr. Yates was quick to find the whiskey," Tina said with a sniff. She released Janny's legs and stood, pretty as a sniffing sunflower.

Dare wondered what in the world she meant by that.

"I'm so sorry Paul caused trouble." Glynna's doctoring attitude wobbled for a moment. "He's been through so much."

Then Glynna steadied herself, turned back to her daughter, and handed Dare the threaded needle.

CHAPTER 15

"You saved her," Glynna sobbed.

Dare found himself alone with Glynna, who'd worked by his side all afternoon and into the evening without shedding a single tear. "Didn't you calmly sew my back up just a little while ago? And you've been working beside me easy as can be for hours. How come you're crying now?"

Dare knew he sounded too harsh. It was possible he was on the ragged edge of his own self-control. Glynna had clearly gone over the edge.

She cried harder. "You saved her hand. Maybe her life."

The cut had the potential to be life threatening if a lot of things had gone wrong, but they hadn't, so Dare wasn't about to claim he'd saved her life.

"I d-didn't have time to c-cry before." Glynna turned to Janny, who was still unconscious. Dare had carefully given her more laudanum, twice during the long day, and she was deeply asleep. Dare feared giving her too much; he'd never dosed a youngster before this day.

"That's just a pure stupid thing to say." Dare couldn't stand much more female fussing. Janny had about been his limit. Just listening to the little one, usually so quiet, scream in pain and fear, fighting Dare and Glynna, was enough to make a grown man cry—if he'd been a weak-bellied girl child.

"I know it is . . ." Glynna cried harder and hugged herself. She looked lonelier than anyone Dare had ever seen. "But I can't st-stop."

They'd stitched for so long, the sun had set on the short Texas day. Paul had come in a few times to see Janny, with Vince close at his side. He'd been subdued and had himself under control. But the hostility was back. Dare had made inroads with Paul over talk of hunting and doctoring, but now it was back to where they'd begun with Paul's anger focused squarely on Dare. Eventually, even with his suspicions, exhaustion had caught up with Paul and he'd fallen asleep in a chair. Glynna had awakened the boy, and he was so groggy he'd allowed himself to be sent to bed.

The whole house was quiet now. Jonas and Tina had gone home with an offer to come back at a moment's notice. Luke and Ruthy were back at their ranch.

Vince said he'd stay but there was nothing to do, so Dare sent him home, too. He was probably out there right now standing guard.

Night had fallen. Four lanterns kept the room bright. Dare could hear Paul snoring steadily in the bedroom upstairs.

Looking at Glynna sobbing was more than Dare could stand. He moved without making a decision to do it.

Glynna, on the far side of Janny's bedside, moved also. With hardly a thought, Dare pulled her into his arms.

No kiss this time. He just held her as she cried. Her hair had started out the day in a tidy braid, coiled at the nape of her neck. The braid hung down now, and Dare's finger slid into the thick rope of hair and knocked away the ribbon that held it.

As the hair unwound, his hands sunk deep into the silky golden waves. He relished the feel of it as he held her tight, her body shaking with sobs. He stood with Glynna in his arms, stunned at the need to take care of this strong, wounded woman.

It seemed like the worthy work of a lifetime, more important than doctoring. More valuable than ranching.

He knew with clear purpose that he wanted the right to protect and care for this woman, to share his life with her. He lifted her chin and looked into those beautiful, tear-soaked golden eyes and it was inevitable that he kiss her.

But as the kiss deepened, he knew it was wrong. He couldn't do this until he'd earned her son's blessing—her son who might've tried to kill him.

Glynna had thought she was beyond womanly dreams, beyond expecting a handsome prince to ride into her life and save her.

And then Dare Riker kissed her. True, that had happened before, but not like this.

His hands sunk deep in her hair and adjusted the angle of the kiss, and she wanted nothing more than to stay forever in the fortress of his arms.

She had a son who was killing mad all the time, and a daughter who barely spoke and was still in life-threatening danger.

Dare had handled her son, though that problem remained. He'd handled her daughter's injury, though she still needed healing.

Now he was handling her, and she couldn't bear to end it. Even if she should.

Her arms swept around his neck as he dragged her deeper into the kiss. She'd been married twice and no man had ever given her this much pleasure, which was a sad commentary.

Dare slowly, gently, slid his hands to cup her face and lifted his head. He moved back just enough to rest his forehead against hers and take an unsteady breath.

She reached one shaky hand up to touch his lips. "Your mustache tickles."

Nodding, Dare said, "I'll shave it off. I'll do whatever you want that'll keep you kissing me."

Glynna smiled, and then her smile quickly faded. "It's not just about me and what I want, Dare."

"I know. We need to figure out what to do about Paul's anger. But I can't pretend I'm not interested in you, Glynna. What are we going to do about this?"

As she ran her finger along his lip, Glynna knew what she'd like to do. She'd like to find a way to join her life with Dare's forever. He was a different kind of man from her other husbands. She knew him, and she'd barely known either of the men she'd married.

"I can't let you into my life while Paul is so angry."

"You may not have noticed"—Dare stole another kiss—"but I'm already in your life."

Glynna had indeed noticed. "If we just had more time . . ."

"I know." Dare stepped away as if he had to force each movement. Glynna stumbled, and Dare steadied her but kept his distance. "I won't make things worse for the boy."

"And it's not as noticeable," Glynna said with a glance at her sleeping daughter, "but Janny is in trouble, too. She wasn't a quiet little girl before I came to live with Flint. Today, screaming and fighting the way she did, was almost a relief. She never disobeys, never even asks for anything. Paul's rage and Janny's silence are damage that's been done to them that I have to heal. But I don't know how beyond giving them time and safety."

Dare laid one finger on Glynna's lips. The touch became a caress. His eyes glinted with sudden determination. "I know we have to be patient, but I like having you near me, Glynna. I like it too much."

As he lowered his head to kiss her, he said, "Nothing has ever felt so right."

"This is so wrong." She muttered the words but didn't break the kiss, which told Dare a lot.

When Glynna was utterly limp in his arms, he let her lower her head to his chest and they just held each other. Like earlier, only without Glynna soaking his shirt.

"What are we going to do about Paul?"

"I'll have a man-to-man talk with him."

Glynna pulled away just enough that Dare had to either wrestle her back or let her go.

"Paul has good reason to distrust men."

"I know Flint was hard on you, but—"

"It's not just Flint."

"He said something about his pa." What the kid had said was he should have killed his pa. That was something mighty ugly for a kid to have inside him. "That marriage was a bad one, too? Is that where Janny learned to be afraid of laudanum?"

"Yes, and Reggie had a fondness for blue ruin, too." Glynna folded her arms across her chest. "That's where I learned my doctoring."

"Your first husband was a doctor?"

"No, my first husband was forever coming home in need of medical treatment, and we couldn't summon a doctor."

"Why not?"

"Because my husband was a deserter from the Confederate army."

That tightened Dare's jaw. He had no use for cowards, but a lot of men had run away. "He isn't the only man who just went home. There were plenty of 'em."

"There weren't plenty who made a career out of it."

Dare tried to figure that out. "A career?"

"There was a bounty being paid to any man who would sign up for the war."

"They had those in the North, too."

"My husband signed up over a dozen times."

Clamping his mouth shut, Dare stroked his mustache to keep from saying anything. Dare had heard of varmints who signed up over and over, finding a new unit to join. In fact, he'd been in Andersonville Prison with those kinds of mangy coyotes. The worst of the Raiders were men who'd only signed up planning to get the enrolling fees, then run off. Some had done it many times. A new name, a new state, a new commanding officer. No one could keep a good tally of everyone who came to fight, or not fight in the case of these sidewinders.

Then these men, if they got taken prisoner before they could run off, had no loyalty to the Yankees and they kept up their thieving ways. After Dare and his Regulator friends had brought peace to the camp, men like Glynna's husband had spent a good chunk of their time trying to kill him. He had three knife wounds in his back to prove they'd come real close.

A chill went through Dare. He fought to hide his revulsion. There were no men he held in greater contempt than those who were disloyal to their own brothers-in-arms. He understood desertion. He understood men who were overwhelmed and heartsick and just gave up the fight to go home—that was a different kind of man, and Dare didn't hold their behavior against them.

Much.

But to take the money and desert as Glynna's first husband had was cold-blooded thievery. It stole money from an already bankrupt war effort. Such a man had no loyalty to his country, his commanding officers, or his fellow soldiers.

"You sewed him up a few times, then?" He forced himself to talk when he wanted to walk out. Glynna had patched her husband up, probably helped him hide, then she'd sent him off to war again. It was pretty clear she hadn't liked the man, but she'd probably spent the money he brought home while Yankees in Andersonville starved and Confederate soldiers marched barefoot with broken-down weapons.

With a humorless laugh, Glynna turned away and spoke with her back to him. "You're just like everyone else."

Dare must've done a poor job of keeping his expression blank. "Everyone else?"

"They hung him. They hung my first husband. Paul Reginald Sevier. My son is Paul Gaston Sevier. Such a proud old name. The marriage was arranged and we'd barely met before the wedding. Reggie was handsome and polished. His father presented us with a beautiful home and gave us a steady income, never asking his son to work. We had Paul right away, and Reggie was so proud to bestow the family name on his own son. He wasn't a bad man, not at first. I thought I had a good marriage. But as the years passed, Reggie was gone more and more. I was busy with my society friends, and most of them had similarly distant marriages, so I didn't mind it overly. And then one night when I was expecting Janny, Reggie came home smelling of perfume."

"Glynna, I'm sorry he was that kind of man. But it's a long way from a wealthy high-society cheat to an army deserter."

"Papa Sevier died. We inherited his fortune. With that money, and now free of his father's controlling hand, Reggie became more flagrant in his infidelity. He was gone more than he was home. I heard rumors that he'd bought a house for a mistress, and he never passed up a poker game. Then my father died and left us more riches. I didn't know how much. It never occurred to me that I should pay attention to our money—there was always plenty. We'd been married nearly ten years when some men came to the door of the mansion we owned in Little Rock to take possession. I laughed. We were rich. It had to be a mistake. I quit laughing when we were thrown into the street."

"Glynna, I'm sorry—"

"Let me finish." Raising a hand with a hard snap of her wrist, still facing away from him, she said, "You don't even know all you should hate me for yet, Dr. Riker. There's plenty more."

"I don't hate you. Don't say that." He should have, at that moment, gone to her, held her, but he couldn't quite make himself.

"We moved into a smaller house we could afford, because my father had secured some investments so they couldn't be taken by bill collectors. The servants were dismissed and I had to learn to cook and clean. Finally all of my father's money had been depleted and our last move was out into the country into little more than a shack. And then the war broke out. Reggie heard money was being paid to soldiers who enlisted, so he left."

"He signed up?"

Nodding, Glynna turned to face Dare finally. Her eyes blazing. She was furious, but at him or at her long-ago husband? "He came home after about two months with money—more money than just what they paid for joining the army."

"Where did he get the extra?" Dare had a good idea.

"He robbed some of the men in his unit when he ran off. Reggie played this game all through the war. Sometimes he'd come home cut up, beaten. Twice he'd been shot. I learned doctoring. The war ended at last. Reggie no longer had the chaos of war to hide his deceit, but he couldn't stop his thieving. He was caught. At his trial, Reggie told everyone I'd pressured him for the money. They didn't charge me, but they hung Reggie and seized possession of my house. I had two children to raise, and I was a pariah in Little Rock, where so many had died in the war." Glynna tilted her head at Dare and gave him a broken smile. "And then I read an ad in the paper for a mail-order bride."

"Flint Greer."

"There were several to choose from, and I picked the man who was farthest away, hoping my past wouldn't follow me out West. Flint came on the stage to Little Rock and we were married immediately. He seemed very nice, but by the time we'd been married a month he'd slapped me for the first time."

There was silence at last. Dare was thankful she'd quit. He felt battered by the story.

"And now I look at you and see you would side with all the good citizens of Little Rock in condemning me. Go to bed, Dr. Riker. I'd prefer to stay with my daughter without your company." She went to Janny's side and sat down, cutting Dare out as if he didn't exist.

"We both need time and rest," he said. Feeling like the

worst kind of coward, he walked toward the back of his house. Glancing over his shoulder, he saw Glynna rest one strong, gentle hand on her daughter's shoulder and bow her head. Dare wondered if she was praying.

It was an idea with merit.

CHAPTER 16

Paul hadn't asked permission to buy a gun. He'd just shown up one morning with it, and Glynna never saw him without it again.

Glynna knew men wore guns on the frontier, men as young as fifteen. And all through the war he'd helped feed their family by hunting. But she still hated seeing that gleaming black pistol holstered on his hip.

And Glynna knew her son was still hostile toward Dare, although it didn't seem to be quite so severe as before. Maybe her son was finally starting to heal. More likely it was because he saw that Glynna was furious with Dare.

Dare still came to the diner for meals and was always polite, yet he rarely looked her in the eye and never said an unnecessary word. She did notice he'd shaved off his mustache. She couldn't look at his face—even though he was none too diligent about shaving—without remembering the moment they'd shared after he'd treated Janny.

The pain was so deep that Glynna thought many times of taking her children and leaving town. She could start a diner in some other little Texas town. Maybe Lana Bullard would come with her. Knowing how to cook was proving to be a big advantage when running a restaurant. In fact, Lana had kept the diner going all week while Glynna focused all her attention on Janny. Truth was, Lana didn't need Glynna at all. That diner could only barely be considered Glynna's. She didn't own the building, she didn't do the cooking, and lately she didn't even show up. And yet by all accounts things were running smoothly.

Glynna worried about the day Lana figured that out.

Instead of working, Glynna spent all her time in the doctor's house. Dare was often called away, and when he was there, Paul made sure to be there, too. While not exactly friendly, Paul did minimal growling.

Janny, on the other hand, was driving Glynna mad.

"I want up!" Janny's voice, which the child had barely used, and then only at a whisper, for much of the year of Glynna's marriage to Flint, was now working perfectly, frequently, and at top volume.

Glynna remembered her noisy, fussy daughter and was overjoyed to see her rediscover her spirit.

"Let me sit in a chair," "I'm hungry," "Read to me, Mama," "My cut itches," "Paul's bothering me," "The bandage is too tight," "I hurt!"

Oh yes, it was a pure blessing to hear Janny speak—at first. Then Glynna wanted the child to hush up.

"I want to see the sewing in my hand again."

Just as Janny made that last demand, Dare returned from the Fosters', where he'd checked on the boy who'd had pneumonia. He gave Glynna his usual distant smile, then turned a genuine smile on Janny.

"Hi, Doc." Janny had taken a liking to the doctor who had dealt her so much pain.

Dare went to her and with his hand he smoothed Janny's unruly hair, pausing to feel for a fever. "You're looking really good today. We're past the time when you should get an infection. You're going to be okay, Janny."

Dare's voice was warm and strong and kind—except when he talked to Glynna.

"I'm bored, Doc. When are you going to let me get up?"

Glynna had almost forgotten that Janny could talk like this. When she was really young, she'd always been full of stories and questions. She'd grown quiet in the last years with Reggie, especially when he was at home. Then during the year with Flint, Janny had become almost completely silent.

Now Glynna was getting her little girl back.

"I'm going to unwrap it and let you see." Dare began gently pulling the bandage away. "Right now the cut is still red and puffy, but it's going to keep getting better and better, so don't be upset if it doesn't look good."

He'd changed the bandage daily. It had looked so vicious and swollen and red that it had terrified Glynna. But Dare had assured her it was doing well. He'd been a perfectly professional doctor in all ways.

But he'd never tried to wrangle another kiss. And the polecat hadn't even given her a real smile. He was just like everyone else, blaming her for Reggie.

Maybe she deserved the blame. She'd never gone to the authorities to turn her husband in. Of course, they'd lived a long way out. There were no authorities.

"I might be able to take some of the stitches out today," Dare said.

It had been over a week, and normally seven days of stitches were enough. But the cut was so dire that Glynna thought it was much too soon. Dare wasn't asking her for her opinion, so she held her tongue.

As Dare tended to the unwrapping, he looked at Glynna, his expression polite and neutral. "Ruthy's in town. She's invited us all to her house for a meal. She thinks a Thanksgiving dinner is in order and wants to have us out next Thursday."

"I've lost track of the days." Glynna tried to remember how long she'd been here tending Janny.

"It's Tuesday. It's been ten days since Janny cut her hand. I think, if we're very careful, we can let Janny get out of this bed and ride in a wagon out to the S Bar S on Thursday."

Then Dare turned to Paul, who leaned near the window that faced the diner, watching every move Dare made. "Do you want to come, Paul? Jonas and his sister are coming. Vince will be there. Ruthy invited the Fosters, but they want to spend their first Thanksgiving in their own home."

Paul shrugged, but he didn't say no—much to Glynna's surprise.

Dare turned back to tending Janny.

"I want to go to the ranch, Ma." Janny was watching her hand be unwrapped like she was anticipating a Christmas gift. "I like it fine now that someone else lives there."

Glynna hated that house and always would, but she had

to make peace with it for the sake of her friendship with Ruthy, and she knew hating a house was irrational and unfair. "We can g-go."

Paul gave her a sharp look. It felt as if Paul was now reading her mind. He could tell things were bad between her and Dare. He could tell she didn't want to go to the ranch. Of course, maybe that was no great trick. Maybe everything showed on her face.

The door swung open.

"How's our little knife juggler doing today?" Ruthy came in, her smile generous and full, her red hair shining in the autumn sunlight.

Glynna was glad Dare had warned her of the invitation so she could say yes to Thanksgiving dinner without hesitation. Ruthy and Tina were the best friends she'd had in her life, the *only* friends she'd had for years. It was important that Glynna show true enthusiasm when Ruthy opened her home.

"Mrs. Stone, Dr. Riker said we can come to your home for dinner." Janny bounced in the bed, and Dare made a scolding noise that kept her still. "He said I'm well enough to be up if we're very, very careful."

Ruthy sat on the bed on the side across from Dare and very gently, not disturbing Dare at work, gave Janny a hug. Then Ruthy took Janny's healthy hand and turned to Glynna, who stood near the door to the back rooms. She kept her distance when Dare was working with Janny.

"Is it all right with you? If the good doctor here says it's safe and we're very, very careful?" Ruthy echoed Janny's words with a smile.

"Yes, that will be wonderful. Janny is tired of being in bed."

"Yay!" Janny bounced and threw one hand high.

Dare had the other one in a solid grip or it would've waved, too. "Sit still. I don't know if you understand what I mean by careful, young lady." Dare's scolding tone was laced with teasing.

Janny laughed. "I'm sorry. I just got excited."

Ruthy leaned down and gave Janny a loud smacking kiss.

"This looks a lot better." Dare had the cut uncovered.

Despite her determination to avoid Dare the Betrayer, Glynna couldn't resist coming to stand beside him as he examined the wound.

"It really does look better." Glynna felt almost light-headed with relief.

Most of the swelling was gone. There would be a terrible scar, but Janny's hand was all right.

"Bend your fingers for me, just a bit." Dare was all doctor as he pressed here and there.

Janny wiggled her fingers stiffly.

"They're all working. Good." He puffed out a breath that Glynna recognized as relief, which told her he'd been a lot more worried than he'd let on. Had he feared Janny's fingers wouldn't move? It had never occurred to her. She said a quick prayer of relief that she hadn't had that to worry about.

"I'm going to take out a few stitches." Dare looked the hand over thoroughly. "A few places, where your hand bends a lot or where the cut was really deep, I'll leave until we get back from the Thanksgiving feast."

Paul came up to Glynna's side and rested one of his hands on Glynna's shoulder. She hadn't known she needed support, but Paul gave it. She expected rudeness, just because of her nearness to Dare, but her son seemed to know Glynna was nearly overcome.

He studied the wound, and if he had something rude to say to Dare, he controlled himself.

Dare glanced up and his eyes slid past Glynna, who'd assisted so often, to settle on Paul. "Can you help me? I need an extra set of hands, and I think your ma and Ruthy could go have some coffee in the kitchen. I made some earlier. You ladies can take a break from all the doctoring."

Dare gave Glynna a look she couldn't define, then he rolled his eyes in Ruthy's direction. Glynna noticed Ruthy's fair, freckled skin had turned ash white and her eyes were riveted on the scar.

Glynna got it.

Ruthy needed to get out of here, and it was past time she knew there was a baby on the way. It looked to be Glynna's job to let her know.

"Is that all right with you to help the doctor, Paul? I could stand to let someone else handle this." The fact that Glynna wasn't perfectly steady said more than words.

"I reckon I can do whatever needs doing." That was about as close to cooperative as Paul was likely to get.

"Let's go have a cup of coffee, Ruthy." Glynna walked toward the kitchen.

Ruthy came along so willingly, Glynna knew she wanted to get away. Glynna swung the kitchen door firmly shut, and both of them sank onto chairs with matching sighs.

The sound they made was so similar, their eyes met and they both laughed.

"Was that hard to look at for you, Ruthy?" Glynna had the feeling that any upset Ruthy felt could be tied directly to an expected child, because Ruthy didn't let much get her down.

"I hadn't seen it before." Ruthy's voice dropped to a whisper, though their voices shouldn't carry unless they got quite loud. "Not since the day she cut it. The poor little girl."

"For some reason it was too much for me today, though it's so much improved." Glynna gathered her wits and got them both a cup of coffee, then sat back down. "Does the sight of something like that always make you light-headed?"

Ruthy gave Glynna a sheepish look. "You noticed?"

"You went pale as milk."

With a little smile, Ruthy said, "I'm not usually such a weakling. It might be because Janny is a child. I reckon that hits a little harder than seeing an adult who's injured. I helped tend Dare when that building blew up on him, and Luke was bleeding, and Vince got shot in—" Ruthy cut off her speech and swallowed hard.

"You mean on the day Flint died? It's all right for you to speak of it."

Ruthy nodded. "I know you didn't care for your husband, Glynna, but that doesn't make talk of him dying easier to hear."

"Of course it's easier—not easy, but nothing like if I'd liked the low-down skunk. It occurs to me I've buried two husbands now. I'm like a black widow spider." Shaking her head, Glynna changed the subject. "Hmm . . . do you think there might . . . uh, be any special reason you got wobbly, a reason *besides* Janny being so young?"

"I can't think what." Ruthy lifted her coffee cup to her lips.

Glynna wasn't quite sure how to go on. It might embarrass Ruthy to have someone else tell her of her baby. But Glynna wasn't going to dwell on the day Flint had died. The polecat had come charging into town, thinking Glynna had run away from him, bent on dragging her home. When Dare, Vince, Luke, and Jonas had stood in Flint's way, the man had shot Vince and had a go at killing Dare. With Luke and Jonas at his side, Dare had won that fight and Flint had died. Glynna had been set free and she couldn't regret her husband was dead, but it had left a wound on all of them that it had come to killing the man.

Ruthy took a sip of the coffee, then grimaced and set it aside. "How long has this been on the stove? It smells burnt."

The coffee smelled just fine, and Glynna decided this was the right moment. "Coffee bothered me a couple of times, too."

"Well, you've learned to make it much better."

Glynna smiled. "Do you mean, I've learned to make it much better now that Lana is making it at the diner and Dare is making it here?"

Ruthy's cheeks flushed pink.

"For me those two times, it wasn't my cooking that made the coffee taste sour." Glynna took a deep breath, then plunged ahead. "It was having a baby on the way."

"Really? That's funny that a baby would have an effect on coffee."

Glynna remembered then that Ruthy's ma had died when Ruthy was just reaching the age of a young woman. Clearly there had been no mother-daughter talk.

"I think a baby is affecting it now."

Ruthy frowned. "You're expecting a baby? Flint left you with child?"

Glynna shook her head and decided only the blunt truth would do. "No, you are, my friend. *You* are expecting a child, not me."

The room fell utterly silent. Ruthy's jaw dropped. Her blue eyes went wide. Glynna waited for Ruthy to think it all through. Finally, in a squeak, Ruthy asked, "How can you know?"

Glynna very gently but honestly told Ruthy just exactly how. By the time Glynna was done, Ruthy's eyes were shining and her cheeks had taken on a glow of pleasure.

"It's true. All of that is happening to me." Ruthy rose from the table. "I have to tell Luke."

Ruthy paused as she reached the kitchen door. "How long do you think it will take to have the baby?"

Glynna told Ruthy what to expect. "I'd be glad to answer questions anytime."

Ruthy's smile turned bashful. "Thank you, Glynna. I suspect I'll think of things to ask, and I appreciate you helping me."

They were too close in age for Glynna to think of Ruthy as a daughter, but it felt wonderful to see her so pleased.

Ruthy seemed to float out of the house. She left without

saying goodbye to anyone. Glynna came into the room with her children, and Dare smiled at her—the first genuine smile he'd shared with her since he'd betrayed her over her traitorous husband.

He didn't speak of Ruthy's expected child, though. Not the sort of thing one discussed in front of children.

"Now," Dare said, breaking up the pleasant moment, "come and see your daughter's hand. I've taken some of the stitches out where I'd stitched the muscle. Then I abraded the wound just a bit and closed the outer layer of skin. I hadn't hoped to do that, but with a bit of help, I believe it's still raw enough that it will heal in a way that reduces the scarring."

Glynna saw a much neater row of stitches than had been there before. Yes, there'd be a scar, but nothing like what Glynna had feared.

"Once it's bandaged again, it'll be safe for her to take a wagon ride." Dare spoke with humorous sternness straight at fidgety Janny. "If she's very careful, she can get out of bed now. And, Miss Janet, if you'll let me carry you, I'll agree to let you go home."

Smiling, Janny nodded. "I'll let you carry me." Janny scooted to the edge of the bed, bracing herself with her hand.

"Watch the hand!"

Janny froze.

Glynna rushed forward. She couldn't blame her daughter. So many simple reactions included using the hands. "We're going to have to be so careful, honey."

Glynna looked up and her eyes met Paul's. He was worried, too.

Dare interrupted the moment by sliding one hand under Janny's knees and another around her back. "Let's wrap her up good with a blanket so she doesn't get a chill. It's mighty cold outside. I'll put her arm in a sling once we're settled, and that will remind her to be cautious."

Janny was in her nightgown. All her clothes had been taken home to be laundered. Glynna rushed for the door. "I'm going to get her bed turned down. Paul, close the door behind the doctor so the heat doesn't leave the house, then get the diner door for him and the door to the upstairs."

She gave one more anxious look at Janny, who was busy grinning at Dare with her right hand curled around his neck and her carefully wrapped left hand cradled in her lap. Glynna knew how fond Janny had become of the heroic, life-saving, handsome, betraying, low-down Dr. Skunk.

Running from him seemed like the best possible plan.

⁂

"You're still standing watch?" Dare had been busy or he'd have thought of this before tonight.

Vince leaned against the back wall of the diner, the shadows half concealing him. He wore a black duster, buttoned up to the throat. His dark hair and tanned skin made him almost invisible in the black night. Except once Dare remembered his friends were standing guard, he'd known exactly where to look. The same spot he'd have picked.

"Jonas has the back." Vince had his arms crossed, looking like he was just hanging around, nothing better to do right before sunup. "He can watch from inside. Luke stood in for Jonas until an hour ago, so Jonas got some sleep. I just took over for Red Wolf."

"You can't stand out here every night." Dawn would be breaking soon. The wind howled and tossed the long coat around Vince's knees. "You'll make yourselves sick from the cold. And there aren't enough of you to keep watch overnight. The shifts are too long. Luke and Red Wolf can't ride in every night. You'll all be worn right down to the bone."

Dare started moving. He hated standing still, and he hated it even more when he was fretting. And having his friends give up sleep to guard him was a fretful business.

Vince nodded. "It'd be a sight more comfortable inside. I've been wondering if Mrs. Greer or Sevier—or whatever Glynna's name is—would let me watch out the back window of the kitchen. I can't ask, though, not if her son and her cook are both suspects. Might as well post a big old sign right here, announcin' we're standing guard."

"Maybe we should do that." Dare had thrown on a coat but not a hat. It wasn't bitter cold—growing up in Indiana taught a man just how cold it could get.

"It wouldn't be real sneaky."

"The only point of being sneaky is to catch someone. If we let the whole town know we've posted a sentry, maybe that'd stop whoever did it. My problems would be solved."

"Nope. Not solved. Just put off a while, cuz the killer'd come back once they thought it was safe."

"Not if it was Paul who set that fire. He's not a killer. He might've done it in a bad moment when he was killing mad, but he seems calmer now. If it's him, I'll be fine."

"Plenty of angry kids in the world, Dare. Not too many that'd set a fire to murder a man. If he did that, he needs to be found out."

"And Lana," Dare said, hating to think that Paul had started the blaze, "if she's as crazy as I think she is, why has she waited all this time? Crazy people aren't patient. I can see why she would've been stopped by me being out of town at the Kiowa village, but I've been back for a long time now."

"Maybe she didn't want to kill Glynna and the kids. Maybe she knows we're watching the house. Maybe she's crazy as a hydrophobic kangaroo rat and we're wasting time trying to make sense of what she's doing." Vince crossed one booted foot across his ankle and seemed so relaxed he might be trying to slip in a nap. Dare knew better. Invincible Vince was always ready for trouble.

"I've decided it was someone stealing drugs. I've had patients wanting morphine before. A couple of 'em passed through not that long ago. If the craving gets too bad, sometimes laudanum won't hardly stay ahead of it. They hid out by town until they saw their chance, stole the drugs— probably half mad if they were locked in a craving for them—then set the fire and ran."

"I dunno," Vince said. "The way that fire was set seemed mighty personal. It wasn't strictly to cover up a crime. Whoever it was aimed to kill you, Dare. If it's someone just wanting morphine, then they probably know you've restocked since the fire. Add to that, if they've been using what they stole all this time, they might be running out."

A rustling sound brought Vince's gun up as Dare spun

around and drew his Colt. A dark shape rounded Dare's house and he squinted, trying to see if it was someone with a grudge and a tin of matches.

"What is she doing out here?"

"She?" Was the moving shadow female? Vince always had eyes like a cat, seeing things in the dark no one else could see. "Is it Glynna?"

"No, it's trouble on two legs."

Dare recognized the aggravated tone. It must be Tina Cahill.

CHAPTER 17

"What is Tina Cahill doin' wandering around at this hour?"
Then Vince realized and suddenly he felt foolish. Tina
Cahill was bringing them—

"Coffee?" Dare sniffed the air.

Vince looked around and saw the night had lightened
and dawn would soon be upon them. Another nightly
vigil was ended. He did a real good job of not letting
Dare see how exhausted he was. It helped that it wasn't
yet daylight.

Tina walked straight for them. Vince saw her eyes locked
right on him. It annoyed him that she'd picked him out so
easy. But then everything the woman did annoyed him.

She rarely spoke a kind word to him—for no reason
Vince could understand. She tended to preach her own
little sermons, mainly about the saloon, which served more
coffee than whiskey most days. And she had a knack for
listening to Jonas's sermons, then repeating them in bits
and pieces to anyone who didn't get away from her fast
enough. She was also a deep well of old chestnuts learned
from her aunt, who didn't deserve to be quoted, considering

231

she'd booted her niece out into the streets when a new man came along.

Vince didn't have time to fool with a woman, and he had enough troubles without worrying about a little filly. But he was used to women, in the rare event he was near one, being real friendly. But Tina had taken an instant dislike to him. She was polite for Jonas's sake, most of the time, but she had a sharp tongue in her head, and she liked to stab him with words every chance she got.

It didn't help that she was the prettiest thing he'd ever seen, and he caught himself on occasion wondering if children born to them would be dark or fair. He could actually picture the little tykes. There would be several, so maybe some blond, some dark. Boys and girls both. Restlessly, because he found the image fascinating, Vince thrust it from his head. He'd accepted that he could never marry nor have children and he'd never spent one second thinking on such a thing before Tina came along.

"The night watch is over." Tina raised one hand with a coffeepot and another with two tin cups.

"You're not supposed to bring us coffee, for heaven's sake." Vince had no idea why he was snipping at the woman. Of course she didn't know she was giving away Vince's position.

"I'd already given away your position, Vince," Dare said. He walked toward Tina and relieved her of the burden of the pot. "She's not doing a bit of harm."

She smiled at Dare.

Vince knew that because her teeth shined white in the half-light. Vince tried to remember if she'd ever once smiled at him. She'd bared her teeth a few times, but it wasn't one bit the same.

A light from behind them drew Vince's attention to the back door of the diner. A lantern had just been lit. Lana was up. That woman was a worker for a fact and one of the finest cooks Vince had ever known. Too bad she was a foam-at-the-mouth madwoman.

"Let's go to my place." Dare started for his house.

"Is Jonas up?" Vince asked, dogging Dare. He had no wish to be left behind with Tina.

"Yes, he got the coffee going," Tina said. She was just a step behind them.

Dare swung his door open and held it for her.

"No one's gonna try and start a fire with four of us awake and the lights on. Another night has passed with no sign of trouble. Besides, if it's Lana Bullard, she's too busy cooking to kill you right now." Vince, remembering his manners, stepped back to let Tina go through. Then he followed.

"I'll tell Jonas to come on over." Dare let the door swing shut behind Vince.

At the sound of the closing door, Tina turned suddenly and Vince stumbled into her and caught her, his hands on her upper arms.

Dare's house was dark. Tina moved, warm and supple under his hands.

"You suspect Lana Bullard is responsible for this?" She sounded surprised.

Vince's fingers flexed on her arms, and he noticed how slender and soft she was.

"Vince!" Tina's tone brought his eyes up.

"Huh?" He decided to keep hanging on for just a few more seconds.

"Lana Bullard—you think she started the fire that almost killed Dare?"

That wasn't what Vince wanted to talk about at all, but he did want to stay right here, and so he forced his mind to work. "Sure, possibly. Probably, in my opinion."

"Why would she do that?"

"Because she's crazy as a hydrophobic kangaroo rat."

Tina shook her head. "She seems fine to me. My aunt Iphigenia always said, 'Don't talk unless you can improve the silence,' and your criticism of a hardworking woman like Lana improves nothing."

Vince ignored almost all of that. "You seem fine to me, too." Vince held her just a little tighter and drew her just a little closer.

Tina opened her mouth, then closed it. For a second it reminded Vince of the catfish he'd pulled out of Lake Michigan while growing up. But this pretty woman's resemblance to a catfish ended right there, and he forgot about fishing when she took a deep breath and he felt her move again under his hands.

"Why?" Tina asked the strangest questions.

"Cuz fishing's got nothing to do with you."

Tina closed her eyes and shook her head as if she needed to rearrange her brain. Then she stepped back.

Vince didn't even consider letting her go and instead tugged, and she stumbled forward right into his arms. The door behind him swung open. Jonas shoved past Vince, who dropped the preacher's sister like she was a blazing hot potato.

Turning his baby sister forcibly around, Jonas herded her into Dare's kitchen. Vince followed, but Jonas firmly closed the kitchen door with Tina in the kitchen, turned, and blocked Vince's path.

Jonas Cahill—Parson Jonas Cahill, good friend, wise counselor, loving man of God—jabbed a finger right under Vince's nose. "You watch your step around my sister."

With narrow eyes Jonas studied Vince a moment too long. Vince remembered his friend had ridden the outlaw trail. He'd been a mighty dangerous man in the war, too.

It helped clear Vince's muddled head right up.

Especially since that beautiful woman didn't even like him. And he didn't like her, neither. Much.

"Uh . . . Jonas, you don't have to—"

Dare, who must've been with Jonas, though Vince hadn't noticed him until now, shoved past Vince. The restless man didn't know how to wait worth a hoot. Vince moved, which broke the awkward stare-down. Jonas headed for the kitchen fast, probably to get there in time to keep an eye on his fuss-budget sister. His beautiful fuss-budget sister. His beautiful fuss-budget sister who'd brought coffee on a cold Texas morning and had arms so soft and strong that Vince still felt them moving under his touch.

Dare threw kindling in his kitchen stove while Tina pulled down a skillet. Vince leaned against the door, to keep watch—and stay away from Tina.

Tina said over her shoulder, "Start breaking eggs, Vince. Make yourself useful."

"No, hold on," Vince said. "Let's go over to the diner for breakfast. I want you to see what I'm talking about with Lana Bullard."

"She's a really good cook," Dare said. "I'd be in big trouble in this town if I had her arrested for attempted murder. I'm going to need solid proof if I don't want to be tarred and feathered and driven out of Broken Wheel." After a moment, Dare added, "They might do it even if I can prove she's guilty."

Vince poured himself more coffee. "You'll be in big trouble if you get your house burned down around your ears again and this time don't wake up in time to get out. Try to remember that when you're worrying about being popular with the townsfolk." Vince went back to his post at the kitchen door.

"True." Dare got coffee for himself and started pacing.

"So you think the cook at the diner tried to kill you?" Tina asked. "Did you insult her pie?"

"No, sir. She makes the best pie I've eaten since I sat at my own ma's table."

A rap on the door drew Vince away. He swung the front door open to find Glynna standing there in the dim light of dawn. "Kinda early for a visit, isn't it, Mrs. Greer?"

"It's Sevier, and yes, it's early." Glynna trailed him into the kitchen, still rubbing the sleep out of her eyes. "I saw the light on when I came down to help Lana. She shooed me out. Can I help you get breakfast over here?"

"No!" Vince, Dare, and Jonas all spoke at once, and spoke a bit too loudly.

"That's just what Lana said." Glynna's eyes got round and leaky looking.

Vince hunched his shoulders and prepared to take a beating—at least that's how a woman's tears felt to him.

"We were planning on eating at the diner." Tina gave the men a confused look. "Otherwise we'd appreciate your help."

Vince stifled a shudder, but Jonas didn't do as well. Dare was always moving, so it was easier for him to get away with jittering around.

"I want to meet your cook. Vince here has said some hard things about her, and I want to judge for myself if she's a troubled woman." Tina frowned at Vince. "It's a hard life out here. If she's really troubled, you might try showing her some compassion instead of insulting her."

Vince rolled his eyes heavenward. "It's not an insult to say a lunatic is a lunatic. It's like saying water is wet."

Tina sniffed and turned her back on him. He sure wished the woman wasn't so pretty. And so bent on hating him.

"Is the diner open?" Dare asked.

"Not quite yet."

"Good, the crowd shows up the minute the door unlocks. Let's go now. I haven't so much as talked with Lana. I want to see how she acts when I walk into that kitchen."

"A kitchen full of sharp knives," Vince muttered.

Dare thought of knives and remembered Janny's hand. He was pacing near Vince, and his friend slapped him on the back and said, "But I'll protect you."

"Hope it doesn't come to that. Let's go."

Glynna had to unlock the diner's front door.

Instead of heading for a chair, Dare walked straight toward the kitchen. "Let's go on back. I want to see her."

It occurred to Dare that he was dealing in a friendly fashion with Glynna—for a change.

Maybe it was because he'd been distracted by Vince standing guard, reminding Dare of the threat to his life.

Maybe it was because Glynna had moved out and he wasn't spending quite so much time brooding over how much he was attracted to her and how disgusted he was with her helping a thieving deserter.

Maybe it was because he knew he was being a confounded fool, and none of what happened to Glynna was her own fault. Might as well blame her for accidentally hitting Greer in the fist with her face.

Glynna went into the kitchen first, Dare right behind her. He heard boots and glanced back to see Vince, followed by Tina and Jonas, all coming in—his friends to guard him, Tina to see if they were treating poor Lana fairly.

Dare stepped into the kitchen to see Lana, her back to him, chopping up a potato with a knife that flashed like lightning. The woman was a hand with the cutlery, no denying it.

"Lana, I'm back," Glynna said. "Can I help?"

"No!" Lana turned around, holding the knife like a weapon—which could be accidental. Then she looked past Glynna and her eyes landed on Dare. He saw her grip tighten on the knife handle. Something deadly flashed in her eyes. She blinked a few times and was just a hardworking cook again.

"I'm not quite ready to start cooking, but the coffee's

hot by now." She jabbed the long, curved blade at the coffeepot. "Pour 'em a cup, Glynna."

It was an order. Lana had truly taken control of Glynna's diner. It made sense that someone would. Glynna clearly had no talent for running a kitchen.

Not surprising, Glynna obeyed the order. The woman had no sense of command.

"Lana, how are you?" Dare figured he wasn't going to be able to prove the woman was a killer just from that flash in her eyes and her skill at chopping. "I haven't seen you for a while."

"I ain't been feeling poorly. No reason to see a doctor." Lana went back to work, reducing a stack of potatoes to shreds. The woman worked magic turning a potato into breakfast.

Her shoulders seemed stiff. She'd turned so he could only see the side of her face.

Dare didn't know how hard to push her. If she wasn't the one who'd attacked him, then she had honest work and a fair amount of skill. Was she fragile enough that he could drive her away? And if so, where would she go?

Dare wanted to send everyone out of the room in the hopes she'd talk more freely with him if they were alone. But Vince-the-guardian wouldn't go, nor Tina-the-reformer, who was determined to guard the rights of the criminally insane.

Jonas wouldn't go, either. He wasn't of a mind to leave Tina and Vince in the same room. Glynna might go. She'd followed an order just a few seconds ago. But that still left the kitchen mighty crowded.

Considering that sharp knife, Dare wasn't sure he wanted them to go. "I've felt bad about how things ended last time you came in."

The clatter of the chopping on the wooden tabletop stopped as suddenly as if Dare's hearing had quit working. Lana flexed her wrist around so the knife went up and down a bit as if she were aiming it. Slowly, Lana straightened from the table, still flexing the knife in eerie silence. Dare should keep talking, but his throat was bone-dry, especially since Glynna was a bit ahead of him, right in the path of the knife.

He caught Glynna by the shoulder and shoved her behind him as Lana began to turn, her knife still tipping up and down. Vince made a fast move and was at Lana's side and wrested the knife from her hand. It happened so fast, Dare hadn't even realized what Vince was doing until he'd done it.

Lana whirled and glared at Vince. "Give me back that knife."

"I didn't like the way you were holding it." Vince wasn't showing one bit of concern for Lana's tender feelings. "You seemed inclined to attack the doctor the last time you saw him, and I didn't see any reason to let you stand there, knife in hand, while you answered his questions. Dr. Riker wants to talk about how upset you were that night you *thought* you'd lost your baby."

Flinching, Dare wished Vince wasn't so blunt. But then why not? If Lana wasn't a crazed killer, she'd apologize for how strangely she acted. Or maybe she'd get upset but in a rational way. If she was a raving lunatic who was currently and tenuously clinging to good sense, it might be better to provoke her when there were plenty of witnesses—and she was unarmed.

"Lana, you understand now that . . ." Dare paused, then glanced sideways at Vince and Jonas. "You need to let me talk with Lana alone. This is private."

"Nope." Vince crossed his arms like a stubborn mule . . . well, a stubborn mule with arms. "I don't trust her, and I'm not leaving. Besides, there are more knives in here."

There was no point in arguing with Vince. Instead, Dare walked right up to the freshly disarmed cook and spoke quietly. "You were confused that night, remember? You were never with child, but that night you seemed to believe there had been a child born and it had died." Swallowing at the glint of rage in Lana's eyes, Dare decided to push harder by mentioning her now-dead husband. "When Simon came to me, he said you'd accused me of killing your son. There was no baby, so you couldn't have had a son. Your thinking wasn't clear that night, Lana. I'm still your doctor. I want to make sure you're all right."

That was the absolute truth, but it wasn't all of it since the extent of how completely she was *not* all right might be connected with murder attempts.

Lana's eyes had a defiant sheen to them, but then she slowly closed her eyes and let her head fall forward.

It occurred to Dare that he couldn't read her expression bowed down this way. He wondered if that was on purpose.

"I know there wasn't a baby," Lana said. There was deep hurt in her voice.

Dare rested a hand on her shoulder. "Your husband is

dead and you lost the dream of having a child. You've lost a lot of weight, and no one knew where you went for several weeks. You do a wonderful job cooking, but you never come out and talk to anyone. How are you?"

Again silence. Dare waited. He wanted her to talk to him, not just say a few words with her eyes averted. As the moments stretched on, Dare felt himself longing to move, to pace, to do something. Patience wasn't his gift.

Finally, Lana gathered herself and looked up, her shoulders square. "I'm fine, Doc. I've found a new man."

Dare wondered who.

"Simon was nuthin' but trouble, and I'm too old to be caring for a baby. I'm better now than I was before I came to this town." She seemed sincere, rational. Not a sign anywhere of wanting him dead, except maybe right at first.

Dare held her gaze for a bit, trying to see if she spoke the truth. If she was lying, she was very good at it.

And considering that she'd spent most of her life working abovestairs in a saloon, there was a good chance she was a dab hand at lying.

"Anything else you need, Doc?" For just a second there was that tone in Lana's voice that had been there before. She'd been in awe of him, devoted, almost worshipful. It had made Dare very uncomfortable.

"No, as long as you're . . . feeling better."

"I'd best get back to my potatoes then, and I need to get the first pan of biscuits out of the oven. It ain't opening time yet, but go on into the dining room and I'll have sausage gravy on biscuits and fried potatoes out for you in a few minutes." Lana looked past Dare. "Glynna, you serve up some coffee while I get the meal on."

More orders.

Dare half smiled when Glynna obediently went for the coffeepot. And why a man who had an unknown killer after him could smile was beyond Dare.

CHAPTER 18

"You're sure Luke got all those stones knocked down?" Glynna watched the upper slopes of the narrow canyon like a hawk. No, she paid better attention than that. What hawk ever had to worry about something falling on its head?

Things still weren't friendly between her and Dare, but Glynna was finding a nice civilized place of peace with him.

She didn't want to marry the mangy, stinking polecat anyway.

Well, not *peace* maybe, but if the no-account backstabbing vermin blamed her for another's sins, she accepted it.

Well, maybe not *accepted* exactly either, but she'd found a way to endure it if the belly-dragging sidewinder wanted to kiss her one minute and then, when she'd taken a terrible risk by being honest about her deserting fool of a husband, decide Reggie's evil was her fault.

Fine then. She had no peace, no acceptance, and she wasn't enduring it well, either. She'd have strangled Dr. Swamp Rat right there on the buckboard seat if the children hadn't been watching.

Nope, things still weren't friendly.

They got through the canyon without a rockslide. Tina, Jonas, and Vince had all piled into the wagon, with Dare driving and Glynna and the children along. They made quite a crowd.

As they climbed down, Glynna saw Vince reach out to assist Tina in jumping down from the wagon. Glynna, in her no-nonsense black calico dress scattered with little white flowers, could climb down herself. But Tina wore a pink dress, the skirt wide with petticoats and flounces. She needed assistance.

Tina frowned at Vince's bright smile as she reached the dropped tailgate. But he caught her waist, and she reached to balance herself on his broad shoulders. Then Jonas shoved Vince sideways and Tina almost tumbled to the ground. Jonas caught her and set her on her feet, while Vince, shaking his head, lifted Janny down, mindful of her injured hand, which now was in a sling.

Glynna hopped down fast before she got a chance to see if Dare would help her. She doubted he would, and the truth hurt.

Ruthy was there to welcome them, wiping her hands on her apron, her red curls escaping from the bun at the nape of her neck. "I just took the turkey out of the oven. We'll eat in no time."

Luke emerged just behind Ruthy and headed out to help the menfolk put the horses up. Paul stayed out with the men. Glynna kept hoping the boy would begin to admire the good qualities of Dare and his friends. Her son needed a man in his life who was worthy of respect.

Glynna headed for the kitchen, drawn by the wonderful aroma. "What can we do to help?"

Ruthy pointed at a stack of plates. "You could set the table."

Tina was soon mashing potatoes while Ruthy whipped up gravy. Glynna frowned but didn't comment when Janny got a cooking job and she didn't. She was beginning to understand just how dimly her cooking was viewed.

Glynna and Tina told the news from town, including their talk with Lana Bullard.

Ruthy said, "Dare should have noticed that woman wasn't with child much faster. He certainly knew I was right away."

"Congratulations, Ruthy." Tina quit mashing and gave Ruthy a one-armed hug.

"He probably hasn't been around women much with his doctoring," Glynna said.

"He told me he'd delivered only one other baby," Ruthy said.

"Only one?" Tina's brows arched. "When was that?"

The back door swung open just as Tina asked her question. The men trooped in.

"It was in Andersonville." Dare looked straight at Tina, so Glynna knew he'd heard.

Dead silence reigned for a moment in the kitchen.

Glynna finally asked the question on all their minds. "How did you deliver a baby in a prison camp full of men?"

Dare looked from one of his Regulator friends to another.

Luke jerked one shoulder. "Of all the ugliness in that place, there was that one spot of hope. Tell 'em, Doc."

247

"While we eat." Dare waved a hand toward the dining room and its perfectly set table.

When the prayer was spoken and the food passed, Dare said, "This was after we got taken out of the prison population."

"Why did you get taken out?" Glynna asked.

Dare shook his head. "A lot of the prisoners wanted us dead, simple as that. We were the Regulators. Heroes to some, the enemy to the Raiders, and a third group considered us traitors."

"Why traitors?" Glynna thought of what a traitor her first husband had been and how cruelly Dare had judged her for that. He had a lot of nerve.

"We put a stop to the Raiders," Vince said. "They were men who beat and robbed other prisoners."

"But that's not traitorous," Glynna said indignantly.

Vince shrugged as he cut his turkey. "It was Yankees stealing from Yankees, and we were charged with putting a stop to it. Some of our fellow prisoners appreciated it a lot."

"Others, who were good men and good soldiers," Jonas added as he scooped up a spoonful of potatoes, "thought we were in league with the Confederate prison guards and considered us traitors. Some of them thought killing one of us was an act of loyalty to the Union and figured God was on their side when they struck."

"And there were the ones who'd worked with the Raiders," Luke said. "Bad men and bad soldiers. We didn't begin to arrest all of 'em. They hated us for stopping their thieving. It made for a mighty mean place to stay once we were teamed up as Regulators. The baby, though, was a bright spot. That's a Thanksgiving story."

"A baby in Andersonville." Ruthy rested a hand on her still-flat stomach and looked properly horrified. "That means there had to be a woman in there."

"No one knew it, though," Dare said. "I heard a sound one night of someone in distress." He took a thoughtful bite of turkey and chewed as if remembering the sound. "That was nothing new. There were people dying daily of every disease imaginable. The moans of the sick and dying were like the wind blowing through the trees. You barely noticed it after a while." Dare hesitated, frowning. "That's not really true. Getting used to it isn't the same as not hearing it. There was a feeling of black, ugly doom over everything, and that mournful noise was part of it."

Glynna saw his mood dip. She didn't want doom at the Thanksgiving table. "What about the baby?"

"Well, I heard this sound and I couldn't help heading for it because it sounded like a woman. I got to this tent made out of nothing but a propped-up blanket, and I found a soldier inside, kneeling beside a second soldier who was writhing in pain. Turned out the soldier in pain was Mrs. Hunt."

Tina said, "I've read about Andersonville Prison, and I heard about the starvation and violence—what villains the Raiders were and what it meant to be a Regulator. Because of Jonas, I took note of what was going on there. But I never heard mention of a woman, and certainly not a baby."

"And Mrs. Hunt wasn't the only one," Dare said. "There were a few others who came to light, maybe more who were never found out. Mrs. Hunt and her husband were on a honeymoon cruise and had nothing to do with the war, although her husband was a soldier on leave who was captured in a boat. When Confederate troops overtook the boat, she was told to go back North, but she wouldn't abandon her new husband. It's said she disguised herself as a man, and she must have—that's the only way I can imagine a woman would escape being brutalized. But there were other women. I learned of them working in the infirmary. They'd get sick and need to be"—Dare glanced toward Janny before he went on—"well, the truth would come out."

Glynna gasped.

"I'd been working in the infirmary for a while. This was after the Regulators had rounded up the Raiders and all of us had been sequestered for our own safety."

"Not completely successful," Vince said.

Glynna thought of the knife wounds in Dare's back.

"I was standing close to a window and could hear the usual sounds from the prison yard. Awful. And then the sound from one tent, one out of so many." Dare shook his head as if to clear it. "I had to check."

"Not too smart going out into the yard with men gunning for you," Luke said. "You should've at least come for one of us."

"I know, but you were all sleeping. It was late enough, most everyone out there was asleep too, and those who weren't, the ones in pain, weren't up to doing much damage. And the worst of the predators had been cleaned out or put on notice."

"A few of 'em still got a chance at you with a knife." Jonas had quit eating, along with everyone else. Glynna had ruined the dinner with her question, and she said a quiet prayer that Dare would finish and still be able to give thanks to God, despite all he'd seen and done.

"I went to the tent, and they were both terrified to realize the noise had brought them outside attention. I saw what was going on and convinced them to trust me. Harry Hunt was the husband's name, and he'd hidden his wife for all those months. Thirteen months they'd been locked up together. Now, after so long hiding his wife, Harry was determined he'd somehow hide the baby. I've never seen a man so fiercely protective of his family. And the men in that prison, many of them had turned into animals. Starvation had about stripped them of their humanity."

Dare swallowed hard. "So I helped. Mrs. Hunt was thin, but she was tough and got through most of it without making hardly a sound. Harry would cover her mouth when she seemed unable to keep quiet."

"That poor woman . . ." Tina said under her breath.

Jonas patted her on the arm. "It's over, Tina. The woman lived, the baby lived. Of all the terrible things that happened in that place, one wonderful thing happened. It was a beautiful miracle."

"And I got to be part of that miracle," Dare said. "I saw life come into the midst of death. Up until then, I'd been working alongside the prison surgeon, Dr. Kerr. It was rough medicine. Mostly I tried to make men comfortable while they died. I helped sever limbs and gave out doses of laudanum—if we had some on hand, which wasn't often."

Dare fell silent and he had tears in his eyes. "When I held that newborn baby in my hands, I started to think of doctoring in a different way. I realized I could save lives, not just stand by while men died. Seeing that baby born, that's when I started to understand what a doctor could be."

"What happened to the baby?" Glynna knew it didn't really matter. It was long ago and far away, and she was frightened of the answer, and yet she couldn't help but ask.

"They kept their secret for a few days." Dare managed a stifled laugh. "But babies are stubborn little things. They cry no matter how careful you are. They were found out, and the camp commander—"

"Wirz was his name," Vince said, cutting off Dare. "He showed the only trace of human decency I'd ever seen from the man. He let the mother and child into the infirmary."

"That's when we got to see him." Luke sat at the head of the long table, and his eyes went to Ruthy, who sat at the opposite end. The look that passed between them spoke of love and another wonderful miracle on the way. "They stayed in the infirmary for a few days before Wirz let them move outside the prison yard and live on the grounds nearby in a tent. He even let Hunt go out and see them every once in a while. Wirz made sure the ma had a better share of food, too."

"Thank God he did," Jonas said. "That baby would never have survived in there. I think some of those men were cruel enough they might have killed it. Not to mention what might have become of Mrs. Hunt."

"The Raiders." Vince's jaw tightened. "They were lower than vermin."

"Why would they be so evil to their fellow Yankees?" Glynna asked.

"They weren't loyal to anyone," Luke said. "They were mostly men who'd just signed up for the Union army to get the bounty the Union was paying to enlist. They had no intention of staying to fight."

"Luke," Dare interrupted. "I don't think—"

"It came out when we rounded up about two hundred and fifty of them." Vince clenched a fist on the table. "They were no-accounts who signed up intending to take the bounty and desert, but they'd been caught before they could. Inside Andersonville they joined with others like them. Men who'd betray their own country for thirty pieces of silver."

"We should—" Dare began again.

"Hard to believe," Jonas said, cutting him off, "they had family low-down enough to take that money. I'd have starved first."

Dare looked at Glynna. "Let's not ruin Thanksgiving with such talk."

She met his eyes and knew this was what he thought of her. The same anger that even kindhearted Jonas felt was burning in all of them. They'd had to fight for their lives against men just like her first husband, Reggie. And if they knew about Reggie and what he'd done, they'd all hate her. Dare was trying to shield her from the knowledge at the same time he hated her himself.

"So what happened to the baby, Dare?" Tina asked. Which at least got them back on a less horrible topic.

Dare tore his eyes away from Glynna and looked down

at his plate. "Wirz put Captain Hunt in better housing, still bad but better. He offered to send Mrs. Hunt home in a prisoner exchange, but she refused to go. Spunky woman."

"She stayed in her tent," Vince added, "outside the camp walls until we were freed by the Yankee army." His grim expression eased just a bit. "Beyond that, we have no idea what became of 'em, but they did survive Andersonville and the war. That's more than a lot of folks."

"Tough woman, tough little baby," Jonas said. "I wonder if his folks talk to him about the way he came into the world or if they've just tried to forget it."

"I hope they don't tell him," Dare said. "Once you know about something like Andersonville, it changes you. There's not much luck forgetting it, no matter how hard you try."

Glynna realized right then that Dare would always paint her with that same tarnished brush, mixed in with his memories of stab wounds on his back, the Raiders, and starvation.

"Finish up," Ruthy said to raise the mood. "I've got pie left to serve. Ladies, can you help me carry it in?"

While the women were out of the room getting pie, Vince jerked his head toward the front door. "After we eat, let's go walk the top of that hill where the avalanche came down."

"You want to go with us, Paul?" Jonas asked.

Dare was surprised when the boy nodded. "I'll come," Paul said. "No sense staying here with the women."

It was the first time Paul had shown any interest in getting to know the Regulators better. Maybe he was easing off on his hostility toward the men, or maybe their talk over the meal had interested the boy. Dare wondered if the boy had indeed set fire to his house. It might be a good thing to see him on that canyon wall, to see how the boy behaved up there.

So when the meal was done, the men set off.

Dare hung back, watching close. Paul acted uncertain of the direction to take. Either the boy was mighty savvy or he'd never been up top of the canyon before.

Luke knew the way and took the lead. He was followed by Jonas, then Paul and Dare, with Vince bringing up the rear. Minutes later, they reached a level spot on the climb.

Dare said, "Hold up for a bit."

The trail was narrow, worn out of the side of a rock with high edges on one side. The blustery November wind was blocked here. It'd blow hard once they got to the top, and it wouldn't be a good place to talk. What should he say to this boy? How could he reach him without making things worse?

"Let's take a breather." Dare sat on a massive rock, which didn't suit him. He never sat still. "The women will want time to visit, so there's no hurry to get back."

Vince arched a questioning brow at him, then found a man-sized boulder to lean against, his arms crossed.

Luke and Jonas seemed to sense that Dare had more on his mind than just resting.

"Can we get going?" Paul's sullen scowl looked right at home on the kid's face. "You're a bunch of old men if you need a rest already."

Luke laughed at that. Jonas and Vince both smiled.

"Paul, you heard us mention the Regulators, right?" Dare asked.

Paul seemed startled at the question. His eyes narrowed and he looked suspiciously from one man to the other. "I was at the table with you. You know I heard."

"In the middle of all that turmoil," Dare went on, "what we learned was that we had to trust each other."

Paul sniffed. "Not much room to trust in a war."

"No, the truth is the exact opposite. In combat you learn to trust your life to the men who fight with you."

"Not likely any real man would trust his life to someone else."

Silence descended on the group. Finally, Dare said, "Well, each one of the men here saved my life. We had to trust each other to survive Andersonville. I don't know much about your pa, except I know you weren't overly fond of him."

"You leave my pa out of this," Paul seethed.

"And Flint Greer," Dare said, "was a worthless slice of manhood if ever there was one."

Paul didn't bother defending Greer.

"You judge all of us"—Dare swept a hand from Luke to Vince to Jonas—"by finding us to be like those two men. You had the devil's own bad luck with the first two fathers in your life. But Luke's wife is best friends with your ma. Tina, Jonas's sister, is almost as good a friend. We're in your life to stay, and you need to trust us. You need to stop thinking every man who comes close is going to hurt you."

Paul stormed straight at Dare. A hard motion of Dare's

hand stopped the kid. But Paul was fuming, his face red, his fists clenched. "I don't want any man close to Ma. I'm old enough and strong enough to protect her, and that makes me a man. She doesn't need any other."

"Protecting your family is part of being a man, that's for sure. But there's more to it than that."

"No, there isn't."

"But there is," Luke interrupted. He stood slightly uphill, as he knew the way to the top of the canyon. "For one thing, a man supports his family." Luke, the prosperous rancher, tucked his thumbs into the front pockets of his breeches.

Paul turned his angry blue eyes on Luke. "I work hard every day."

"I know you do, son." Luke walked the few steps to Paul and rested a hand on his back.

"That's not all of it, though," Vince said. He stood straight and moved a step closer to Paul. "You need to be a leader, something that's hard for a boy with no pa. Your ma runs things, and yet a man has a natural desire to be head of the house. It's a hard place for you to be."

Dare knew that of all of them, Vince was the best leader. When there was a decision to be made with different ideas about the right path, Dare found himself going along with Vince.

"I can't tell Ma what to do. I've tried, and she won't put up with it." Paul didn't sound so angry for once, like he knew exactly what Vince was talking about and couldn't see just how to handle his ma.

"And a man needs to be the spiritual head of the family,

Paul." Jonas said it with such solid conviction that Dare felt his own shoulders square.

His brow furrowed, Paul asked, "What does that mean?"

"You can make sure your ma knows you support her in her faith and that you share it." Jonas came up on the downhill side of Paul.

Paul looked down at his boots. "I ain't seen much proof of God in my life."

"Sure you have," Jonas said with a smile.

Paul looked up sharply, startled.

"You've gone through some hard things," Jonas went on, "but life has challenges for everyone, no matter who they are. You've come out the other side healthy and whole. God didn't smooth out all the bumps, but He got you through."

"So that's it?" Paul sounded belligerent, as always. "To be a man I need to work hard, be a leader, and become the spiritual head of the house?"

"You have to *act*." Tired of sitting, Dare stood and faced Paul directly. If the boy would just see it, he'd realize he was surrounded by men who'd help him and be kind to him and teach him.

"Act?"

Dare nodded. "Being a man is about taking action. A man makes decisions, acts on those decisions, then takes responsibility for his actions. It's a mighty good reason to do the right thing, because you want to stand up tall and be proud of what you've done." Dare thought of the boy's pa. "You want an example of how to be a man, you watch Luke work his ranch. Or watch Vince step forward when there's trouble and take the lead. Or watch Jonas practice his faith in God. And watch me take action."

"I've had enough of others telling me how to live." Paul practically spit the words.

"Paul," Dare said carefully, "we're trying to help."

"You're not trying to help. You're after my ma."

"Paul, calm down, I—"

"I've seen you with your hands on her." Paul shoved Dare then, and the kid was strong enough that Dare staggered back against the boulder he'd been using as a chair. "You want her just like every man wants her." Paul leaned forward, and Dare saw the kid was very close to his height. Fifteen years old. Paul wasn't a kid anymore by a lot of measures.

"I would never hurt your ma. No real man would—that's what we've been trying to tell you. Just because you knew two coyotes—"

"No decent man"—Paul's chest heaved—"puts his hands on a woman like you did with my ma, after she's sworn to me she'd get my blessing first." His hand clenched close to his pistol. One wrong move, one wrong word, and things could turn deadly.

The moment stretched as Dare waited to see if the boy was going to back down or make things a lot worse. The day this kid started wearing a gun, he had to be treated as an adult in some real serious ways.

"Paul, we mean you no harm. We count your ma as our friend, and any friend of a Regulator earns our protection. We can be trusted not to hurt any of you." But Dare had already hurt Paul's ma, and the guilt over that twisted now in his gut. Yet he didn't let it show on his face, because that might be the last straw to drive Paul to some desperate act.

Paul held Dare's gaze. The tension coiled tighter. Dare saw confusion in the boy's eyes. He wanted to trust someone. He wanted help. Caring for his ma and little sister had been too much for him.

Suddenly Paul's hand moved away from the gun and again he shoved Dare, hard, with both hands on Dare's chest. "You stay away from my ma! You come sniffing around her again and I'll show you how a man protects his family." He whirled and stalked off back down the slope.

The men stood watching as the boy walked away. The kid reached the bottom of the slope, his stride long and fast, propelled by rage. He was heading straight for Luke's house, back to his ma.

They all stared in silence for several long moments. The wind gusted, even in the sheltered spot in which they stood. Then Vince looked at Dare and said with a sly tone, "So you've had your hands on Glynna, huh?"

"That ain't a surprise to none of us," Luke said.

"Well, I'm surprised." Jonas frowned at Dare. "Just how much of that kid's anger is justified, Dare?"

"None of it is justified, and you know it," Vince answered before Dare could. "A man's got his eyes on a woman, it don't mean that kid's got any business making death threats. Dare wouldn't do anything that wasn't honorable."

That brought on another moment of silence, which saved Dare from having to punch anyone or admit that the way he'd treated Glynna might count as mighty dishonorable.

"I'd still like to know about the part where you had

260

your hands on Glynna. And don't worry about giving us too many details." Vince started chuckling.

Before he could decide to start swinging, or admit something that'd make him want to punch himself, Dare turned to the canyon they'd been climbing. "Enough. Now let's go see if that avalanche was man-made."

CHAPTER 19

"Look at this." Luke crouched down, pointing to deep gouges in a rock. Raw scrapes showed the bright red of the canyon stone. "Right after the avalanche, before I hauled the rocks out of the pass, I came up here to make sure there were no more loose rocks. I didn't notice this, but at the time I wasn't even thinking about someone starting the avalanche."

Dare looked around. They were at the highest point. The chill wind gusted, cutting through his heavy buffalo-hide coat and sneaking down his collar.

"It looks like it was pried up by a crowbar." Luke was the tracker among them. "I've got tools in my barn that could be used to do this." The wind at the top of the canyon was sharp, and when Luke looked up, his blue eyes were a match for the cold air. This proved the avalanche had been deliberate. Someone had tried to kill Dare. Luke studied the terrain. "Someone did this to you, Dare, and on my property."

Vince had wandered farther down the length of the cliff top. In a clump of short bluestem grass clinging to the rocky ground, he reached down and straightened with a length of iron in his hand. "A crowbar like this?"

Luke rose, his eyes riveted on the tool. "That's mine." His expression hardened. "They didn't just do this on my property—they used my tools."

Luke grabbed the long, heavy crowbar and turned to look at a copse of mesquite trees bowing and dancing in the wind. "And look at the ropelike branches on this tree." He strode over to the tree and touched one of the branches. "It wouldn't've taken long to lever up a row of stones, prop them in place with smaller rocks or sticks, string the branches together, and let a woven-together length of them hang down. That kid would've just had to jerk on the dangling branch as he rode through the pass."

Suddenly the tension swamping Dare eased some. "Well, that lets Paul off the hook. He wouldn't have done this, because Glynna was still in the canyon. To set this avalanche off, he'd've been aiming to kill both of us, or at least not care if both of us got hurt."

Jonas actually managed a tight smile. "You're right. It can't be the boy. Not much comfort in knowing someone tried to kill you and Glynna, but it's a relief to eliminate the kid from our suspects."

"Which leaves us with some unknown outlaw who maybe wanted to steal drugs from you, or—"

"Lana Bullard." Dare thought of how she'd acted yesterday. Mostly not crazy. Not like she hated him. But maybe all that proved was that the woman had a talent for lying. What woman who had to convince men she wanted their attentions in exchange for money didn't have that talent?

"Unless of course these aren't connected," Jonas said thoughtfully.

"You mean there might be more than one person trying to kill me?" Dare shoved both hands in his pockets. "You know, I really try to be a good person. How come I'm the one with all the scars?"

Vince clapped him on his scarred-up back. "Let's figure on it being one person for now. We'll keep a closer eye on Lana and maybe we can convince her to give Glynna cooking lessons. If she'd take that on, she won't have time to murder you."

Dare remembered wanting to punch Vince earlier, but just like back then, he settled for rolling his eyes. "Let's get out of this wind. No sense freezing to death and cheating someone out of the fun of killing me."

They headed back down the trail.

Vince slipped out through his back door and eased around the south end of town. He saw Luke standing guard at the back of the diner. Vince made enough noise that his sharpshooting friend knew he was coming.

"Head on home," Vince told him.

Luke shuddered. "You know, it's getting too cold to stand watch all night long."

"Right." Vince gave a nod. "It's time we find a lookout post inside somewhere. Maybe we could watch from inside the general store."

"Jonas said to tell you he'd keep coffee on. I'm going to get a cup and take another out to Red Wolf, then get on home. Reckon you could grab a cup a few times without risking Dare's life, especially now that he's on guard himself."

Vince nodded again and then settled in. A while later a slight creaking of leather followed by hoofbeats told him that Luke was on his way out of town. Then nothing moved and no one made a sound for a long time before the cold got to him.

Easing from shadow to shadow, he made his way to Jonas's back door and rapped with one knuckle four times. He waited to a count of five, then rapped three times, then waited and rapped four more.

The door swung open, but instead of being greeted by his redheaded friend, Tina stood in the doorway glowing like no woman had a right to. Vince hurried inside and closed the door behind him, even though he didn't think Jonas was awake yet. The house was too silent.

Or maybe being in the presence of the prettiest girl he'd ever seen made it so he couldn't see or hear anything but her.

"Keep your voice down," Tina whispered as she stepped aside to let Vince pass. "Did you come for coffee?"

That chilly question helped him to start thinking again. "Yes, I'd appreciate it."

"In the kitchen."

"Where's Jonas?"

"He's in that room he uses as an office. Some man came to the front door a while ago, upset about something. That's why we're whispering. Jonas is talking with him. I told him I'd keep watch for a few minutes."

"And he agreed to that? He trusted Dare's life to you?" Vince almost flinched. He hadn't meant to sound quite so doubtful.

"He had no choice, Mr. Yates. His job is to counsel people in trouble, and my aunt Iphigenia always said, 'Do what is right, come what may.'"

"Your aunt Iphigenia sounds like an old crank."

"That describes her pretty well. You, of course, did have a choice, and you chose to abandon guarding your friend so you could fetch yourself a cup of coffee."

And Christina Cahill was a young crank. Vince didn't say that out loud.

"I suggest you get your coffee and then get back to standing watch. I suppose we should be grateful that it's only coffee you're drinking."

Vince snapped. "That's about the tenth time you've made some ugly reference to me drinking. I'm tired of it, woman."

"The references," she asked, "or the drinking?"

Vince took two long strides, realized he was getting ready to start hollering, and stopped. He'd've gone right ahead and started hollering at her, except Jonas was trying to help some poor soul. Whoever it was didn't need to be interrupted by him and Tina fighting outside his office door.

Instead he bent down until his nose almost touched hers and whispered, "We'll talk about this away from Jonas's office." He grabbed Tina's arm and dragged her into the kitchen—except he didn't drag her, he suddenly realized. She came right along with him, as if she were spoiling for a fight.

He got her into the kitchen, closed the door, and spun her around to face him, never releasing her arm. "I am tired of your snooty—"

"You keep your hands off me." She wrenched her arm free. "I'm not putting up with the bad manners and unwanted touches of a drunkard."

"Where did you get the idea I'm a drunkard?"

She made a noise so rude, the top of Vince's head nearly blew off. "Don't waste my time with excuses and lies, Mr. Yates." Then, raising a forefinger, she jabbed at his chest with great force. Even wearing his coat, she might've gouged deep enough to break the skin. "My aunt Iphigenia always said, 'A drunkard is like a whiskey bottle, all neck and belly and no head.' And I've no wish to converse with a man who has no head." Jab, jab.

"Don't quote that old bat to me."

Tina gasped. "Get your coffee and go." Another jab.

"Stop poking at me." Vince shoved her hand aside, and the feisty little thing shoved right back.

Vince grasped her shoulders and she fought against his hold, backing up to the kitchen door. He followed right along.

He saw that pointy finger coming at him again and caught both her wrists in a manacled grip.

"Let go of me." She twisted in his grasp.

"I haven't had a drink since before the war."

That stopped her wrestling. "But—"

"And then I drank about one mouthful of gin, once, when I was trying to prove what a man I was. I emptied my stomach on my father's fancy imported rug, and between the mess and the punishment my father handed out, that swallow was enough to know I wasn't interested."

Vince noticed that she'd shut up at last. And quit struggling. She still looked skeptical, but why had she thought he was a drinker to begin with? He looked her in the eyes. "You said something about 'the other morning.' What morning? What did you hear or see that made you think I was drinking?"

"The first morning I arrived in town. You stumbled in the street and fell flat on your face."

A twist of embarrassment reminded Vince of that moment. So she'd seen him make a fool of himself. Clearing his throat, he said, "I didn't know you'd noticed that."

"It wasn't the act of a sober man." Tina arched one of her lovely blond brows, and Vince suddenly realized he was very close to her. Her wrists were firmly caught in his grip still, and he could feel her pulse, feel her life and strength and sass. Most women would've been intimidated, a little scared to be in the hands of a man, alone.

Instead she stood there glaring at him, her eyes—the bluest, brightest things he'd ever seen—flashing with suspicion, still demanding he prove himself. He didn't mean to run his thumbs over the soft underside of her wrists, but his thumbs were there and her pulse made him aware of how alive she was, and it reminded him he was very much alive, too. He was looming over her, and then he loomed closer, and in some place in a man's mind where he didn't really make choices but instead just followed his instincts, his eyes flickered to those rude, pink lips. He couldn't help himself. He leaned even closer, and darned if she didn't, too.

Then she butted him in the face with her head.

Really slammed into him hard. He turned away, feeling to see if his nose was bleeding.

"Why are you blocking the door, Tina?"

Jonas.

She hadn't head-butted him; she'd been shoved into him by her overprotective big brother.

Even with his face half broken, Vince knew to head straight for the steaming coffeepot as if that was what he'd come in there for all along.

It was true.

Vince prided himself on always thinking fast, and he did so now. "Jonas, would you please tell your sister that I'm *not* a drinker? She seems determined to bleat at me about temperance."

Vince hoped Jonas would see that he and Tina had been wrangling—which they had been, except for right there toward the end.

"If you say you're not a drinker, then I'll take your word," Tina said. Bless her heart, she had all her sass right handy to slap at him. Music to Vince's ears, since she could have told her brother, a man who knew his way around firearms, that Vince had shoved her up against the door and been about to steal a kiss.

Not that she hadn't seemed inclined to hand that kiss right back, no stealing involved.

"Get your coffee and get back to your post, Vince." Jonas sounded worried, not mad. "We stirred that youngster up. If he's the one who burned Dare's house down—"

"Which he isn't," Vince interjected.

"I agree." Jonas stepped up to fill his cup of coffee, while Vince, not sure whether he had a big old bruise forming on his face or not, turned and headed for the door.

But it struck Vince that Jonas had made a real good point. "If there are several people with a motive to kill poor old Dare, then I suppose it's possible there are several people trying to kill him." Vince then left the kitchen, not interested in standing still in front of Jonas's eagle eyes.

As he walked out, he heard Tina say, "What's the matter with the doctor that people want to kill him?"

Jonas ignored the question and said, "When did Vince get here? You shouldn't be alone with a man at this hour, Tina. It isn't proper."

Then Vince was too far away to hear any more, which was a blessing, unless Tina gave some half-witted version of events that made Vince's good friend want to kill him.

Vince returned to his post, leaned against the back wall of the diner, and crossed his arms to stay warm. He looked at Dare's house . . . the front door. Something was wrong with it.

Not waiting to think it over, Vince strode forward. He got close enough to see the door was ajar. Had Dare come out to see him and gone back in, forgetting to close it? Not likely on a cold night like this.

When he was near enough, Vince saw black on the ground by the door and paused for an instant to look at the line, darker than the surrounding night. He crouched just long enough to know it was blood.

He lunged to his feet, pushed the door open, and rushed into the house, his gun drawn.

He found Dare facedown on the floor. A knife sticking out of his back and a pool of blood on the floor around him.

With a quick sweep of the room, he made sure there wasn't someone waiting to add another victim before hurrying back to Dare. Vince checked for a pulse and found one. That was the outside limit of Vince's doctoring skills.

Dare groaned. The knife. Vince reached to pull it out and stopped.

He only hesitated a second before he ran for Jonas. Whatever they had to do, Vince couldn't do it alone—not when some knife-wielding lunatic was still around.

After pounding on Jonas's door with his fist, Vince heard footsteps thundering toward him. "Dare's been stabbed."

Vince had left his friend unguarded. There would be time later on to hate himself for that, but for now, the next closest thing to a doctor was Glynna.

"He's in his house," Vince told Jonas. He wasn't going to wait and have a talk with Jonas. "I'm going for Glynna."

Vince whirled and ran. He reached the back of the diner just as he heard Jonas leaving for Dare's place. Banging on the diner's back door, Vince gave Glynna ten seconds to open it, battering it with the side of his fist the whole time.

He pulled back a foot to kick the door in, then heard commotion inside. He shouted through the door, "Glynna! Dare's hurt and needs help."

The door swung open and the boy was there. His chest heaving, gun in hand.

"We need your ma. Dare's been stabbed." Vince noticed the kid was dressed. Had he been up and about? Had he done the stabbing?

Glynna appeared in a nightgown, barefooted. "What's happened, Vince?"

"You've got to come. Dare's hurt."

"Where is he?" She dashed past her son, who made a move to stop her but he was too slow.

"At his place."

She raced past Vince too, running flat-out for Dare's house.

"Ma," Paul called after her, sounding furious, "you can't go out dressed like that!"

CHAPTER 20

Glynna charged into Dare's house to see Jonas firing up a lantern. Tina knelt on the floor at Dare's side. A knife stuck out between his right shoulder and his backbone at a downward angle, as if the assailant had held the weapon high and slashed from above.

Instantly Glynna was on the side across from Tina, also on her knees. "Where's his doctor bag?"

Vince sprinted for it and thrust it into her hands.

When she took it, she wrenched it open and pulled a fistful of clean cloths from it. "That knife has to come out—now." She handed the bag to Tina. "Find the carbolic acid. Dare believes in the stuff."

Vince moved to where Dare's head lay. "Tell me what to do."

Furious, Glynna's head snapped up and she glared so hard that Vince took a half step back. "You go find who-ever did this."

❧

Vince was dying to do just that.

Dare was in good hands now, but whoever had attacked

275

him was a backstabbing coward and there'd be no second attack, not even if only defenseless women were alert and working over Dare.

Paul came into the room. Vince considered asking a few hard questions about the boy's whereabouts. He was fully dressed, boots on and everything. But they'd ruled him out. "You stay here and watch over your ma and Tina. Jonas, let's go."

Vince knew exactly where he wanted to check first.

Jonas followed without a single word of protest. For a preacher, Jonas was mighty angry and mighty eager to exact some justice.

Once they were out of earshot, Jonas asked, "Are we going after Lana Bullard?"

"Yeah, she's in the boardinghouse." Vince strode for the darkened building that stood on the far south side of town. There were twenty yards or so between it and the diner. Asa's boardinghouse was at an angle to town and off by itself a bit, but plenty close for someone to sneak around and catch Dare alone, especially if Dare was trusting his friend to be standing watch.

To stop from punching himself in the head for leaving Dare, then staying away too long, bickering and . . . *not* bickering with that pill Tina Cahill, Vince charged up the front steps and tried the door. Unlocked. Asa Munson wasn't a trusting man, but this was Broken Wheel, and most doors weren't locked. Most doors didn't even have a lock. Asa ran the place, another salty Texan who'd stuck it out in this tough corner of Indian Territory.

"I don't know which room she's in," Vince said. If any strangers were in town, this was where they slept.

The boardinghouse was where Vince had taken Lana after she'd screamed her threats at Dare. Lana had thought she was expecting a baby. For a while Dare had believed her. As the months went by, Dare finally had to tell the woman she was mistaking a change of life for a baby on the way. Lana, whose devotion to Dare was a kind of madness, twisted her love into hate.

When a woman made a man into a god, then watched him turn into a devil who'd kill a child, how could she not go mad?

She'd sent her husband, Simon Bullard, after Dare. Simon was Flint Greer's foreman and a known gunslinger. Flint, Glynna's now-dead husband, had been eager to rid the town of the doctor who'd found out about Flint's cruelty to Glynna. Bullard and Greer had come to Broken Wheel with a band of gunslingers to face Dare and retrieve Flint's runaway wife. But Dare wasn't standing alone. Instead they'd found Luke, who'd come back to reclaim the ranch Flint had stolen. Also at Dare's side stood Vince and Jonas, who'd come to town to back their friend.

In the chaos of that fight and the cleanup afterward, Lana vanished. Only recently had she turned up and was cooking now for Glynna at the diner. None of them had known where she'd gone during that time, however. Apparently she'd gone crazy.

"There aren't that many rooms here." Jonas had his gun out. "We'll check 'em all."

Vince really had to sit his friend down sometime and discuss gunslinging and preaching and how the two didn't

277

mix. He'd do that right after they dealt with Lana. For now, Vince was glad for the backup.

They went up the stairs fast, but as quietly as they could manage. Asa lived on the first floor, and Vince saw no reason to announce themselves to the crusty old coot.

There were four bedrooms upstairs. Vince went to the first one and tried the door. It swung open to show an empty room. It looked cleared out, not like its inhabitant was skulking around with a knife.

The next room was locked. Vince pulled back his foot, but Jonas grabbed his arm and said, "It takes a skeleton key, and I've got the one from my house."

He produced it from his pocket, and they opened the door to find a man lying on the bed, snoring. An empty bottle of whiskey on his bedside table told the story of why he was sleeping through this visit.

They closed the door and went on down the hall. Vince reached for the next doorknob just as it swung away. Lana stood there gaping at them. She was fully dressed. Vince reached for her, and she squawked like a startled chicken. Then her knife came up.

"I'm going to pull out the knife." Glynna glanced uncertainly at Tina. "If I do it smooth and steady, I shouldn't do any more damage. At an angle like this, I'm hoping it didn't go in too deep. If it didn't get his lung or h-heart, he has a chance." Glynna quit talking then before she had herself in tears.

"I'll press a cloth to the wound as soon as the knife is out." Tina knelt close by, ready.

With a quick, ruthless yank, and a sickening hiss of metal on flesh, Glynna removed the knife. She recognized the knife, let out a gasp, and then she set it aside.

Dare groaned in pain. His first sign of consciousness.

Tina quickly pressed the white cloth she held onto the gushing wound.

Dare groaned louder.

Pray.

It came to Glynna like words whispered on the wind. She had little training and only the roughest kind of experience as a doctor. She needed God to guide her hands.

Dare's eyes flickered open.

"You, Dare Riker, are going to stop needing so much medical attention. I'm fed up with you being hurt all the time." Glynna took refuge in sternness.

Dare's eyes focused. They flashed with humor, which Glynna would've bet was beyond him at this moment. "Yes, ma'am."

She liked the sound of those two words. Maybe she should give up owning a diner and start practicing medicine.

"Who did this, Dare?" Glynna asked.

"I didn't see. Couldn't sleep. Came out to talk to Vince. Couldn't find him and headed back in."

Which made no sense. Why was Dare going to Vince's in the middle of the night?

Tina, with most of her weight pressing down on Dare's wound, narrowed her eyes to slits. "That man is completely irresponsible."

Glynna, her hands temporarily empty while Tina kept

pressure on the wound, held up the knife she'd removed from Dare's back.

Tina said, "That might be a clue. It's not a normal kind of knife for a man to carry."

"That's because it's from the diner," Glynna said. "It's one of only four sharp knifes we keep in the kitchen. It was there when I locked up today."

"When you locked up with only you and your young'uns inside?" Tina asked.

Glynna glanced at her. "What do you mean by that?"

"You're the one who said no one had access to the knife except you and your . . ." Tina stumbled over the next words and looked over at Paul, who now stood, his back pressed against the door as if he wanted to be anywhere but here.

Glynna's mind went mushy. Tina couldn't think she'd done this. And to accuse Janny was outrageous. And there'd been the uncomfortable glance at her son.

Glynna's heart clutched until she thought for a moment it'd quit beating.

Jonas moved so fast that Vince was stunned. He dodged past Vince and shoved Lana's hand straight up before she could plunge the knife.

A scream fit to curdle a man's blood ripped from Lana's throat. She slashed her nails across Jonas's face and wrenched her knife hand out of his grip.

Vince dived into the fracas. He grabbed at her knife hand. She was fast and slippery, and the knife remained in her control.

"What's going on up there?" A roar from belowstairs was accompanied by the sound of a lever-action rifle getting ready to shoot. They had to get this shrieking woman under control before Asa shot them.

Vince got her right hand but still grappled with her left. Jonas tried to help, but the two of them were getting in each other's way, and if they weren't careful, this little woman was going to best them and slit them open like prized pigs.

Asa thundered up the stairs.

Lana let loose with the kind of scream that sunk into a man all the way to the bone. The drunk in the next room had his snoring disrupted. The fourth bedroom door, the room they hadn't inspected yet, slammed open.

"We mean her no harm," Vince shouted, hoping to head off any gunfire.

Lana landed a punch to the side of his head that made his ears ring. A mean, dangerous woman, but who'd believe that?

"It's Parson Cahill," Jonas yelled. Tacking the word *parson* on was a good idea. "We're here to question Lana about a crime."

Jonas got her other hand finally, and now their only trouble was being kicked or bitten. Vince had to give the woman credit, as she wasn't about to let herself get dragged away quietly. He respected that.

Then she gave a good kick to his knee and his leg buckled.

In just that second, Asa made it to the top of the stairs and came at them with his rifle. The other sober man in the building stepped out of his room with two six-guns trained on the two of them. Vince was surprised to recognize Mitch Porter, who used to be the sheriff of Broken Wheel. The no-account weasel had been a loyal friend of Flint Greer. Flint Greer—now dead, thanks to Dare and his Regulator friends.

Another man with a motive for murder.

The crack of a cocking gun cut through the temporary break in Lana's screeching. Mitch Porter said, "Let her go."

⸎

"Don't sew me up."

Dare drew Glynna's attention from thoughts she couldn't bear. She couldn't do a thing about Tina's suspicions right now. She needed to doctor the doctor, and then she'd straighten out the mistaken notions about her son.

"Why not? I did a fine job of it last time. I think we decided I'm the second best doctor in this town. You can't fix this yourself."

"Yeah, you did the sewing just fine, but I see a look in your eyes that's scaring me."

Glynna, drawn to him, her gaze locked on his, knew he'd gotten Tina's unwilling accusation, and Dare wanted to buffer Glynna's pain because . . . because . . . with a barely suppressed shudder she realized it was because Dare thought it was true, too.

Well, the both of them were dead wrong. What they thought wasn't possible, and she dismissed the very idea. She slid her eyes back and forth between the two of them. "We'll talk about this later."

Dare's gaze sharpened. Tina nodded.

"Paul, help us get Dare off the floor." Glynna had to worry about first things first. "Tina, you concentrate on keeping that cloth hard against Dare's wound."

As gently as possible, they moved Dare. He managed to stand, but he was so wobbly that it took all three of them—well, four counting Dare—to get him up and on the bed.

Glynna got the carbolic acid. "Paul, get some water. There are hot wells on Dare's stove. If there's not water in them, start some heating."

"No, I can run to my place," Tina offered. "We don't have time for heating water."

"You're not going anywhere alone, Tina." Dare was mighty bossy for a man who was bleeding and semiconscious.

Paul hurried out to the kitchen and called back, "There's water in here." He soon returned with a sloshing basin.

"I'm going to need more rags." Glynna looked up at her surly son, who quickly grabbed a stack of them off a shelf.

When he'd brought them to her, Glynna said, "Go back to the diner, Paul. Janny's there alone, sleeping. I don't want her to wake up and be afraid."

Paul looked like he was going to defy her.

When Dare didn't protest Paul's going off alone, Glynna's stomach twisted. Dare thought Paul had done the stabbing, so he wasn't in any danger.

"Do it!" Glynna snapped, her anger at the implications of that knife coming out in her voice. If he wasn't so stubbornly hostile, no one would suspect him of stabbing a man.

❧

In the split second of distraction from Mitch Porter's six-guns, Lana yanked her wrists free and hurled that blasted knife straight at Vince and Jonas. They both dove for the floor. Lana ran, screaming, straight at Asa.

Asa wasn't a man to shoot a woman, so he jumped aside. Vince wheeled to grab her.

"Stop right there or I'll shoot you dead." Porter's voice carried such dire truth that Vince stopped and turned to face the former sheriff. The man stood there with two Colt revolvers drawn and cocked.

Porter was the back-shooting type. Now that Vince was facing the coyote, the danger was probably past, even though Porter had his guns drawn and Vince's was still holstered.

Lana thundered down Asa's stairs. The door to the outside opened and slammed shut.

"She stabbed Dr. Riker in the back," Jonas said, shoving past Vince. "Now she's getting away."

Something mean, maybe evil, shifted in Porter's eyes. Vince couldn't put his finger on it, but Porter didn't look like a man protecting a woman. He had his own reasons for pulling those guns.

"I haven't heard much but snoring from her tonight." Porter started straight for them. "She didn't stab anyone. She's been right here."

Then Porter, the arrogant little banty rooster, got too close. Jonas made a smooth, fast move and wrenched both guns from Porter's hands.

Vince didn't wait to talk sense into Porter, but instead turned and ran after Lana. Asa was still standing there, armed, but he pointed the muzzle of his rifle toward the ceiling and let them go. Asa probably didn't care much what happened so long as they got out of his boarding-house to do it.

Jonas's footsteps pounded right behind Vince.

"You get back here!" Porter shouted. He was coming, too. Vince ran outside, took a quick look toward town, and saw nothing.

"She'll go into the woods." Jonas dashed toward the back of the building, which stood near a clump of cottonwood trees. Vince saw that Jonas was now carrying both of Porter's guns. Beyond the trees were jagged boulders and scrub mesquite, arroyos and mesa—some of the wildest land Vince had ever seen. A thousand places to hide if a woman was savvy, and there was reason to think Lana was just that, since she'd disappeared into this land for nearly a month.

And they'd just let her escape into that rugged wilderness.

"She lived off the land after Bullard died," Vince said. "She knows what she's doing."

"Let's split up and listen for her," Jonas said. "She should be running still. We got her knife, and she didn't have a gun, so even if she waylays us, we should be able to overpower her."

"A rock to the head might slow us down some," Vince said. He went to the right of the cottonwoods, while Jonas headed to the left. Soon they were swallowed up by the night. An hour left before sunrise, Vince figured. A woman could get herself mighty well hidden in an hour.

❧❦❧

Paul didn't budge. "You'd like that, wouldn't you? You want to be alone with him."

The more her son talked, the more Glynna knew why Dare and Tina suspected him of this. She could see the regret on their faces; they didn't want to suspect him. But his hostility was so overwhelming, it gave them pause.

But not her. She had to get him out of here so she could talk sense into them. Glynna dug deep to find her motherly voice. "I'm not alone with him and you know it. Miss Cahill is here."

"She won't be for long." Dare's voice cut into Glynna's effort to be strict.

Tina lifted her head, surprised. "Why not?"

"Because I don't want Paul going out alone, either."

A terrible tension eased in Glynna. Dare was letting Tina go with Paul. Tina didn't seem to want to leave, but not out of fear of being alone with Paul. No, she wanted to stay and help.

Glynna drew a deep breath. Yes, they had to suspect him, but they clearly didn't really think he'd done it.

"Tina, you're going with him," Dare said firmly. "Whoever stabbed me, unless somehow Vince and Jonas caught . . . him, is still out there. I shouldn't have Glynna here with only the two of us to keep watch, because I'm not worth much. But Janny shouldn't be alone. Bring me my gun, Tina. That way, at least we're in pairs."

Tina said, "I'm stanching your bleeding back, Dare."

"Glynna, take over." Dare rapped out the order like he'd just gotten promoted to General.

Tina narrowed her eyes at him, unimpressed with his orders, but then she looked at Glynna and nodded.

So Glynna took over pressing on the wound.

Tina got Dare's gun out of the holster hanging from a peg by his front door and brought it to him. When Tina was close, Dare said quietly, "Take the Winchester over the door for yourself. Lock the diner up tight. I'll send Jonas over just as soon as he gets back."

A lot passed between Tina and Dare in a single glance. Tina went and got Dare's rifle.

She moved to the door, but Paul stood there with his arms crossed, planted. "You're not staying here alone with him, Ma."

Glynna was fed up. "Dare's got a knife wound in his back, for heaven's sake. To say I want to be alone with him is foolish. Janny will be terrified if she wakes up alone." Glynna couldn't keep up her bossy-mother tone. Maybe that was the root of all their problems. Too much pleading, and not enough of Glynna being in charge. "She's made such progress lately, Paul. A lot of it because of Dr. Riker's care of her. Instead of insulting him, you should be thanking him. Now go."

Paul gave her a look so dark, Glynna faltered inside. What was her boy capable of?

Finally his eyes dropped from hers and he whirled away, tore the door open and stormed out, slamming it behind him. Tina dragged it open and hurried after him. If she didn't want to be out alone, she needed to keep up.

When the door clicked shut again, Glynna turned to Dare, who was watching her with kind eyes.

CHAPTER 21

The moonlight came and went as clouds scudded across the night sky. In one moment of brightness, Vince saw a shadow slip around a boulder in the distance.

It all came back to him.

War.

Vince had been a spy. Not just a sneaking-around kind of spy, though he'd done that, too. He'd also been a dab hand at a Southern accent, learned from his mother, who'd married a wealthy Chicago businessman and brought her Southern charm to the North with her.

Vince had gone behind enemy lines, acting like a Reb. He'd enlisted in their service, gathered information, and gone back up North with it. It'd worked right up until he got caught and landed in Andersonville.

He'd lived to tell the tale, and now he found his old sneaking skills all right here at hand. He moved silently and kept to the shadows, watching for any movement.

There she was. She had on a dark dress, but it was a lighter dark than the shadows and boulders. He caught only a tiny glimpse of her every so often. She was good. He'd give her that.

Moving slow and steady, in utter silence, he closed the distance as she appeared, then vanished, rounding man-high boulders, sliding behind scrub brush.

With his eyes on the last spot, forward and to his left, a sudden motion to his right gave him a start. He clawed for his gun, then froze. A chill shot down his spine as something low, more animal than man, slid away, floating like a ghost on his left again. Definitely Lana. His night vision was as sharp as an owl's, and he saw her crawling. But she was too far from where he'd seen motion from his right. So who had he seen? Jonas wasn't this close, but what if he'd veered this way? It made Vince leave his gun firmly in its holster. He wasn't pulling the trigger at anyone or anything unless he was sure beyond any doubt of what he was shooting at.

Of course, that was always his rule, but Lana's unexpected, ghostly appearance told him just how on edge he was.

Had Porter come out here? What about Asa? Vince couldn't very well holler for everyone to identify themselves.

Vince faded back against a towering cottonwood, studying the terrain, listening, mindful with each breath to remain silent. Then, coming from his right, something dark rushed straight toward him.

Honestly, Dare was as tired of getting stabbed in the back as a man could be. "Finish bandaging, then we'll talk."

Dare could see that Glynna wanted to tear someone's head off. Too bad his was the only one handy.

He spent every second of her bandaging time trying to figure what to say to keep his head on his shoulders. But more than he was worried for himself, he didn't want to hurt her.

When finally she finished, she released a tight breath as if she'd fought every second for control while she worked on him. "Maybe now you'll explain to me why you think my son's guilty of knifing you in the back."

"I . . . let me tell you what's been happening, and why we've wondered about Paul but decided he wasn't involved in the trouble." He added that last part real quick, before she could start yelling at him.

"Trouble? What trouble?" Glynna probably hadn't even connected the avalanche, the fire, and this stabbing.

Dare was sorry he had to help her out. "It was a man-made avalanche." Dare very gingerly rolled onto his side so he could look at her better. His back didn't thank him.

"What?" Glynna interrupted him, which gave his back a second to adjust to the new position.

"Someone started that avalanche." Dare propped himself up on one elbow. He needed to have this talk with Glynna where he could hold her, comfort her, keep her from escaping . . . or attacking. "There's no doubt about it."

"Paul was in the avalanche. He couldn't have started it." She wobbled as if her knees were about to give out.

"It started just as he was leaving the pass, and we figured out how he could have done it." Dare reached up and caught Glynna's hand and pulled her to sit on the bed beside him. "But it put you in danger, so he couldn't have been involved. Everything he does is aimed at protecting you."

He loosened his grip on her wrist and caressed her rapidly pounding pulse. "Then my house burned down. That fire was set. Someone was mighty careful to start a blaze that trapped me inside."

"You think my son tried to burn you to death?" Glynna screeched the question, lurching to her feet.

Glynna struggled, and Dare's arm was killing him, so he let her go. "He's threatened to kill me before and even attacked me, remember? And Paul's carrying a mighty big grudge against any man who gets close to you."

He looked at Glynna, and their gazes locked. The close moments they'd shared were still there between them.

Dare spoke softly. "We counted Paul out when we realized the avalanche was rigged because that endangered you."

"We?" Glynna sounded sharp with hurt. "So you and your Regulator friends have been discussing whether my son is trying to commit murder?"

Dare didn't answer. She knew it was true. "We assume all three attacks were done by one person. So if he didn't set off the avalanche, it stands to reason he didn't start the fire, and he didn't stab me."

He tried to sit up, but the attempt to do so made him dizzy. How much blood had he lost? "I could use a drink of water." He was too weak to speak clearly, let alone be persuasive. "I need to start rebuilding my blood supply, and I need something to eat. A little broth maybe."

"There's some soup left over in the diner," Glynna said. "I can go skim some broth off and bring it here."

"No, I don't like you out alone," Dare said, knowing his voice cracked with command. He ran his fingers through his hair and noticed his hand shaking. "I think whoever's after me is only after me, but until we know for certain, we can't take any chances. The broth can wait until Vince and Jonas come back. Water's good for now."

Glynna headed for the kitchen. Dare lowered himself to lie flat on his stomach, weak as a newborn kitten. Here he was, stuck in bed, with a killer to find.

"Any more orders for me, General Dare?" Glynna came back with a tin cup brimming with water. She was as mad as a wounded badger. Dare didn't blame her, yet it didn't change anything.

"I've got just one."

He couldn't drink the water lying facedown, and he couldn't roll over and lie on his back, propped up by pillows. So with fierce effort he sat up.

Supported by Glynna, he swung his legs over the edge of the bed and managed to not fall on his face. She guided the water to his mouth and it tasted like heaven. Then a few seconds later his stomach threatened to empty. He had to turn his head aside.

"Just one?" Glynna glared, but she didn't dump the water over his head like he thought she might. "Well, what is it? To h-have Paul arrested?"

"No, not that." When her voice broke like she might start crying, Dare was quick to try to head that off. "That's the last thing I want. I don't think it's him, but if no one could get to that knife except you and your children, I'm not sure what to think."

Glynna ran her hand the length of Dare's arm, and it took him just a small move—about all he was capable of—to catch her fingers.

"What are we going to do, Dare?"

She might not have realized it, but she said *we*. She was asking for his help. It made Dare feel about ten feet tall. He knew then that she was through handling her son herself. She wasn't up to turning the boy into a man.

"There's really only one thing we can do. . . ." Dare was going to say it and the thought made him even dizzier, and that had nothing to do with the loss of blood.

"Paul didn't do it," Glynna repeated. "I know he's not capable of it. He's mostly talk. Just because he's had two fathers, both of 'em low-down dirty skunks, doesn't mean he'd try to kill someone."

Dare nodded.

"I should never have married either of them." She tore loose from Dare's grasp and wove her hands together as if she were in prayer. "I was too stupid to be able to judge their character."

"You weren't given a chance to judge their character. Your first marriage was arranged, your second you were a mail-order bride. Where in all that were you ever given a chance to learn the truth about them? It's a waste of time beating on yourself, Glynna. You can't undo the past." He meant to offer comfort, but a stab of pain coarsened his tone and he sounded harsh again.

Glynna caught her breath.

He cleared his throat. "We just have to go forward with what needs doing."

"I don't know what needs doing. I can't seem to reach him. He's so angry all the—"

"Your son," Dare said, cutting her off, "needs an honorable man in his life." He sounded grim and that wasn't how he'd wanted this, yet he couldn't think what else to say.

Sweeping aside thoughts of Glynna's traitorous first husband and how she'd helped him, he took a couple of deep breaths and forged on.

"Your son needs someone to teach him how to grow up straight and strong. And the way we're going to help him do that"—Dare reached out and caught her hand again, tighter this time so she couldn't escape—"is to get married."

The warrior in Vince kicked in hard. Instead of ducking out of sight, he turned and dove at whoever was coming at him.

Slamming into the moving form, he knew a woman when he tackled one. This wasn't one.

It wasn't Jonas either, which left one person. Vince drew back a long overdue fist and punched Mitch Porter in the face. Trust Porter to make a sneak attack. They'd made enough noise to bring Jonas running, which meant Lana was getting away.

Vince stood while Porter lay flat, clutching his jaw, mewling in pain.

"What's the matter with you, Porter?" When Vince asked, suddenly it was more than just a passing question.

What *was* wrong with this man? Lana had said something about seeing someone. "You're not involved with Lana Bullard, are you?"

Porter hesitated for too long. "I-I'm just protecting a woman like any decent man would."

Decent man left Porter out, which meant Vince had guessed about right.

Jonas ran up. "Did you get her?"

"No, Porter tried to dry-gulch me. It's a good thing you took his guns or he'd've shot me in the back."

"I would not!" Porter sounded like a ten-year-old boy accused of stealing a pie off the windowsill.

"I'm tired of having to watch out for him." Jonas dragged Porter to his feet. "And now Lana's gotten clean away. Maybe Luke can come in and track her once it's light. Let's lock Porter in the jail and get back to Dare. He shouldn't be alone with Lana still running loose." Jonas shoved Porter toward town.

"I'm not going to jail." Porter stumbled forward, all the fight drained out of him. Now all he had was whining. "It ain't fittin' to lock up a lawman. And I ain't done nuthin' wrong. I was just lookin' out for Lana."

"Guess what, Porter? I'm the law in this town now," Vince said. He put his hand on Porter's shoulder and shoved him onward. Locking this varmint up was going to be the only good part of a miserable night. "And I'm accusing you of aiding an escaping suspect." He'd read his share of law books and he was sure about this one. "That's against the law, in case you didn't know."

"How come you're the law in Broken Wheel?"

"A Texas Ranger swore me in as his deputy."

"That low-down Ranger who shot two decent men? Simon Bullard and Flint Greer?"

"Bullard and Greer, decent? And Lana Bullard, you defend. But I don't remember you being overly concerned with a woman's safety when it was Glynna Greer who came to you for help."

Vince had heard the story of Glynna running off from her brute of a husband and coming, children in tow, to Broken Wheel. Porter had held her until Greer got to town.

"You put up with Glynna being abused without a second thought. How come all of a sudden you're so concerned with a woman getting proper treatment?"

"I trusted Greer. He struck me as an honest man, and I took Glynna for a liar."

"A liar?" Vince was almost sputtering. "She came to town all black and blue."

"No, she didn't. You weren't in town when that happened. There wasn't a mark on her. All I saw was a fussy city gal throwing a fit at her husband."

"Dare went out to doctor her twice." Vince took a step toward Porter. "Greer was brutal to her. She turned to you for protection and you threw her back into purgatory. This whole town bears the shame for leaving a polecat like you as sheriff after that."

"A man ain't got no pride if his woman runs off. That woman dishonored a good man in front of the whole town."

"A woman is a rare and fine thing." *Except maybe for Lana Bullard,* Vince thought. "No man can call himself a man if he sees a woman in need of protection and turns his back, leaving her to an ugly fate."

"A man's got a right to keep his woman in line. All I saw was a woman running out on her husband with horses she stole. I refused to help her."

"You're a coward." Vince took the last two steps toward Porter and clenched his fist. "A coward and a liar and a sidewinder."

"Vince, stop." Jonas cut into the fight just when Vince was beginning to taste the satisfaction he'd get by slugging Porter in the mouth. "We won't solve this now. We need to find Lana."

Vince, seething at Porter's cowardice, reined in his temper with a Texas-sized effort.

They got back to town and locked Porter away in the badly damaged cell. Greer had used blasting powder to break his hired gun Bullard out of jail, and there was no money to fix the dreary little building. But they'd managed to bolt the bars back together and cover the hole blown in the floor and the back wall.

"I'm keeping the key," Vince said, dangling it so Porter could see it. "I think Lana is working with you, and I don't trust her not to come in here to try and set you free."

Jonas headed for the door. "Now let's get back to Dare. If Lana stabbed him once, she might come after him again."

Vince was right on Jonas's heels.

CHAPTER 22

"Dare, we can't get—"

Dare cut her off by kissing her. He ignored the pain in his shoulder and dragged her into his arms. He was steadier and stronger with her there. He tilted his head and deepened the kiss.

She didn't resist for a second, and he knew this was his answer, not her weak *"Dare, we can't."*

He raised his head and looked down into those golden eyes. Everything about her was golden. She moved to be closer to him, and every shift of her body increased his longing for her to be his. "You have to marry me, Glynna."

She raised her hands to rest on his cheeks. Her golden eyes shifted back and forth between his. "I do. I have to marry you. I can't want you like this and not marry you. But what will we do about Paul?"

"That's the question, isn't it?" Dare was suddenly aware of the door behind them and that anyone could walk in. Paul, Vince, Lana . . .

"We should have locked the door after Tina. Go. We can't have this talk if we don't have privacy."

Parson Jonas was walking around town right now. They could have this wedding immediately. As Dare glanced at the door, he made a wrong move and his back seemed to stab him all over again. Might be best to get married in a few days' time, he decided, when he could do justice to the honeymoon. At the moment he was more patient than protector. And they needed to tell Paul, let the boy adjust to the idea of the marriage.

Glynna stood. Her hair looked for all the world like someone had run their hands deeply into it. He didn't want Paul to see her like this, although it was almost morning and her hair being messy could be laid down to a lot of things.

"Dare, I know how it was when I told you about Reggie. I could see your anger at him for being such a traitor. And you blamed me, too." Glynna gave a short, humorless laugh. "Reggie blamed me for my father's money running out, even though it was him who spent it all. He blamed me when we ended up living on that pathetic farm. And Flint blamed me for being a poor cook and a disappointment at . . . at meeting his husbandly needs. And then here you were blaming me for the actions of my first husband. When we first met, you even blamed me for being hurt."

"Don't compare me to those yellow-bellied coyotes you were married to." Dare knew he'd felt those things, but not anymore. What little niggling he felt wasn't stronger than his need to claim Glynna as his wife. They'd work out any confused feelings on Dare's part later.

"How long before you start scowling and complaining? How long, Dare?"

The woman had a point. They'd put the wedding off

a while until they'd settled all of that. Then he imagined Vince walking in on him kissing Glynna. His friend would needle him about that forever. They really needed to lock that door. But more than that, he had to get Glynna to forget how he'd reacted to her traitorous scum of a first husband. Risking being caught, Dare reached for her to kiss her to distraction.

"Stop!" She laid both hands flat on his chest. "What if there was nothing wrong with either of my husbands, nor my son? Maybe it's me. Maybe, even if you're the most honorable of men, you'll turn bad because I bring that out in a man."

"That's ridiculous, Glynna. Your other husbands were bad from the first. And your son will be just fine. He needs a strong, honorable man for a pa, is all."

"And that's you, right? The ridiculous little woman can't handle her own son, but the big strong Regulator war hero doctor can? Right . . . ?"

"Stop putting words in my mouth." Dare had a feeling that growling at a woman while you proposed to her was all wrong. He tried his best to stop. "Glynna, I'm not marrying you to save your son. I'm marrying you because I can't be near you and not want to be married to you in every way you can imagine."

At last her hands on his chest relaxed. Her beautiful golden eyes opened wide as she stopped struggling. There was a long moment as they sat together, then she nodded. "I feel the same, Dare. I do."

"We don't have to get married right away." Although Dare wanted to badly. He wanted her pledged to him before God and man. But Paul was going to be a hard one to handle, and they all needed a bit more time to work things out. "Go lock the door. We're getting married. We can decide when later, but for right now, I want that door locked."

Glynna, with flattering reluctance, eased away from him and stood. She hurried to the front door, plucked the skeleton key off the nail by the doorjamb, and locked it.

"I'm pretty sure I locked the back door," Dare said, "but can you check it?" Just then another wave of dizziness swept over him and he felt the need to lie down and sleep for a while, but he had to resist it and stay alert. "You know, it's been way too long since Jonas and Vince left. I don't like it that they haven't come back saying they found Lana."

"Is there a key hanging up by the back door, too?"

"No, I use the same key on both doors."

Glynna looked down at the key in her hand. Then, with her eyes blazing like the rising sun, she said, "This key would probably work in the diner's door. That means someone besides my own family could've gotten in."

"Most keys work all too well in doors they weren't made for."

"Which means someone had access to my knives besides Paul."

"And Lana knew that kitchen and your knives better than anyone." Dare wasn't thinking like a patient now, nor a doctor. He was thinking like a soldier who'd faced danger and judged risks and used logic to find answers. His head cleared as one more piece in this puzzle slipped into place.

"I'll get the back door locked, then we'll wait for your

friends. You should lie down." Glynna rushed toward the kitchen. Dare wobbled a bit but somehow stayed upright. He wasn't going to rest, so he'd take this time to finish settling things with Glynna.

Still, he looked sideways at the bed. It was inviting. And his back hurt like blue blazes. Maybe he could—

"Dare?"

The tone in Glynna's voice brought his head around hard. She stood, ashen-faced, in the hallway to the back door. Dare rose unsteadily to his feet.

Lana Bullard, her hair gone wild and her eyes gone mad, was right behind Glynna with an arm around her neck and a knife only inches from her throat.

"My boardinghouse key works in pretty near every door in town," Lana said. "Your old house. The diner. Your new house."

Dare took a half step forward. "Lana, stop!"

"You killed my son, Doc. Now I'm gonna kill someone precious to you."

❧

Vince led Jonas down the steps toward the main street. "Sun's finally comin' up."

"Glad to get shut of this night." Jonas sounded exhausted, but Vince knew this wasn't going to be a day to catch up on sleep.

"One of us needs to ride out to get Luke."

Jonas and Vince strode side by side toward the row of buildings where the diner stood shoulder to shoulder with the general store and the saloon. The door to the diner swung open and Vince went for his gun by reflex. Paul stepped into the doorway, glaring at them, of course. Vince's hand trembled on his gun and only then did he realize how on edge he was.

Jonas muttered, "Didn't we tell him to stay with Dare and the women?"

"I want to see how Dare's doing. We'll deal with the kid later."

But Paul wasn't waiting until later. He stormed down the steps of the diner and strode straight for them. Vince and Jonas could walk over the grouchy youngster or they could stop. They stopped but, for Vince at least, it wasn't that easy a choice.

Paul started complaining before he stopped walking. "I'm sick of your friend—"

Vince cut him off. "Why aren't you with Dare?"

Paul's fists clenched. "My ma wanted me to go back to the diner so Janny wouldn't wake up alone, but that's not why—"

Jonas cut him off. "Then what are you doing out here?"

"Tina is with her. Stop interrupt—"

"So you left a sleeping child and my sister alone after Dare got stabbed?" Jonas sounded too angry for a preacher. "I'm going to make sure they're all right." Jonas took off for the diner, which stood with its front door wide open where Paul had come out.

Vince turned on the kid. "You know there's danger. You saw Dare had been attacked. But you're too stubborn to help out by watching over them?" His voice grew deeper, louder. "Instead you came out here to complain about your ma and our good friend and think we'll take your side? Listen, you little pup, we got you out of a bad situation with Flint Greer. We saved your ma's life in an avalanche. Dare was right there risking his life."

Paul's chin came up in defiance. "You only did that to get Luke Stone's ranch back."

"No." Vince slashed a hand. "From the minute Dare realized Greer was responsible for your ma being hurt, Luke's land wasn't the most important thing anymore. Not to any of us. We pushed as hard as we could to get you out of there. That's because we're men. And men don't stand by while a woman or child is being hurt. Dare would never hurt your ma, nor any of your family. I don't blame you for remembering the hard lessons you've been taught, but use some common sense. Dare Riker is a good man and you're close enough to an adult to see that."

"I *am* an adult, and my ma don't need another husband."

Vince swerved around Paul, then stopped. Mad as he was at the boy, he couldn't leave him out here alone. "Jonas is with Janny and Tina now, so you come along with me back to Dare's house. I'm not going to stay out here yappin' when there's a would-be killer loose in town."

"I thought you just came from the jail. I figured you locked someone up."

"You figured wrong, kid. And not for the first time. Let's go make sure your ma's all right." Vince didn't leave the boy, despite the urgent need to check on Dare. Paul wanted to be back by his mother, so it didn't take long for him to come along. Vince prayed that they didn't walk in on Dare and Glynna smooching, but instead walk in and find nothing the least bit interesting. He'd had a bellyful of the young'un complaining, and walking in on his mother in another man's arms would most likely keep the racket going all the way till the noon hour.

Dare had a gun inches from his hand. Lana was a little taller than Glynna, and in the normal run of things, Dare figured he could hit what he aimed at.

But that razor-sharp knife was too close to Glynna's neck, and Dare's hand too shaky. Glynna being in danger made the stakes so high that Dare couldn't risk it, even though he wanted to reach Lana Bullard and rip her apart with his bare hands.

How did it come to this? She'd adored him when he'd first come to town. He'd never been comfortable with it, but he realized now that her adoration was as irrational as her hatred.

"Lana, put down the knife and let's talk. Let's talk about that night when you came to my office and you thought a baby died."

"It happened! Don't try and deny it." Lana's teeth bared, and her bloodshot eyes flashed. The knife wobbled and Glynna flinched. A line of blood welled and a rivulet flowed down Glynna's neck. Dare knew he might have to do it. Take the long, ugly chance that he could shoot Lana before Glynna was killed. Another death on his conscience. And if he failed and Glynna died, Dare might well die too, from grief.

Only now, as he saw that gleaming butcher knife, did Dare realize he was in love with her.

God, please give me wisdom. Give me the right words. How do I talk to someone who's crazed with grief for her child?

It came to him as if God had opened the pages of a book for Dare to read.

"Do you know what God did when His son, Jesus, died?"

Shaking her head, Lana seemed to truly be listening.

"God forgave the men who'd killed Him." Dare risked a quick glance at Glynna. She was ready to move, to fight, to do whatever needed to be done. But Glynna was listening, too.

Maybe Glynna needed to be reminded about forgiveness. Then Dare wondered if he didn't need the reminder just as much.

Shaking her head, the knife came back up, close again to Glynna's neck. "No, He didn't," Lana said. "No one could forgive that."

"Jesus's last words as He died at the hands of evil men was, 'God forgive them, for they know not what they do.'"

"And God did it? Just like that? He let them kill His son? He didn't even care enough to be killing mad?"

"The Bible said that there were earthquakes when Jesus died. The sun went dark. A temple, that's a church, was ripped up inside. Graves opened and dead people were seen walkin' around. I'd say God was mighty upset."

Lana's eyes seemed to focus for the first time. She glanced at the knife, then at Glynna.

"Just like you're upset, Lana. But look at me. You know me. You'd come to see me many times. You know I'm not a man who would harm a child. But whatever you believe, you need to forgive me like God forgave those who killed His son. You need to put down that knife and let Glynna go."

Lana's eyes shifted to the knife. Slowly, a fraction of an inch at a time, her grip relaxed on Glynna's neck. Finally her restraining arm fell to her side.

Glynna stepped away as if afraid a sudden move might stir Lana up again. When Lana didn't grab for her, Glynna walked the few steps to Dare and turned to face Lana. Dare sank down to sit on the bed while Glynna stood at his side.

Dare should probably walk over and take that ugly knife from Lana, but he wasn't sure he could stand.

"I reckon I can forgive you, Doc. And Glynna's never been nuthin' but good to me, so you're right that I shouldn't hurt her." Lana looked at the knife as if she were under a trance. It came up as Lana drew it toward herself. "But all I'm left with is the grief of my child dying and my husband running off. I'm left with nothing, just like I've always had nothing."

Tears trickled down Lana's cheeks. The knife turned to point inward, straight at Lana's heart. "I am so tired of living with nothing." Her tears fell faster. "I forgive you, Doc."

Dare tried to stand, but his knees buckled and he fell back to where he sat. Glynna had started to move toward Lana when Dare grabbed her by the wrist and held her back.

Lana looked again at the knife and her expression was pure sadness, hopelessness. "Bury me beside my husband and son."

A shift of shadow in the hallway behind Lana drew Dare's attention.

Vince.

She pulled back the knife to strike herself.

With a single motion Vince quickly reached around Lana and knocked the knife from her hand.

A scream of grief ripped from Lana's throat. The despair in her eyes shifted to pure madness. She whirled on Vince and attacked.

CHAPTER 23

Vince went down under a clawing madwoman. He kicked aside the knife and caught both of her wrists at the same time she started walloping him with her feet.

"Am I gonna have to fight this woman every day for the rest of my life?" Vince shouted.

Just then she caught him with a cruelly placed knee, howled right in his face, and spit on him. Next she went for his throat with her teeth.

But a second later, Lana was yanked away from Vince. Paul had entered the fight and he had the woman wrapped tight in his arms, pinning her hands to her sides.

Glynna stepped forward and stuffed a kerchief in Lana's mouth, which dropped the noise level considerably.

Dare began stumbling toward the ruckus.

"You sit back down!" Vince told Dare. He staggered to his feet and caught Lana's legs, wrapping both arms around her ankles.

"Lana, please calm down," Glynna said. She was going to handle this with kindness.

Lana bucked in their arms. Vince had wrangled long-horns that didn't kick like this woman.

Lana continued to scream, muffled by the gag.

"Lana, we're not going to hurt you. Don't be afraid." Glynna's pretty brow was furrowed with worry. She looked up at Vince. The uncertainty had him confused at first.

"I don't suppose I can get her calm enough to cook breakfast at the diner, can I?"

Vince thought he saw foam coming from the corners of Lana's mouth. "Nope. Don't reckon she's gonna be able to fry eggs today."

"We're really going to miss her."

Nothing more than the plain truth.

"I'm not going to miss her that much." Dare drew Vince's attention as he backed up a couple of steps and sat down on the bed. Honestly, it looked more like he collapsed, but at least Dare didn't end up facedown on the floor again. Vince was too busy to catch him or to pick him back up.

"Glynna, get over here." Dare, sounding exhausted, still put a lot of command in his voice.

Vince looked at Paul. "Go ahead, Glynna. We've got her."

The boy nodded. "Yep, I've got a solid grip." Paul seemed less surly than usual. Maybe he was feeling useful.

"You've been cut," Dare said. "Your neck's bleeding." He looked almost frantically at Glynna's neck as she approached the bed where he sat.

Her hand went to her neck and she pulled away bloody fingers. The color seemed to fade from Glynna's face.

"Don't even think of fainting," Vince snapped. He'd

ordered around men who were a lot bigger weaklings than Glynna. He'd found he had a voice that could clear most anyone's head.

Glynna gathered herself, looked away from her hand, and straightened her shoulder. Vince's voice was as good as smelling salts.

"Her neck's not hurt bad, Dare. Leave it for now. We need to get Jonas over here. Go find him, Glynna. Janny will be safe now. Tell Tina to start cooking for the town, so we won't have a bunch of men spittin' mad that Lana's been arrested."

Glynna nodded. "I'll be right back." She patted Dare on the shoulder and left.

"Now, you need to lie down and rest, Dare."

Dare tipped sideways so easily, Vince figured his friend had been holding himself upright through pure iron will.

"Paul, you and I need to get her calmed down somehow so we can question her."

"How're we gonna do that when neither of us can let go?"

A few minutes passed before Glynna came rushing back in. Vince was glad to see her. He thought having a woman present, considering this wrestling match with Lana, was the right thing to do.

The woman in their arms gave a particularly wild wrench of her body and almost got away.

"Maybe give her some laudanum." Dare spoke barely above a whisper. "Just a spoonful from the bottle. That should help her regain control of herself."

It was a good idea, but Vince considered upping the

313

dosage and dumping the whole bottle of the stuff down her throat.

"It's on that shelf there," Dare said, pointing a listless finger. The man truly needed some rest.

"Bring her over to this chair," Glynna said. She got some long strips of cloth out of Dare's stack of rags. "We'll restrain her."

"We need to send a wire to Big John and tell him we've got two prisoners to transport."

"Two?" Paul asked.

Vince ignored the kid. "And when that's all done, Dare, I'll slap a bandage on that scratch on Glynna's neck."

He thought he heard Dare snoring.

Jonas came in seconds later. Heaving a sigh of relief, Vince said, "Good. I'm glad you're here finally."

Jonas arched a brow at Lana, who was twisting in the arms of Vince and Paul. He didn't look all that eager to get involved in holding her prisoner.

"We've got a crazy woman in custody and we have to interrogate her."

"Are you sure?" Jonas asked.

Vince had looked through the front window of Dare's house and seen Lana holding Glynna in time to change course and come instead through the back door. Paul had been halfway to crazy himself to see his ma with a knife to her throat.

"I'm sure," Vince said with a nod.

Paul barely missed clunking heads with the lunatic as Vince toted Lana to the nearest chair. "I think the hard part is yet to come," Vince said.

"That woman makes the best eggs over easy I've ever had," Dare said from where he lay on his belly on the bed.

"Her fried potatoes put my ma's to shame," Jonas added. "And my ma was a mighty good cook."

Vince and Paul sat Lana on the chair. "This town is gonna miss her cookin' and that's a fact," Paul said as she wrested one arm loose and clawed at his face.

"Some of us'll miss her more than others," Dare mumbled.

Vince let go of Lana's feet, and he and Paul each grabbed an arm as she lunged from the chair. They sat her back down.

"I don't know if I can get close enough to tie her up." Jonas, a long strip of white cloth in one hand, dodged a slashing foot.

Vince looked at Glynna. "Get in here and help us. If she keeps fighting us like this, she's gonna end up hurt, and we don't want that."

Privately, Vince wanted to see this woman severely punished for stabbing Dare. But he'd leave that for the law. Although these days, unless their Regulator friend was in town, Vince was the only law in Broken Wheel. Big John Conroy made his home in town, but he spent most of the time traveling. He was overdue to come back home, though. They could get Lana locked up and figure out what to do with her until Big John got home.

Working together, Jonas and Glynna finally got Lana bound to the wooden chair.

She still had the gag in her mouth, so things were pretty quiet. Of course, they couldn't keep her tied up forever.

Vince grimaced. "It's gonna be noisy when I take that gag out of her mouth."

"She's a raving lunatic." Jonas shook his head at the completely out-of-control woman.

"No, she's not," Paul replied. "She's been working for us for a while now, and she seemed real sensible."

"She was good at chopping potatoes," Glynna said. "It was impressive, but I admit it made me a little nervous to see her flashing that knife with so much skill."

"Lana!" Vince crouched in front of her. Since her feet were bound, he was able to get pretty close. He tried to penetrate her frothing struggle.

Glynna came up beside Vince. "She's scared to death."

"This isn't panic." Vince rose. "She stabbed Dare. She held that knife to your throat. She attacked me when I knocked it away from her. This is rage, not fear."

Vince reached down and removed the gag from Lana's mouth. Instantly her muffled screams became full-throated screams.

"Let's try the laudanum," Glynna said.

Suddenly Lana stopped screaming and sat up straight, looking at the bottle Glynna held.

"Looks like *laudanum* is the magic word," Vince said. He studied the now calmer woman. "Can you answer some questions for us, Lana?"

She turned on Vince. Her face was slick with sweat, and her hair was a tangle. Her eyes were so bloodshot, all the white had turned to red. She panted and tugged against her bonds, but she didn't go back to the shrieking.

"If you answer my questions, I'll give you a dose of the medicine." And if that wasn't a temptation worthy of the devil himself, Vince didn't know what was.

He glanced over to Dare, who looked to be fast asleep at last. A man didn't often fall asleep, no matter how weary, with a woman screaming a few feet away, so Dare was probably more unconscious than asleep. Vince needed to finish with Lana so his wounded friend could get some much-needed attention.

"Whaddya want to know?" Lana asked. Her voice was hoarse from all her screaming, but despite her rational question, Vince wouldn't have untied her for a million bucks.

As she waited, breathing as if she'd run all the way from Fort Worth, Jonas moved forward and crouched down in front of Lana.

"What did you do to Dare?" Jonas began.

Vince was pretty sure any confession Lana blurted out in her current state wasn't exactly fair. He thought he'd read that somewhere.

"He killed my son." Lana's head lifted and Vince saw hatred in her eyes. Her voice rose, though not to a scream. Just hard, cold words.

"No, he didn't," Vince interjected. He was wasting his breath, but he felt honor-bound to waste it. "There was no baby, Lana. You're mixed up about that."

"He killed my husband."

Technically, Big John Conroy had killed him, but considering Lana's addled state, it was probably more wasted time to point that out. Still, it needed to be said. "No, he didn't. That's not true, either. Dare was inside the livery stable, and Simon died outside—in a shootout with a lawman."

Vince decided not to mention Big John by name, just in case he convinced Lana he spoke the truth. No sense luring a murderous lunatic away from one friend only to point her to another.

"I lost my home because of him."

"Lana—" Vince started, again.

Jonas's hand came up. "Let her talk, Vince."

"Everything I cared about was taken from me by the man I trusted to save me!" Lana's voice rose to the cry of a wounded creature.

There was a long silence. Jonas looked for all the world like a man who was absolutely stumped. He opened his mouth several times, then closed it again. What did a person say to a woman who was so furiously mad?

Then Lana looked straight at Jonas—Vince's friend, a truly decent man of God. Her eyes glittered with hate. Her cheeks flushed red with rage. With a growl that was more animal than human she turned to the bed where Dare lay unmoving. "And now he's dead."

She looked from Jonas to Vince to a dumbfounded Glynna.

"So you killed him." Jonas, speaking quietly, didn't correct Lana's assumption that her attack on Dare had been fatal.

How Jonas kept calm, Vince couldn't imagine. Just hearing the sentence declaring Dare dead made Vince mad enough to swing a fist. And under the veneer of calm, Vince heard the anger Jonas was masking. Lana was real lucky to be in the hands of civilized men.

"I'm not sayin' another word until you give me that medicine," Lana said. "I hurt all over."

They asked and prodded, but she stubbornly refused to comply. Finally, Glynna said, "Surely a sip won't hurt."

Jonas and Vince looked at each other. Glynna made the decision for them by lifting the bottle to Lana's lips. Lana made a sudden dipping motion with her head and managed to suck down a few good gulps before Glynna jumped back.

"She got half the bottle." Glynna held it up with alarm.

Lana smacked her lips and gave a satisfied sigh.

"Better get your answers quick, Jonas. Something tells me our prisoner is going to take a long nap here pretty soon."

Jonas spoke the same words he had before. "So, you admit you stabbed Dr. Riker?"

"He's dead. He had it coming." She began lifting her head as if she was gathering her senses a bit, the medicine making her calm maybe. "Untie me."

"I'm not turning you loose." Vince only had to feel the bruises on his own body and see the scratches on Jonas's and Paul's faces to know they were better off with Lana restrained.

"Go on, Lana," Jonas cajoled, "you were telling us about attacking Dare."

Lana glared at Jonas for a few seconds, then her eyes lost focus and her head slumped forward.

Jonas lifted her chin and she snorted, then settled into snoring. "I think the laudanum got to her already. She's fast asleep, and before we got a full confession."

⁂

The jailhouse had been reconstructed. Well, mostly it was still a wreck, but when Vince kicked Porter out of the cell and dropped a sleeping Lana down on the tattered cot, she shifted onto her side and tucked both hands under her face like an innocent child. An innocent child with prison in her near future.

Jonas had stayed with Dare.

"You should've never wrecked my jail like this." Mitch Porter was a poor excuse for a man, let alone a lawman.

"I didn't wreck it. Greer did when he blasted Simon Bullard out. And it's not your jail. I'm the law in Broken Wheel now." It was a job with no pay because no one wanted to chip in, but Big John had sworn him in so it was official.

Porter got a look at Vince's determined glare. "This ain't over. You aren't Broken Wheel's sheriff."

"Big John Conroy, the Texas Ranger, deputizes me whenever he's on the road." Over Vince's fierce objections. He didn't want to be sheriff. Right now, though, Vince had to admit it'd come in mighty handy. And fun besides to thwart this coyote.

"You know, Porter, a lawman would question you about what happened last night. Should we do that now? You were next door to Mrs. Bullard. Did you hear her get up and move around?"

"I was asleep. And I don't have to answer any questions."

Vince ignored Porter's refusal to be questioned. If Porter didn't want to talk, he could leave. "You came out of your room dressed and wearing your boots."

"I heard you coming up the stairs. I knew someone was out there. I got ready for trouble."

"You got fully dressed mighty fast and quiet." Vince decided he had a knack for prying questions that came in handy at a time like this.

"Yep, now that you're a *lawman*," Porter said, "you'll learn how to get ready for trouble fast and quiet, too."

"If you want to stay on the outside of that cell, Porter, get out of here." Vince headed for the door, shoving Porter ahead of him, now that his prisoner was under control. "If I told my story right and convinced a judge you were covering for a would-be murderer, you might end up seeing things through bars for a lot of years."

Tina cooked for the diner that morning and she did a good job of it. Glynna wondered if she'd be available to work for her full-time. Lana was a better cook, to be sure, and Tina wasn't half as skillful with a knife, but both women definitely had Glynna beat in the kitchen.

Glynna had helped a little with serving breakfast, yet the job of checking on Dare had fallen to her and that was what occupied her thoughts right now. Or maybe she'd grabbed the responsibility and refused to let go. Vince and Jonas were splitting their time between the jailhouse and Dare's side, though Glynna didn't trust them to be as careful as she would be.

However it had happened, she had to check on Dare throughout the morning, leaving Paul, Janny, and Tina shorthanded at the diner.

She hurried back to work whenever she got a free minute, until she went in and saw Dare awake. Sitting up in bed. Vince and Jonas were sharing a cup of coffee with him.

Dare turned to look at her. Pain etched lines in his face. He was pale and shaky, but he was all right. He'd proposed last night. Maybe in the heat of the moment, Dare had thought marrying her was a good idea. Maybe now he was sorry. Maybe . . .

"You two get out of here for a while." Dare cut into her worries. "And, Jonas, don't go far. You're going to need to speak some vows between Glynna and me in a little while."

Vince grinned bright enough to blind a woman. She knew in a detached way that Vince was one of the most handsome men she'd ever seen, but it didn't seem to affect Glynna overly. She only had eyes for Dare. His hair, always in need of a trim, and his scruffy face that always needed a shave touched her heart in a way no man, certainly neither of the ones she'd married, ever had.

Jonas said, "I read a book that said a couple should be betrothed for a while before they marry, Dare. And I've done some studying about the things a man and woman ought to talk about before they wed. I don't think you should rush in to this."

"Get out."

Jonas smiled over that rude order, for some odd reason. "I think you two, and probably Paul and Janny, should counsel with me for at least a couple of months before you get married."

Even Glynna could see Jonas was just teasing.

"The wedding is before we eat the noon meal. Now leave us alone."

"I'm not speaking any vows until you've had this out with Paul." Jonas had turned dead serious all of a sudden. "It's the right thing to do and you know it—to tell the children what you're planning to do and then give them at least a little bit of time to adjust to the idea. And I'm not going far. I'm not leaving the two of you alone in here for long. It ain't proper."

"What kind of improper thing do you think's gonna happen with my back slashed open?" Dare fairly growled the question.

"I don't underestimate you, my friend." Jonas turned and followed a grinning Vince out the door. When it swung shut, Glynna heard them both start laughing.

"Your friends are—"

Dare stood up.

"Stop!" Glynna rushed to his side.

"I'm not in the mood to be lectured about my friends right now." Dare let Glynna ease him back onto the bed. Sitting side by side, he said, "I suppose he's right. We should have a long talk with Paul."

Glynna knew that was exactly what they should do— they should tell her son. She smiled, then shook her head slowly. "Let's get married, Dare. I think this is too big a decision for a child to make."

Dare sat up straighter. "What? I don't get it. What about your promise to him not to get married without his blessing?"

Glynna slid her hand around Dare's back, down low so she wouldn't bump his wound. "I think the way he worked with us last night is his blessing, don't you?"

Turning to face her, Dare leaned over and kissed her. The kiss lingered for a long time. He didn't seem all that injured anymore.

"If he's ready to accept us," Dare said, "then he'll take

323

the news well. I'm not going to ask for his blessing—at least I'm not going to change my mind if he withholds it. You're right. It's too big a decision, even for a mostly grown boy."

"The breakfast crowd has thinned out. I'll go get Paul right now." Glynna stood and then was dragged right back down beside Dare.

He smiled at her, and she was amazed at how attractive a shaggy man could be. "There's no rush, is there?"

"I thought you wanted to get married right away. I thought you were in a hurry." The man confused her, but that didn't stop her from smiling right back at him. Of all the things they'd gone through together, deciding whether they were in a hurry to get married seemed like a very simple choice, mainly because neither answer changed anything. They would marry. And soon.

Dare leaned in closer to her until he blocked out the whole world. She closed her eyes and saw him inside her head. His lips warmed her all the way to her soul.

The door banged open in the way only one person in the world ever banged it.

"Ma!"

Glynna pulled back, shrugged one shoulder at Dare, and stood. He struggled to stand too, but she pressed a hand on his shoulder to keep him seated. Then she faced her frustrated, confused son.

"Come on over here, Paul." Glynna turned her back and sat again, figuring Paul would come around to vent his anger.

He did just that.

"Dare and I are getting married," she told him.

"You promised!" When he spoke, he sounded like a child. Glynna's heart ached for him. "You swore you'd ask for my blessing."

She looked at her son, a boy in a man's body. "I'd love it if you were happy about it, but I should never have made that promise."

"You don't need another man, Ma. You've got me." He wasn't a child, but he was still far from an adult. There was a chair close to the bed, and he stomped over to it and took a seat. "We're doin' fine in the diner. We don't need anyone else to take care of us."

It struck Glynna that this was the most rational anger her son had shown in a long time. He was actually talking.

"We're not getting married because your ma needs a roof over her head, Paul." Dare's deep voice came out rocky, but it soothed, like a brook rumbling over stone. "We're getting married because I love your ma and she loves me. I love you too, Paul."

Paul shot Dare a glance loaded with such suspicion that Glynna despaired of her son ever trusting anyone again.

Dare went on, "You've had some mighty bad luck in your life, and I don't blame you for having doubts, real serious doubts. But I'll be a good pa to you. I'll always be kind to your ma. I'll treat Janny like she was my own child. I want to be in your family, and I'd love it if you welcomed me in, son."

Paul opened his mouth, his eyes flashing with anger. Glynna knew what he'd say. *I'm not your son.* He wanted to blast those words out like bullets. Then, to her surprise, he clamped his mouth shut. He was listening. She thought that maybe she even saw the smallest trace of longing in his eyes. What boy didn't want a good man for a father?

Paul looked down between his splayed knees. Glynna noticed his pants were too short. Again. The boy was growing faster than long-stemmed grama grass.

"I reckon you'll do as you want," Paul finally said.

Dare leaned forward and rested a hand on her boy's sagging shoulders. "I'll take on the job of caring for this family and lift the weight off your shoulders. I think the day will come soon when you're glad to have me around."

Paul raised his head and studied Dare. "I heard what you said about forgiveness. I was behind Lana, listening. It's a hard truth. God forgave all those people who killed Jesus. . . ."

Frowning, Paul was silent for a long stretch, and neither Glynna nor Dare broke the silence.

"Is it right that I'm supposed to forgive a man like my pa, who was a thief and a traitor? Are you saying I'm supposed to forgive Greer, who hit my ma? He never asked for forgiveness. If I'd have said 'I forgive you' to him, he'd have spit in my face. Does God really want us to forgive a man like that?"

At that moment, Glynna realized she'd never forgiven either of her husbands, and she'd never wanted to, never even considered it. Didn't a person have to ask? Didn't they have to be sorry about what they'd done?

"I was locked up in prison for a long time," Dare said. "The camp commander took pleasure in our suffering. The guards too seemed to take pleasure in causing us pain. I think there's a difference between forgiving and trusting. If an unrepentant man is around, I don't think God expects us to trust him. For someone like Greer, the forgiveness is more for you. It does a lot of damage to carry hate around inside."

Paul sat up a bit straighter. "It does?"

Dare nodded. "Giving up the hurt and anger would leave space in your head for something better. You work hard at the diner. You take care of Janny and protect your ma. Hating those men poisons your thinking, Paul, and takes up too much of your time and energy. I think if you can forgive those men, you can have room in your heart to be happy."

Dare gave the boy a choice between the angry life he'd been living for so long and simple happiness.

After a while a hesitant smile bloomed on Paul's face. There were still shadows, still doubts, but the smile was genuine.

Awkwardly the boy reached out his hand and offered it to Dare to shake. "Welcome to the family, Doc."

CHAPTER 24

Dare's eyes blinked, startled by the extended hand and the shy smile. He grabbed hold of Paul's hand, feeling like he'd passed muster. "Oh, I forgot to tell you, I'm gonna stop being a doctor."

Paul shrugged. "Stop if you can, but I think you're probably stuck with healing. You can't seem to resist it."

Dare turned to Glynna. "Now that we'll be married, I won't have to buy Greer's land. You can quit worrying about selling it. We can just move out there. I think the cabin is a shack we'll have to—"

"No, I'm not moving to Flint's place," she said, cutting him off. "I can't believe a man who wants to marry me doesn't know me better than to believe I'd ever live on land that man owned."

Dare, aggravated, exchanged a look with Paul. The boy seemed to commiserate with him, and Dare realized the boy knew this woman better than he did.

"Ma, I thought we were supposed to forgive Greer."

"I'm not going to profit from a marriage to that rat snake of a man."

"Now, Glynna, honey, calm—"

The door behind them swung open, and Vince strode in carrying a stack of papers and books. "Your latest medical publications arrived, Dare. Guess what it says here?"

"Stop reading my mail."

"I was bored waiting for you to talk things out with Paul." Vince wasn't an easy man to shame. "Don't you want to hear what it says?"

"I'm not in the mood to read right now."

"Not even an article that says you're an honest-to-goodness doctor right like you are now?" Vince rounded the bed and slapped the paper in Dare's hand. "You don't have to go to school at all. Turns out the experience you had in the war is enough."

Dare's eyes landed on an article with the title *Irregular Doctors*. He read the first few paragraphs and immediately felt his spirits soar. He shoved the article at Glynna. "They say there are all sorts of doctors. I qualify. My service counts as an apprenticeship if a doctor who's a commanding officer—which the doc at Andersonville was—recruits me and watches over my work for long enough a time. I'm well over the requirements."

"Does this mean we don't have to move to that awful shack and starve until you learn how to rope a longhorn?" No doubt about it, his soon-to-be wife had a sarcastic streak in her.

"Let's split the land between Luke and the Fosters. It borders both of them. We'll give it to them, and it'll be at least a little repayment for the damage Greer did."

The smile that spread on Glynna's pretty face made Dare

forget about doctors and ranches and knife wounds and even sullen young men. He would've dragged her into his arms right then and reminded her of just how happy he was to be marrying her if he hadn't had so blasted much company.

"Vince!" Dare hadn't meant his voice to crack quite like such a whip. "Go get Jonas and let's get this wedding over with."

"What about Luke? He'll want to come, too."

"Don't you think we should tell Janny first?" Paul arched a white-blond brow.

"Dare, lie down before you fall over. We can let you heal up for a few days before—"

Dare shot a look at Vince. "Find Luke. You've got two hours to get back here. Now go."

"Yes, sir." Vince gave a casual salute, flashed a grin and headed out, the door slamming shut behind him.

"Paul, go get Janny."

"I think she's busy pouring coffee."

"Get her over here."

Paul rolled his eyes and then left the room.

"Now, Dare, you can't just order me to . . ."

Silence reigned in the room while Dare did his very best to demonstrate that he was fully up to the task of getting married—so long as he got to sit down during the ceremony.

Glynna was clinging to him by the time he left off kissing her.

Dare smiled. "I'm a decent cook, too." Decent compared to her, at least. "I can work in the diner. Heaven knows you make more money than I do."

Smiling back at him, she gave him a nice thank-you kiss. "I'd appreciate the help."

Of course the customers were going to have to stop staring at his wife. Dare intended to make that as clear as glass. He hoped that didn't hurt business any.

Dare decided he should probably rest until Luke got back. He needed a nap and some food and a lot of water to replace his blood supply and to get his head to stop spinning—though he blamed some of the spinning on Glynna's warm kisses.

Before he could ask Glynna to get him some water, the door swung open again, this time with a lot more force.

Vince came back far too soon. He'd left smiling, but now his face looked like a storm cloud getting ready to shoot lightning all over everyone.

"I thought you were going for Luke."

"I sent Jonas."

"What's the problem?" Dare knew his friend too well to think it was anything small. Vince didn't let little things bother him.

Vince held up a sign that Dare hadn't noticed him holding. It said *Don't Put a Thief in Your Mouth to Steal Your Brains*. He turned the sign, and on the other side it said *Demon Rum*.

"Where on earth did you get that?" Dare asked. He changed his mind. This was mighty small indeed.

"Tina Cahill has decided we need to close the saloon," Vince answered.

"Isn't she busy cooking?" Glynna asked, casting a worried glance in the direction of her diner.

332

As if Glynna would be of any help if she went over there.

"It seems she's capable of cooking and making trouble all at the same time."

"Talented woman," Dare said quietly. "I don't see why you care. You don't ever go in the saloon."

"It's the principle of the thing!"

Dare shook his head. Maybe Vince just made no sense, or maybe Dare was honestly dizzy. "And what principle is that?"

Vince scowled. "Don't be stupid."

Tina came rushing in. "Give me back that sign!"

Vince dodged around the bed so he was in front of Dare. Tina chased after him as Vince raced out the back door, Tina hard on his heels.

"Well, I'd better get myself back over to the diner." Glynna was halfway to her feet when Dare pulled her right back down beside him.

"Go close up for the day. You can take your wedding day off, I'd think."

Glynna grinned. "Good idea. I'll get the children and we can talk about our new life together."

"I like the sound of that. Have I mentioned yet that I love you?"

Glynna's smile faltered, and for a moment Dare was afraid he'd said the wrong thing.

Women could be very confusing.

Then her smile turned into a glow so bright, the sun looked dim by comparison.

"No man has ever said that to me before." She threw her arms around his neck and almost knocked him over.

He almost let her. Then she kissed him hard, and with her eyes brimming with tears, she said, "I'll go close the diner and we can get on with being husband and wife just as soon as Jonas gets back."

He kissed her again. "If Luke's not riding right along with him, he's gonna miss the ceremony."

Speaking against Dare's lips, Glynna said, "He is indeed."

She was slow in going after Janny and Paul. So slow, in fact, that Luke and Ruthy were back in plenty of time for the ceremony.

Janny and Paul had time enough to cook the noon meal without Tina's help, as she was too busy painting a new sign when Vince got away with her other one.

And Dare found kissing Glynna got his strength all fired up. In fact, he gained enough strength to participate fully in the wedding, and had plenty left over for the wedding night.

Mary Connealy writes romantic comedy with cowboys. She is the author of the acclaimed KINCAID BRIDES, LASSOED IN TEXAS, MONTANA MARRIAGES, and SOPHIE'S DAUGHTERS series. Mary has been nominated for a Christy Award, was a finalist for a RITA Award, and is a two-time winner of the Carol Award. She lives on a ranch in eastern Nebraska with her very own romantic cowboy hero. They have four grown daughters—Joslyn, married to Matt; Wendy; Shelly, married to Aaron; and Katy—and two spectacular grandchildren, Elle and Isaac. Readers can learn more about Mary and her upcoming books at:

maryconnealy.com
mconnealy.blogspot.com
seekerville.blogspot.com
petticoatsandpistols.com

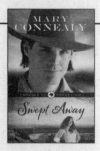